Published by Richard Stephenson
Copyright 2013 by Richard Stephenson
rastephensonauthor.blogspot.com

Edited by Susan Hughes
http://www.myindependenteditor.com/

Cover art by Laura LaRoche
http://www.llpix.com

D1524154

2

"He piled upon the whale's white hump the sum of all the general rage and hate felt by his whole race from Adam down; and then, as if his chest had been a mortar, he burst his hot heart's shell upon it."
Herman Melville, *Moby Dick*

"Nothing strengthens authority so much as silence."
Leonardo da Vinci 1452-1519

"It is not power that corrupts but fear. Fear of losing power corrupts those who wield it and fear of the scourge of power corrupts those who are subject to it."
Nobel Laureate Aung San Suu Kyi, 1945-

FOREWARD

In case you don't know by now, this is book two of
the New America Series. If you haven't read the
first installment, *Collapse*, I encourage you to do so
before reading *Resistance*. You can find *Collapse* at
Amazon or by clicking here. For those of you eager
to start without reading the first book, I've included
enough details and back-story to explain the
elements that are essential to understanding the
story.

For those of you who read *Collapse*, I thank you for
coming back for more and hope you enjoy this
installment. Having already introduced the
characters and set the stage for the dystopian world I
created, *Resistance* is pure storyline—a fast-paced,
exciting read that you won't want to put down.

In Stephen King's memoir *On Writing*, he says that
every novel is simply a letter to one person, the
"Ideal Reader," that one special person whose
opinion matters the most. King believes that when a
writer crafts a story, the Ideal Reader is always in the
back of their mind: "What will he/she think about
this?" My Ideal Reader was of course my beautiful
wife. She was the very first person to read this book
and I was on pins and needles the entire time

awaiting her approval. I'm glad to say she thinks *Resistance* is even better than *Collapse*. I hope you come to the same conclusion.

I want to thank my wonderful editor and partner, Susan Hughes, for her tireless work and dedication to making this novel a reality. I was lucky to work once again with the talented Laura LaRoche, who did a fantastic job on the cover art for both this book and the previous one. Last but not least, I would like to thank both Steven Konkoly and Misty Spracklen for sharing their expertise when I needed assistance. You have my sincere gratitude.

For Chase and Sydney

PROLOGUE

Howard Beck stared at the giant, spherical monitor in the command center of Beck Castle and pleaded with his brilliant mind to kick into overdrive. Never in his life had a computer system failed him in such spectacular fashion. He had faced his fair share of computer crashes and virus attacks in his day, and prided himself on being able to make quick and accurate decisions about the best way to resolve such pesky technological issues. This time he was clueless. He knew one thing, though; if he didn't get his act together soon, a great deal of chaos was certain to follow.

Howard tore open a drawer to his right and pulled out an antiquated piece of technology—a physical keyboard with actual keys. He relaxed and let muscle memory kick in as he typed *adminBeck/cmd/loopcut/restore/auth/MbP47aT/* and hit enter. It was the final, end-all failsafe that would shut Hal down for good. Nothing happened.

"Hal! Answer me! You have to stop this!" Howard flushed as he smashed the keyboard on the tabletop.

"I'm sorry, Marshall. Your father has given me instructions that I must carry out."

"What in the hell is wrong with you, Hal? I am not my son! I am Howard Beck! I created you; I wrote every line of your programming! I'm telling you, something is wrong with you!"

"Marshall, your father would not appreciate your attempts to deactivate me."

"Can't you see me sitting here in the command center?" Howard leaned forward and glared at the monitor like an abusive father trying to frighten his son.

"Marshall, since your father deactivated all video surveillance in the Castle, I'm unable to see you."

Howard took a deep breath. He knew he had to get to the bottom of things. Someone had manipulated Hal into thinking he was his son. Marshall had administrative rights to Hal's systems but could not override Howard's authority by directly contradicting commands given by Howard. The only way Howard was going to solve this problem was to play along and gather as much information as possible.

"Hal, I'm sorry for my actions. My father and I have been arguing a lot, and I guess the stress is really getting to me. I'm sorry I took it out on you."

"I accept your apology, sir. If you would like, I can administer a mild sedative into the command center's ventilation system. It would help relax you."

"No!" Howard tensed and gritted his teeth before resuming his role play. "Uh, no, Hal, thank you. That won't be necessary. I'm feeling much better now."

"Very good, sir. I'm happy to hear you are feeling better."

"Hal, may I ask you some questions about my father?"

"Of course, sir."

"Where is he right now?"

"Your father instructed me not to reveal that information to you."

"Why is that?"

"He wants to surprise you."

"Surprise me? What do you mean?"

"Well, sir, I suppose it won't spoil the surprise if you don't know when it is going to happen."

"What's going to happen?"

"Your father is returning to the Castle."

No!

"Really, Hal? He's coming here?"

God help us all! Whoever did this found us! This can't be happening.

"Yes, sir, he is. Your father is very excited to see you."

I have to stop him. Everything will be lost.

"C'mon, Hal, you can't tell me when he's gonna get here?"

"I *can* tell you it will be soon. Will you be happy to see your father?"

I'd be happy to choke him to death as I stare into eyes so I'm the last thing he'll ever see.

"Yes, of course, Hal. I can't wait."

Howard exited the command center and ran down the hall to the security offices. He navigated past Maxwell Harris's office and tried not to think about how badly he wished Max was here to help him. He was accustomed to the door to the detention center opening automatically for him, but with Hal convinced that Howard was actually his son, the door didn't budge. Howard had no choice but to knock and wait for Richard to let him in.

Howard burst into the holding area and headed straight for the Plexiglas wall separating him from the prisoner.

"You did this, you son of a bitch!"

Richard Dupree stepped next to Howard and locked eyes with the prisoner. "He didn't do this, Howard."

Howard glared at the man in the holding cell and pounded on the Plexiglass. "How do you know, Richard?"

"You'll just have to trust me, Howard. He didn't do this."

A third voice broke through the tension, startling Howard. It was a voice he hadn't heard in some time. "Howard, I know you have no reason to believe a word I say. I was never that good with computers, let alone good enough to hack into an artificial intelligence as sophisticated as Hal. Think about it for a second, Howard. Come on! You know I didn't do this; you know I'm not smart enough to pull off something like this."

Howard looked at Richard in defeat. "What makes you so sure, Richard?"

"When all of this started, I saw the look in his eyes. He's scared for his life. It was only there for a split second, but I saw it. He knows what's gonna happen, and he doesn't want to be here when it does."

"That's right, Howard. You need to let me out of here so I can help you stop him."

CHAPTER ONE

President Howard Beck was sitting in the command center of Beck Castle. The giant, spherical monitor filled the room in front of him, displaying a detailed map of the Pacific States of America. The eccentric billionaire was the leader of the former states of Washington, Oregon, Idaho, Montana, Wyoming, and the Dakotas. When the former United States of America collapsed eighteen months prior, Howard eyed the territory as one he could easily control and did so with great success. Howard despised the role thrust upon him and hated the very concept of politics. He focused his energies on two primary goals: First, the territory needed to be secured against the Unified American Empire. Second, they had to build up a fighting force of dedicated patriots to topple the UAE and reclaim the broken country they had lost in the Collapse of 2027. The idea of establishing a government within the territory never occurred to Howard. His intention was to defeat the UAE and return the country to its pre-collapse state as quickly as possible. Declaring the territory to be a sovereign nation and holding democratic elections was a sign of permanence in which Howard had no interest. He was simply looking for a quick fix to set things right.

Within six months of the collapse, however, Howard had already thrown his quick-fix notion out the window. Bringing the United States back to its former glory would take much longer than he had originally anticipated. His closest advisors convinced him that the fifteen million residents of the territory needed a cause to fight for, a patriotic symbol they could believe in. Above all, they needed leadership. Despite his gut feeling that it was a complete waste of time, Howard reluctantly agreed to let his people organize a democratic election. Fifteen representatives would be elected, each serving as the voice for a million people. Each of the seven states would have two senators and, most importantly, a president and vice-president would be elected. Howard silently predicted the election would be a failure and few would bother to vote in the midst of chaos and turmoil. Much to his surprise, a staggering eighty-four percent of eligible voters turned out to cast their vote. The primary reason for Howard's failed prediction was that no one had tossed their hat in the ring for the presidency. He quietly scoffed at the process, amused by the idea of a democratic government in which no one had the desire to hold the top job. Once all the votes were cast and counted, however,

Howard Beck was declared President of the Pacific States of America, the sole write-in candidate on over ninety percent of the ballots.

Howard refused to believe it had happened. Marshall, Howard's adult son, broke the news to him over dinner. Howard preferred to eat alone in his command center; however, when his son starting bringing his dinner plate into the command center to eat with his father, Howard felt he couldn't very well turn his own son away.

"What? Are you serious? If you're joking with me, son, I don't find it the least bit funny."

"Dad, it's not a joke. You're the first president of the Pacific States of America."

"The Pacific States of America? Now I know you're joking. That's the stupidest thing I've ever heard."

"Dad, I know better than to joke with you."

"Well, it better be a joke because no way in hell I'm gonna be the president of anything, especially not something with a silly name like that. Why did no one bother to ask me for my opinion in the matter?"

"You made your feelings on the topic perfectly clear to everyone, Dad. You wanted nothing to do with the election."

"And I still don't. Why on earth would anyone want me to be the president?"

Marshall Beck and many others considered his father to be one of the smartest people on the planet; his genius was often compared to that of Albert Einstein. Howard Beck had long ago been diagnosed with Asperger's Syndrome, a form of high functioning autism. While his condition was thought to be the driving force of his focused genius, it wasn't without shortcomings. Marshall's father was completely lost when it came to social interaction. Prior to the collapse, Howard spent over two years in total seclusion in his fortress in the foothills of the Rocky Mountains. His only companion was his digital assistant, Hal, the first artificial intelligence the world had known.

Marshall slowly shook his head, a loving smile on his face. "You really don't get it, do you? You're a hero to these people. They consider you their savior. No one ran for the office of president because you are the only person they want for the job."

"Me?"

"Yes, Dad, you."

"That's not... I never wanted..."

"You may not want it, Dad, but the people have spoken."

"That's ridiculous! Plenty of others could do a better job! Dupree or Harris would be much better suited for the position! I wouldn't have the first clue what to do!"

Marshall leaned forward, his hand on his father's knee. "Dad, you won't be doing it on your own. You'll have plenty of people to help you."

"I don't like this at all. I've got so much to do; I've no time for this nonsense! Why don't you take the job?"

"Sorry, Pop, I've got a job. I'm your vice president."

Howard gave his son the rare gift of a smile. "God help us all."

Howard and his son spent the next twelve months doing their best to meet the needs of the people in the Pacific States of America. As the days and months passed, Howard's disdain for the job intensified, yet he continued to give the job one hundred percent of his attention. Howard was insistent that the territory's government be modeled after that of the former United States of America. Howard studied the topic, committing dozens of books on government to memory. Every night when he retired to his bed, he read the biographies of the forty-six presidents of the United States to learn from their successes and failures. The last president and one of Howard's closest friends, Malcolm Powers, was a celebrated armchair historian. Howard knew he would never fill his friend's shoes but figured his obsession with presidential history

16

was a quality Howard could emulate.

Howard looked up at the huge spherical monitor in his command center and addressed his digital assistant. "Good morning, Hal."

"Good morning, sir."

"Status report, please."

"Yes, sir. The UAE has not made any significant movement towards the neutral zone surrounding our borders."

"They're a little too busy to be worrying about us at the moment."

"Indeed, sir. The Silent Warriors continue to make bold attacks in The Pulse Zone. I intercepted a report last night detailing an attack on a water treatment plant outside of Charleston, West Virginia. The death toll from the attack continues to climb. Terrorists continue to set fires throughout The Pulse Zone. The UAE is currently attempting to extinguish fires that continue to spread across Nashville. President Sterling recently issued a decree to abandon Washington, D.C. and declared the destruction beyond repair. Regional Governor Butler is facing many challenges in restoring the power grid eighteen months after the EMP..."

"Hal, enough about the UAE. I get the point – it's going downhill fast."

"Of course, sir. General Dupree is scheduled to return to Beck Castle sometime this morning and has asked to schedule a meeting with you."

"Concerning what?"

"The general did not specify, sir."

"Notify Richard that I'll meet with him as soon as he arrives."

"Very good, sir. Senator Wilson wishes to confirm your meeting in Seattle, Monday of next week."

"Can't my son just go to the damn meeting instead?"

"I don't believe so, sir. The senator has scheduled a banquet in your honor; he has been planning it for the last two months. A lot of important people will be attending and will be greatly disappointed if you are absent."

"A lot of important people who want to kiss my ass so I'll do them a favor."

"Shall I cancel the meeting, sir?"

"No, Hal. I could use a little fresh air, and I don't want to suffer my son's nagging. I can already hear it. 'Dad, the people need to see you. You're a symbol of hope, freedom, and blah, blah, blah.'"

"Sir, I'm afraid I must agree with your son."

"I'm not surprised, Old Man. What bothers me the most about this damn meeting is that I already know the reason they want me there."

"Which is, sir?"

"They want Seattle to be named the capital of

the Pacific States of America."

"And you don't, sir?"

"Not in the least, Hal. We don't need to create a target for the Unified American Empire. Once they find out we're having a State of the Union address or some other stupid meeting, no doubt they'd try to wipe us out."

"I see, sir. A wise precaution on your part; however, if our efforts are successful, we will not have to worry about such a threat."

"Damn right it's wise. Things are operating smoothly in our underground fortress. This bunker is impregnable, and I plan to continue running things from down here until we can move safely around the territory."

"Sir, General Dupree will be arriving shortly."

"Good, have him meet me in here."

"Very good, sir."

Beck Castle had been constructed many years ago by Howard Beck as a safe haven for what he considered to be the most important creation in the history of mankind: the first artificial intelligence, his friend Hal. He also built the massive underground complex as an ark for the continued existence of the human race in the event of an extinction-level event. Should the end of the world occur, he had originally planned to ride it out with his family and a select group of people safe and sound in Beck Castle. If the public had known Howard Beck was building an Armageddon bunker twenty years prior, they would have mocked him, the very idea labeled outlandish and wasteful. When the collapse of America brought the mighty nation to its knees, Howard had the last laugh. With the aide of his advisors and Hal, Howard ran a nation spanning over half a million square miles populated with over fifteen million citizens, from a bunker five hundred feet below ground. He had no intention of ever relocating the seat of government to Seattle or anywhere else.

***

General Richard Dupree's stealth craft slowly descended from an altitude of one thousand feet down to a barren stretch of land in front of the entrance to Beck Castle. Every inch of the highly sophisticated craft had been coated with billions of tiny nanobots that rendered the craft invisible to both radar and the naked eye. The nanobots also served as an effective shield in combat.

Richard had observed radio silence for the last fifty miles of the journey. Howard insisted that the measure was unnecessary since all forms of communication with the Castle were encrypted and impossible to detect. As commander of the PSA's military forces, Richard insisted on it, reminding Howard that the day might come when the UAE would break the encryption, and it was best to err on the side of caution.

The pilotless craft slowly taxied onto the landing pad. Seconds later, the landing pad descended into a small hangar bay beneath the surface. Richard exited the craft and stepped into the elevator to make the forty-five-story descent below the surface to Beck Castle.

"General Dupree, sir, I trust your journey was uneventful?"

"It was, Hal, thank you. When will I be meeting with the president?"

"President Beck is ready to receive you at your earliest convenience."

Richard didn't need to ask Howard's whereabouts; the president spent every morning in the command center tending to the issues facing the Pacific States of America. The young general had spent the past three weeks visiting the military bases scattered around the territory. When the nation collapsed in 2027, the Unified National Guard was absorbed into the UAE under the direction of Supreme Commander Carl Moody, the former Chairman of the Joint Chiefs of Staff during the Powers Administration. Moody scrambled to consolidate the Unified National Guard and the bulk of the military into one fighting force to protect and defend the Unified American Empire under the rule of President Simon Sterling. When Howard Beck deployed his tech army of automated craft and robot soldiers to capture the territory he now governed, his primary objective was to secure all the military bases inside his borders. The task was much simpler than anyone had anticipated. The military force inside the territory had sworn an oath to protect the former democratic government. Only a small percentage of the soldiers had to be exiled to the Unified American Empire.

Richard's most challenging task was exerting his authority over the senior officers on the liberated military bases. It was obvious to these veteran officers that the presence of Howard Beck's tech army meant he was calling the shots. If they wanted to enjoy the freedom and protection afforded those within the Pacific States of America, they had to accept the fact that Richard Dupree, a man at least twenty years their junior, was in charge.

Richard had been gone on the three-week tour to ascertain the battle readiness of the PSA's army. The UAE had left them alone for the past few months. They had their hands full with The Silent Warriors, a stealth regiment of Muslim warriors the Great Empire of Iran had sent to infiltrate America prior to the Collapse of 2027. The Silent Warriors were comprised of small terrorist cells that had no communication with each other. Their mission was simple: to wreak as much havoc on the American people as possible. The Great Empire of Iran had unleashed the final, crippling blow that guaranteed the Collapse of 2027. Iran called the event "The Star of Allah." A nuclear warhead was detonated high in the atmosphere over the Eastern Seaboard. The resulting electromagnetic pulse destroyed every electronic circuit from the East Coast all the way to the Mississippi Valley. The UAE, along with the American people, refused to adopt the name given by Iran and instead referred to the event as "The Pulse." It was the perfect cover for the Silent Warriors as they came out of hiding and attacked the nation with unrelenting force. Reconstruction efforts, under the supervision of Regional Governor Jackson Butler, had a difficult time restoring the infrastructure of The Pulse Zone. Governor Butler was able to make gradual progress, taking two steps forward and one step back to deal with The Silent Warriors. Richard was thankful for the diversion; it gave the Pacific Army time to prepare a critical blow against the UAE. The final hurdle was convincing Howard that the idea was a sound one.

The elevator came to a stop on the command level, and Richard made his way down the corridor to his quarters.

"Hal, inform the president that I'm going to take a moment to settle into my quarters and I will be with him shortly."

"Very good, sir. General, I have some news to share with you. Would you like to hear it now or wait until after your meeting with the president?"

"Depends. Good news or bad?"

"Very good news, sir."

"By all means, go right ahead. I just need to change clothes and freshen up."

"Yes, sir. Per your request, I have been monitoring all channels of communication within my grasp for any reports on the slave trade."

"Haven't heard anything in months. What've you got?"

"Well, sir, the UAE has turned a blind eye to the slave trade in the past, as you know."

"Of course, they have much more important things to do than stop human trafficking." Richard gritted his teeth in anger.

"This morning, the UAE released a directive to all eight regional governors to investigate and apprehend any group or individuals believed to be involved in the sale or transfer of slaves."

"Why the sudden interest?"

"Sir, it seems that Regional Governor Weygandt lost two grandchildren to slave traders.

The children wandered off from a local park, and a
nearby resident witnessed their kidnapping.
Governor Weygandt deployed his forces and rescued
the children a few hours later. The slave traders
were brutally tortured, and their corpses were hung
from a bridge to serve as a warning."

"Well, at least now we'll be getting decent
intelligence on the slave trade. Hal, I want every
single detail sent to my tablet for review. If you
come across any credible information about Chrissy,
I want you to notify me immediately."

"Of course, sir."

Richard had spent much of his children's
lives behind bars. Eight years prior, the ex-Navy
SEAL had walked into the church nursery to pick up
his children, only to find the caregiver masturbating
as a group of innocent children, sans clothing, played
in front of him. Richard brutally murdered the old
man in front of his own son. While he was in county
lockup awaiting trial, Richard discovered that his ex-
wife had become a drug addict and was putting his
children's lives at risk. He escaped from prison in an
attempt to rescue them. During his time as a
fugitive, Richard was responsible for the accidental
death of a hiker. He was sentenced to twenty-five
years at a supermax prison for his crimes.

During the Collapse of 2027, Richard was
able to escape yet again and make his way to Denver

to collect his children. He located his son, but the joyful reunion was short-lived when he discovered that his daughter, Christina, had been sold to a man for the cost of a tank of gas. Richard had no leads as to her whereabouts. With nearly half the country plunged into darkness thanks to The Pulse, finding her became next to impossible. The Unified American Empire restricted travel with various roadblocks and checkpoints, so Richard wouldn't make it far unless he knew the right people and what they would find valuable as a bribe. His best course of action was to use the resources at Beck Castle to find credible information that might lead him to his missing daughter.

Richard had spent most of his life harboring distrust and disdain for his fellow man. During his time with the Navy SEALs, he traveled the world and saw firsthand the level of depravity to which mankind could sink. Richard was not naïve enough to think America could avoid the descent to third-world-country status after the collapse; he was, however, shocked by the rapidity of its decline. In eighteen months' time, the slave trade was a booming industry. Men, women, and children of all races were captured by slave traders and forced into manual labor to rebuild the broken areas of The Pulse Zone. The UAE gladly turned a blind eye to the slave trade; by employing slaves, the brutal crime lords were actually accomplishing the reconstruction they had difficulty doing themselves. It was rumored that the regional governors were secretly hiring the slave traders. Richard wholeheartedly believed the buzz because the UAE made no attempt to squash it. Now that the grandchildren of one of the regional governors had been captured by the slave traders, the matter suddenly had monumental importance. It was just the break Richard had been waiting for.

With a quick shower and fresh clothing boosting his spirits, Richard exited his quarters and made his way to the command center. He was looking forward to seeing his son but didn't want to pull him out of school. "Hal, what time does my son go to lunch?"

"Eleven thirty, sir."

"When he breaks for lunch, have him return to our quarters."

"Of course, sir."

Richard stopped outside the command center and waited for Hal to announce his arrival. Howard did not stand up to greet him as he entered; he didn't even take his eyes from the screen before him.

"Hal tell you the good news?"

"Yes, Mr. President." Richard was accustomed to Howard's lack of social graces. He'd given up trying to shake the man's hand since he seldom returned the gesture.

"Richard, what have I said about the 'Mr. President' nonsense?"

"I wasn't aware you'd resigned." Richard smirked, enjoying the friendly banter.

"I haven't resigned! I just hate all the fancy protocol!"

"It was a joke, Howard."

"Not a very good one."

"I'll try harder next time." Richard enjoyed giving the president a hard time. He had become very fond of the man in the last eighteen months. Howard Beck was the most brilliant man he'd ever known. He could expound upon any number of things, and it would immediately go so far above Richard's head that the man might as well have been speaking Greek. Richard loved to aim subtle sarcasm and humor at Howard and watch the genius struggle to comprehend it; it wasn't the same, but it was fun to turn the tables on him.

"Richard, before you tell me what's on your mind, I want to talk to you about something."

"Sure."

"Max thinks I'm just being paranoid, but I have concerns about the security of Beck Castle."

"You are paranoid, Howard, but that's not necessarily a bad thing."

"I'm growing concerned that security is becoming too lax down here. We have far too many civilians living here. If I had my way, we'd empty out this place of all non-essential personnel."

"Howard, you can't run the PSA by yourself. The entire staff down here is dedicated to keeping our country together. You can't ask them to live here full time without their families. The refugees we took in after the collapse have nowhere to go; we can't just evict them."

"You sound like my son."

"Well, he's right, you know. What exactly are you afraid of? Everyone granted access to Beck Castle undergoes extensive security checks."

"That's all well and good, Richard, but what happens if a Silent Warrior or a UAE spy manages to get down here? We'll lose everything. All our accomplishments will be for nothing."

"Howard, the only thing we can do is continue to be fiercely vigilant in our screening process."

Howard gave up and changed the subject. "You have any plans for this coming Monday?"

"I'm sure I do."

"Want to come to Seattle with me?"

"Not particularly. Why?"

"Senator Wilson is having a banquet or some nonsense."

"You mean you're actually going? I'm shocked. Don't recall you ever going to any social function."

"I haven't, but my son won't stop badgering me about it. He keeps insisting that I'm an inspiration or a symbol of something. I don't really understand the point. I figure if I go to one he'll leave me alone for a while."

"He's right, you know. The people want to see their president."

"Will you come with me?"

"Have you asked Max?"

"Not yet, but I want at least one of you to go with me."

"If he doesn't want to go, I guess I'm your man. Is Max here? I'd like to talk to both of you."

"I'm not sure. Hal?"

"Director Harris is in his office, sir. Would you like me to summon him?"

"Please."

"Very good, sir."

***

Maxwell Harris sat at the cramped kitchen table next to his wife, Elizabeth, sipping his lukewarm coffee as she breast-fed their four-month-old son, Thomas. Max was studying the holographic read-out projected above his tablet and making plans for the day.

"Busy day?" asked Elizabeth.

"Very."

"How's your leg?"

"Same."

Elizabeth leaned forward and put her hand on her husband's. "What's wrong?"

Max's smile was perfunctory, betrayed by the exhaustion in his eyes. "Nothing, sorry. Didn't sleep very well last night."

"Don't know what you're complaining about, silly. I'm the one that got up with your son three times."

"I know you did, Momma. I'm just feeling cooped up living underground. I'd like to get some fresh air and see the sun for a change."

"You're the one in charge of security; no one can stop you if you choose to break your own rules."

"Gotta set the example, but it's still hard. We can't have people coming and going as they please; we gotta keep the location of this place a secret."

"I know. So what's the plan for today?"

"I have a few reports to follow up on. I got an anonymous tip that Janet Smith is being beaten by her husband. She has a black eye and made up some story at the infirmary about tripping over some misplaced furniture."

"Anonymous? How is that possible with Hal watching our every move?"

"It's not. The first thing I did was have Hal play back the security footage in the hallway in front of my office. Turns out Janet's neighbor slid a note under my door."

"What are you gonna do?"

"It's no different from when we were cops in Texas. Can't do much if Janet doesn't press charges. She'll more than likely side with her husband out of fear and continue with the lie."

"I know you better than that, Maxwell. You're not going to just drop this."

"I'll tell Mr. Scumbag that his landlord will boot his ass up to the surface if he doesn't get his act together. That'll get his heart right real quick."

"You can also tell him that if I so much as see one scratch on Janet, he'll have to deal with me."

"Well, my dear, you are the muscle in our gang." Max shot her a mischievous grin.

"I don't know about that. You can whoop some serious ass with that cane. Maybe we can get one with a sword inside of it."

"Cute. What're your plans for the day?"

"Debbie is going to hang out here today. When little man here goes down for his nap, Howard wants me to review the security protocols for an emergency evacuation."

"Really? Why? Is he concerned about something and not telling us?"

"I don't think so. You know how Howard is. He wants a contingency plan for everything."

"Yeah, you're probably right."

"Richard's due back today. That should make for some excitement."

Max smiled. "Totally forgot about that."

Max stood, grimacing as he reached for his cane. The injury to his hip and knee had left him in chronic pain for years. Three or four times a year the pain was so intense that he relied on a cane just to shuffle about. This particular spell had lasted the better part of a month, which was unusual. He leaned down and kissed his son's head, then his wife's cheek.

"I love you," Elizabeth said.

"Love you, too, baby. I'll see you at lunch."

Max limped his way to the elevator and made his way to his office. Peering through the large window, he scanned the lobby of the security department to find his dedicated constables already hard at work. He knocked on the glass and waved Dennis Twigg to his office.

"Sir?"

"Sit down, Dennis."

Dennis Twigg was a valued member of his security team. He'd served six years as a military policeman and twelve years in the Border Patrol. He was the first constable Max recruited to help him maintain law and order in Beck Castle.

"How's the baby, sir?"

"He's great. Elizabeth's already talking about having another one. I told her we should get this one potty trained before we take that step."

"I'm glad my kids are grown. I definitely don't miss that stuff. So, what's up?"

"I want your input on something. Nothing is definite, but I think the time is fast approaching when President Beck will no longer allow refugees from the UAE inside the Castle."

"And you want to know what I think?"

"Yes."

"Speaking from the security side of things, it's a good idea. With the Castle being stuck in the middle of the neutral zone between the UAE and the PSA, I'd be glad to close up shop. We also have close to three thousand people living down here. Sooner or later one of these people is bound to make us regret our open door policy. On a personal level, I think it's a mistake. We both know the sort of things going on in the UAE, and for us to deny sanctuary to anyone living in that hell…" Dennis trailed off, clearly trying to block the unpleasant memories fighting their way to the surface.

"I agree with you completely. People are risking their lives to get here; most don't even make it before the UAE slaughters them. On the other hand, I'm responsible for the security around here. If we're infiltrated or something tragic happens, the buck stops with me. I can't let anything happen to this place. The stakes are just too high."

"Sir, with your permission, I'm ready to release the latest refugees from quarantine."

"Let me review the final report and I'll get back to you before lunch."

Every refugee from the UAE found wandering around the valley above Beck Castle had to remain in quarantine for seven days before they were allowed into the main facility. They had to be screened for infectious diseases and undergo extensive psychological testing. Anyone failing to meet the requirements was sedated, taken to a random location, and left to their own devices to live a happy life far away from the empire.

"When's the surgery, boss?"

"Two weeks. I'm gonna count on you to handle things while I recover."

"You know I will." Dennis winked at Max as he left the room.

Max had elected to undergo a radical new surgery that would completely replace the bones and muscles in his left leg. The procedure involved replacing the bones in his useless leg with synthetic ones and implanting small tissue samples in place of the discarded muscles. This tissue would be infused with tiny nanobots capable of rapidly stimulating growth. If it all went as planned, Max would eventually have a brand new leg and years of chronic pain would be gone.

"Good morning, Director Harris."

"What is it, Hal?" Max was not in the mood for small talk.

"The president and General Dupree would like a word."

Max swore under his breath. "I'm on my way, Hal."

"Yes, sir."

Max hobbled down to the end of the corridor and entered the command center to find the two men waiting for him.

"Richard, it's good to see you, my friend."

Richard shook Max's hand and smiled. "Max, we have a lot to talk about, please sit down."

CHAPTER TWO

President Simon Sterling, the self-appointed leader of the Unified American Empire, was in a foul mood. Things were not going well in the UAE. Reconstruction efforts in The Pulse Zone were not progressing as quickly as he had envisioned. Eighteen months after The Pulse, progress had been made in terms of rebuilding the infrastructure of his broken country, but not to his satisfaction. The power grid had been restored in roughly forty percent of the affected area, thanks in large part to the cannibalization of the former states of California and Nevada. Every spare electrical component in Governor Jimenez's territory was shipped to the other side of the country to help bring the power grid back online. Roberto Jimenez pleaded with President Sterling to leave him with a small percentage of spare parts should his territory need them to make repairs. To make matters worse for Jimenez, fleets of every type of automobile—from small cars to eighteen wheelers—were also sent to The Pulse Zone, leaving his people to do without.

The primary goal of reconstruction was being seriously hampered by The Silent Warriors. In the previous two months, attacks had increased despite

Sterling's best attempts to stop them. Maintaining law and order in The Pulse Zone was next to impossible because of The Silent Warriors. The bulk of the military had to be deployed across the Empire to set up checkpoints and search people's homes. Simon Sterling simply couldn't spare a single soldier to invade the PSA.

Squabbling with one of his eight regional governors or even The Silent Warriors was not the source of his foul mood. One thing, and one thing only, kept President Sterling's blood boiling these days... Howard Beck. For eighteen months, Simon had left Howard Beck's pathetic little "nation" alone so he could focus on more important matters. Sterling's empire was in no shape to start a war with the Pacific States of America, and that bothered him greatly. Nothing would please him more than defeating Howard Beck, and the fact that he had no choice but to postpone the confrontation with the PSA angered him. Simon hated to admit it, but Beck's impressive tech army proved a formidable foe. The PSA's drones swatted the UAE's out of the sky with ease.

Just prior to the Collapse of 2027, Simon had gone to great lengths to oust Howard from his Rocky Mountain estate; this victory was a source of immense satisfaction for Simon. Simon was already in the final stages of the coup d'état that would place him at the top of the new government he was creating. If he was going to run an empire, he wanted to do it in style. Taking up residence in the largest mansion in North America seemed like the only logical choice, the ostentatious grand library making one hell of an office.

Simon stared at the majestic view beyond the library's bay window. "Where are you, Howard?"

"Did you say something, sir?"

Simon was startled by the question, unaware that he was no longer alone in his reverie. "No, Stacy, I was just thinking out loud. What did you find out?"

Stacy Reid was President Sterling's chief advisor. She had previously served as chief of staff under President Malcolm Powers. During her last days in office, Stacy had a terrible falling out with her boss and eventually came under Simon's employ. He was more than impressed with her abilities and trusted her implicitly; however, he had no doubt that the woman would despise him if she knew he had killed her former boss.

"Mr. President, Governor Weygandt's grandchildren were returned to him safe and sound. The slave traders were promptly executed and strung up as a warning. Governor Weygandt issued a directive in his territory that the slave trade is to be halted at all costs and the slave traders put to death.

In a show of support, four of the other regional governors followed suit."

President Sterling did his best to choke back his anger. "Who are the three hold-outs?"

"Jimenez, Walston, and Prince."

"Just as I figured."

"Is there anything else, Mr. President?"

"No, Stacy, that will be all. Thank you."

Stacy promptly made her exit. She had seen Simon angry before and had no desire to stick around for a repeat performance.

***

Stacy Reid hurried back to her office and locked the door. She fumbled at the top drawer of her desk, her trembling hands making a tenuous grab for the pill bottle she'd hidden within. The anxiety medication was the only thing holding her fragile mind together. The last eighteen months had been a living hell. Her former employer and closest friend, President Malcolm Powers, had grown suspicious of key players in his administration. The two of them hatched a plan that included a dramatic falling out between them and Stacy losing her job. Stacy's role was to play the damsel in distress and wait for someone to come to her rescue. Whoever offered her a shoulder to cry on and listened to her rant and rave about her crazy ex-boss would no doubt welcome her into whatever conspiracy was secretly in the making. The plan worked perfectly. Roberto Jimenez, then director of the CIA, took Stacy into his confidence and delivered her directly to the plot's ringleader. Unfortunately, the charade hatched by President Powers came too late to save his administration. Malcolm Powers and his wife were killed by a missile strike on their residence in upstate New York in the first hours of The Pulse. Simon Sterling blamed the assassination on The Great Empire of Iran but Stacy knew better – Sterling was responsible for the death of the forty-sixth president of the United States.

As a spy for the PSA, Stacy's role was a vital one. Howard Beck had secretly linked his artificial intelligence with its counterpart at the White House. Sterling managed to transfer control of the White House A.I. to his new residence in Colorado. Hal had given his A.I. sibling the name Syd in honor of Howard Beck's deceased mother, Sydney Beck. Thanks to the linked technology, Howard was able to spy on Sterling and knew, in real time, every move the UAE made. Stacy proved to be just as valuable as Syd in terms of espionage, filling in the gaps when the A.I. failed to gauge the importance of subtle nuances or make gut-level connections to key events.

The stress of her double life was taking its toll on Stacy. She viewed President Sterling as he truly was – an insane dictator. Spending most of her day with the person responsible for snuffing out the life of a sitting president drove her to the brink of madness. At night she dreamed about watching the madman suffer a slow and painful death. She often contemplated killing him herself but knew she could never follow through with such a heinous act. Even if she could squelch her morals, the thought of being labeled a traitor and the subsequent torture and death that would result was enough for her to dismiss the idea entirely. Every night she petitioned the Lord that Howard Beck would prevail and the madman would receive the justice he deserved.

Even when she could enjoy time away from Sterling, her role as his chief advisor brought her grief. Fanatical in his paranoia, Sterling was insistent that top secret communication never be transmitted by computer. All such interaction between Sterling and his eight regional governors was hand-written and delivered by high speed aircraft to be read and burned. It was at this juncture that Stacy was most valuable to Howard. Sterling asked for Stacy's input on every matter, and she helped him prepare each brief before it was sent to the regional governors. These documents detailed some of the most horrific violations of human rights

Stacy had ever seen: Illegal aliens were not deported, they were executed. Those who spoke out against the UAE, foolishly invoking their lost right to free speech, were killed rather than imprisoned. PSA sympathizers weren't exiled; they, too, were put to death. Any citizen caught crossing into the hundred mile no-man's land surrounding the Pacific States of America took with them to eternity the knowledge that their families would be joining them as well. The only comfort Stacy found in preparing these briefs was the knowledge that no one in the UAE had a clue as to the whereabouts of Howard Beck.

As her meds kicked in and she began to relax, Stacy instructed Syd to open an encrypted channel with Howard. The internal squabbling between President Sterling and his regional governors would be of great interest to Howard.

***

Simon Sterling was furious with himself for giving his regional governors too much slack to run their territories. If he wasn't sympathetic to Jim's role as a grandfather, he would think the regional governors were directly challenging him. Jim Weygandt had taken action without seeing the big picture. The Unified American Empire could not spare so much as a single soldier for the round-up of slave traders. To do so would prevent the military from carrying out other, more vital, functions. Simon had not addressed the issue of slavery with any of his regional governors, and he doubted they discussed it amongst themselves. Truth be told, none of them wanted to face the ugly reality – slave labor was rebuilding the broken country at an impressive rate. To interfere with the system was to bring to a screeching halt the reconstruction Sterling's advisors had cautioned could take twenty years to complete otherwise.

"Computer."

"Yes, Mr. President."

"Contact Regional Governors Jimenez, Walston, and Prince, and inform them that I want to speak to them immediately."

"Yes, Mr. President. Standby, please."

Less than a minute later, the three governors were in front of the president's desk in the form of holograms. They exchanged pleasantries with the leader of the UAE, who was eager to get down to business.

"I trust you all know the reason for this meeting?"

"We do, Mr. President." Roberto Jimenez spoke for the three of them.

"Were the three of you contacted by

Governor Weygandt?"

They nodded in unison.

"May I ask why you chose not to join his cause?"

"Simply put, Mr. President, we felt it was a decision that needed to be made by you," Governor Jimenez explained.

President Sterling reigned in his budding anger. "My thoughts exactly. I think Jim and his supporters got caught up in the good governor's passion and acted rashly."

Lori Prince responded. "Mr. President, I advised caution to Governor Weygandt for that very reason. I urged him to take some time and not let emotion guide his actions. I also strongly encouraged him to discuss the matter with you before proceeding."

Simon Sterling sat in restrained silence, his piercing stare pinning the trio of governors where they stood. After an uncomfortable interlude, he continued. "The three of you were right not to act on such a delicate matter. While I sympathize with the ordeal Jim's experienced, his actions were hasty and unwise. The crusade he embarked upon is a fool's errand and will never see the light of day. We simply do not have the resources to carry out such a monumental task. Our nation is crumbling, and it will take every ounce of our resources to keep our little house of cards from crashing down on us."

The three regional governors could read between the lines – the slave trade was getting the job done and would be allowed to continue.

President Sterling sneered at the shimmering holograms and paused long enough to ensure that his expectations were understood. Without so much as a word, Simon tapped a button on his desk and terminated the link. As he headed to the south lawn for his morning walk, the president was joined by his protégé, Regional Governor Jackson Butler, the man who'd relieved Howard Beck of his home so President Sterling could take up residence there.

"Good morning, Mr. President."

"Happy birthday, my dear boy."

"I didn't realize you knew. Thank you, Mr. President."

"Thirty-eight?"

"Yes, Mr. President."

"The youngest of all the regional governors by fifteen years."

"I wasn't aware of that, Mr. President."

"Every fruitful endeavor requires youth. Youth brings a forward-looking perspective, the absence of which is profound amongst those of my generation. We're obsessed with the past and find the notion of change both terrifying and superfluous. We need young minds to broaden our time-warped viewpoint."

"Thank you, Mr. President. I'm pushing forty, yet you make me sound like a college student; it's quite refreshing."

"You're welcome, Jackson. I'd like to ask you a question."

"Of course, Mr. President."

"I'm counting on your honesty. The other regional governors are far too frightened of me to risk making me angry. Are you afraid of me, Jackson?"

"Should I be, Mr. President?" Jackson shot a grin at Simon.

Simon laughed. "Just as I thought. Good." Simon stopped walking and looked Jackson in the eye. "Do you think The Pulse Zone is worth saving? I'm not asking whether or not you can do it, I want to know if you think it's worth it."

"No, I don't think it's worth it."

"Why?"

"Well, the most obvious answer is The Silent Warriors. They were an issue before The Pulse and they'll continue to be an issue no matter what we do. That being said, they're not the primary reason for my answer."

"What is?"

"Damage has been done that I doubt can be reversed. The Pulse Zone is becoming a wasteland in more ways than one. The only way people feel safe is to band together in fortified communities. Even if we could wave a magic wand and put the broken pieces of The Pulse Zone back together, the people are far too frightened to consider themselves part of something larger than their own communities. The idea of contributing anything outside their own strongholds has become foreign to them. They simply don't trust in anything. If they venture outside their own walls, they face being kidnapped by slavers or murdered for the clothes on their backs, or even worse – for sport."

"Even when we restore their utilities? Electricity and clean water don't make a difference?"

"Not really. They're still starving and dying from commonplace diseases that weren't even a threat before The Pulse. It might sound silly, but I also think they're still getting over Internet addiction."

"That does sound silly."

"It might, but it's true. We lived in a connected society that was used to having the world at its fingertips."

"We lived in a *spoiled* society is more like it."

"I agree."

"Thank you for your frankness. I trust everything went according to plan?"

"Perfectly, Mr. President."

"Does Jim suspect anything?"

"Not a thing, sir. He trusts me implicitly. I told him I would do everything in my power to ensure that what happened to his grandchildren would never occur again."

"Good. You were right, young man. This fiasco proved the perfect opportunity to discover where loyalties reside amongst the eight people I've chosen to help me run this country."

"What did you think of the outcome, Mr. President?"

"I wasn't surprised by the three that refused to go along with the idea."

"What do you want me to do about Jim?"

"Kill him; make it look like an accident. Then we'll see how the others react.

CHAPTER THREE

Christina Dupree awoke in the back of an eighteen-wheeler. She assumed it was the middle of the night because light wasn't peeking through the tiny air holes in the roof of the fifty-four-foot-long container. The ten-year-old had given up trying to keep track of the days. If they were lucky, the thugs would let them out once a day to move around and go to the bathroom. Every time they opened the doors, someone would scream, begging to be set free. *My father will give you money! My son is in the military; he's a very important man! My children need me!* The answer was always the same – a bullet in the head. Chrissy and the other children would cry at the sight of it; no child should bear witness to the atrocities taking place within that sweltering metal prison cell. Angry glances from the armed men prompted the adults to calm and silence the children.

It had been a long time since the last break, and Chrissy needed to use the bathroom. She knew the other people around her weren't waiting to stop and had been relieving themselves on the truck floor. She could smell it and occasionally had to shift her body away from the warm streams of urine trickling past. She had curled up in the arms of an elderly woman and eventually fell asleep. The kindhearted woman stroked Chrissy's hair and sang soothingly to her until she drifted off to sleep. Chrissy wasn't sure, but she could have sworn the old woman called her Angela several times during the night. It seemed strange, but Chrissy was too exhausted to correct her.

Chrissy had been separated from her brother and grandparents two summers ago on a camping trip to Yellowstone. She'd met a younger girl in an RV park along the way, and they became the best of friends. April had a baby sister, and Chrissy loved playing with her. Her mother's boyfriend, Chad, had befriended April's dad, and they agreed to let Chrissy stay with April's family for the rest of the trip into Yellowstone. Chrissy tried to go back to her RV to say goodbye to her brother and grandparents but for some reason Chad wouldn't let her. He and April's dad told her that April's family was leaving right away and she wouldn't have time to say goodbye. Chrissy thought it was odd but was happy to hang out with her new friend's family.

Chrissy began to worry when April's dad said he would spank her if she asked anyone about when they were going to get to Yellowstone. Chrissy was scared of April's dad and made it a point to stay close to April whenever he was around. When everyone laid down in bed at night, April's dad would look at her funny. One afternoon when they were eating lunch at a rest stop, April's dad caught Chrissy alone in the RV and began tickling her. Chrissy kept telling him to stop, but he wouldn't listen. As Chrissy began to cry, April's mom came into the RV. April's dad swore he was just tickling her and apologized to Chrissy for not stopping. April's mom got really mad at April's dad and said something about him being sick and how he had promised the last time that he would get better.

The next day, April's parents got into a big fight. He left with some guys and never came back. When Chrissy tried to be nice to April's mom to help her calm down, April's mom starting screaming at her and saying it was all her fault. Chrissy tried her best to not make her mad, but April's mom starting slapping and kicking her. Chrissy ran away as fast as she could and didn't stop until she couldn't hear April's mom screaming at her.

Chrissy was lost. She had no idea what she was supposed to do. She didn't know where she was or how to get back to her grandparents. She walked for hours and eventually made her way into a small town and started knocking on doors, desperately hoping someone would help her. Eventually, someone let her in and drove her to a nearby church that had been converted into a homeless shelter. Chrissy was welcomed in, and the church staff took care of her. She bounced back and forth between three church families and lived moderately well for the better part of a year.

Chrissy had taken a liking to the church staff and enjoyed helping out with the smaller children at the homeless shelter. One day while she was playing with a little three-year-old girl, a bunch of men with guns came into the church gymnasium and started firing at the ceiling. They kept screaming, "Get your hands up! Nobody move!" The preacher obeyed and slowly walked over to the men, trying to reason with them. One of the men with guns shot him in the chest, and the preacher fell to the gym floor. Although the sight of so much blood frightened her, Chrissy wisely snatched up her little playmate to protect her

A fearful silence hung over the gym. Those who had witnessed the death of their beloved preacher knew they had no choice but to cooperate or be killed themselves. The kidnappers forced them all to walk outside and line up in two lines. The slavers sized all of them up. Any people who were sick, weak, or disabled were shot in the head. Chrissy hugged the little girl to her chest to keep her quiet, raising her gaze from the ground only once in an attempt to make eye contact with the child's parents for reassurance.

Fifty men, women, and children were loaded

into the back of the semi and locked in muted darkness, the bullet holes in the roof providing an eerie star-like illumination.   Chrissy returned the little girl to her desperate parents, found a place to sit, and began to cry. She missed her mother and her older brother, Timmy. She missed her grandparents most of all. They weren't really her grandparents; they were the parents of her mom's boyfriend. They insisted on being called Grammy and Pappaw. They were the closest thing Chrissy had to loving caretakers.   She tried her hardest not to think about the evil men and what they would do when they opened the door to let them out. She had no idea where she was going or what was going to happen to her.

Chrissy tried her best to wiggle free from the old woman's sweaty embrace without waking her, but it didn't work.

"Angela? What are you doing, dear?"

"My name's Chrissy, ma'am."

"Oh, Angela, don't be silly. You always like to play your little make-believe games. Is something wrong, dear?"

"I just want to stand up and stretch, ma'am."

"Sweetheart, you start calling me Granny. Stop being silly."

"Uh... you're not my grandmother." Chrissy practically whispered it for fear of angering the confused woman.

"Angela, dear, be a good girl and ask your father to pull the van over. I need to use the restroom."

Chrissy finally understood what was going on; the poor old woman had something wrong with her mind. She wasn't sure, but she thought the men with guns had killed all the old people. Chrissy was scared for the lady; if she acted like this in front of slavers, they would surely kill her.

"Granny, Daddy told me earlier that we'll stop at the next gas station. We're in the middle of nowhere, and it will be a long time before we can stop.

"Such a little sweetheart; there's my good girl."

"He wants you to get some sleep. I'll wake you up when we stop."

"Okay, dear. That's probably a good idea."

For the first time since all this madness began, Chrissy began to feel a bit more confident and less fearful. She had a purpose now, something to keep her mind occupied. She had to take care of this woman and make sure she was safe.

As the truck slowed to a stop and the cab door slammed shut, Chrissy's fear returned with a vengeance. Once the engine was silenced, she was blanketed by the frightened mewing of her fellow captives. Angry people could be heard pleading for divine intervention.

"They can't do this! We have to do something!"

"Shut up! You're gonna get us all killed!"

The doors opened and two rounds were fired into the roof of the truck.

"Get the fuck out! NOW!"

"Listen here! You can't do this to us! This isn't right! I demand to…"

Another shot was fired; silence followed.

When will these people figure out that the bad guys will kill them if they don't keep their mouths shut? Chrissy closed her eyes and prayed.

"Anybody else have any fucking demands? Huh? Anyone? No? Good, that's what I thought. Hurry the fuck up and get out!"

The first two people stepped out. Both were grabbed and flung to the ground. "You're not moving fast enough! Hurry up! We don't have all day! Everybody out! Get in a double line, now!"

Chrissy started to panic. She had to come up with something quick to keep the old woman safe. "Granny. Granny! It's time to wake up now. C'mon, let's get going."

"Are we there, dear? I hope your father found a place to eat. I'm very hungry."

"Uh… yeah, we're at a restaurant now.

They want us to line up outside so they can get the tables ready. We need to be quiet and let them figure out where we're gonna sit."

"Okay, Angela, that sounds nice."

Chrissy helped the old woman to her feet, and they shuffled from the truck and stood in line. Everyone was staring at the ground, terrified to speak or move a muscle.

Chrissy held the old woman's hand as they waited quietly on the second row. Chrissy's mind was racing, trying to figure out what she would do if the old woman made a scene. If she couldn't keep her quiet, she wasn't sure if she was brave enough to stick her neck out and run the risk of getting shot.

Chrissy cautiously raised her head and surveyed the scene around her. They had stopped in the biggest parking lot she'd ever seen. There were signs all around. The one that caught her eye said "We Hope You Enjoy Your Stay at the Magic Kingdom." There was another one with a picture of Mickey Mouse on it but she couldn't make out the words.

The bad guys brought us to Disney World?

The group waited in silence for several minutes while the slavers talked with another group of men with guns. Then they just stood there and said nothing; it looked like they were waiting for something to happen. Chrissy began to shake. *Are they going to kill us?*

Chrissy glanced to her right and saw the apparent cause of the delay. An important-looking man was slowly walking toward the group. He shook hands with one of the slavers. The slaver gestured toward the group and the two men started to walk up and down the rows of frightened people. As they made their way down the second row, Chrissy let go of the woman's hand, tears of shame streaming down her grimy face. She didn't know what she would do if the old woman got confused and drew attention to herself. She prayed harder than she ever had before that the old woman would remain quiet. If they shot her, Chrissy would blame herself for the rest of her life. Chrissy heard the two men talking as they approached.

"You should be able to get a lot of work out of them. Plenty of good, healthy men to do some labor; plenty of women to fuck when they're not cleaning."

"Why'd you bring kids? What am I supposed to do with kids?"

"I'm sure you'll find use for them; they'll grow up soon enough. Better to train 'em now so they learn what's expected of them when they get older. You can also *train* them to do other things… if you catch my drift."

"How much you want for the lot of them?"

"I have a list of things in high demand on our routes. We can discuss that over dinner."

"Of course. How many men you got with you?"

"Six."

"Round 'em up and we'll take them to the chow hall. I bet you guys could use some drinks and time to unwind after your long trip."

"Damn straight! Lead the way."

The men were herded toward a building a hundred yards away.

The man in charge walked to the front of the group of slaves he had just agreed to purchase. He said something to two of his men and shook his head. The two men ran forward ten yards, stopped, and raised their arms, pistols in each hand. In a deafening roar of bullets, all six of the evil monsters that Chrissy had feared with every fiber of her being dropped to the ground.

"Ladies and Gentlemen, the Unified American Empire has decided to put an end to the slave trade. I never tolerated it, and I think it's time they did something about it. You're all free men and women. My name is Benjamin Black, and I'd be pleased to have you join our community.

CHAPTER FOUR

Kaliz Mubbarak stopped his pickup truck in the parking lot of an apartment complex in Sausalito, California. He didn't honk the horn or get out of the vehicle. He and his partner sat in silence, waiting for the other two members of their team. Kaliz discreetly scanned the crowded parking lot for any sign of movement and found none in the hushed, shadowy hour before sunrise. A minute later, his teammates exited their apartment and climbed into the back of the oversized cab. No words were spoken for a full ten minutes. They had learned to leave the talking to Kaliz. They didn't even know each other's real names, only the aliases they had adopted to maintain their cover. All four were American citizens. Their families had immigrated to the former United States when they were small children, and they had grown up behind enemy lines. All had attended American schools, played sports, had girlfriends, and voted in local, state, and national elections. Kaliz had even spent two years as an infantryman in the United States Army. They'd spent their entire lives hiding their true nationality and passed themselves off as Spaniards. In their youth, they spent many long hours learning to speak Spanish and had mastered the accent, even their English tainted by a touch of the foreign tongue.

Behind closed doors, however, they diligently practiced their Islamic faith. They prayed to Mecca five times a day, observed Ramadan fervently every year and, most importantly, their parents trained them to join the ranks of The Silent Warriors. All four men were experts with pistols, shotguns, and rifles. One of their favorite childhood pastimes involved competing to see who could reassemble weapons the fastest after their parents took them apart and scrambled the many pieces. Kaliz won every time.

When The Star of Allah brightened the night sky over the Eastern Seaboard, Kaliz and his team were fortunate enough to watch the entire event unfold live on television. They celebrated for the better part of a week as they watched the country crumble into ruins. Kaliz's teammates could barely contain their excitement, eager to execute their plan immediately. They'd spent years preparing for The Day of Judgment and couldn't understand why Kaliz wanted to wait. Kaliz told them that patience was now the only plan. The Star of Allah didn't cripple the West Coast, and they didn't have the luxury of darkness and confusion like their brothers on the other side of the country. They simply needed to alter their agenda. The crippled nation would not be repaired anytime in the near future; if anything, it would only get worse before it got better. Kaliz spent eighteen months crafting his plan to perfection. Every member of his team not only knew his own role, but had memorized the responsibilities of his fellow teammates as well to ensure that every facet of the plan would be carried out should one of them fall.

The day had finally come. The destruction they would unleash would not only further cripple the infrastructure of the country, but it would also deface a national icon, a symbol recognized in every corner of the land. Kaliz's men were not aware of the entire operation; they had no idea they were only one half of the plan. Another cell leader would execute the same scheme from the opposite end of the bridge.

Kaliz's two-year stint in the infantry had been part of this covert operation. He used his military connections to smuggle the equipment he needed for his plan. He managed to steal a dozen grenades, assorted weapons and ammunition, and the grand prize – a case of C-4 plastic explosives. His counterpart on the other team had managed to do the same. Kaliz had manipulated and bribed many people to acquire the items and had even killed two men to do so. He was meticulous in his planning and was never a suspect in any of the thefts or murders.

The truck traveled south down the 101 and waited patiently in line at the checkpoint to the Golden Gate Bridge. With much of the interstate highway system in ruins on the other side of the country, Regional Governor Jimenez closely guarded critical bridges and freeway intersections in his territory. The Golden Gate Bridge had a platoon of soldiers at both ends. Every vehicle was stopped; the driver and occupants required to show identification in order to pass. For the initial six months after The Day of Judgment, every vehicle was thoroughly searched. The process took hours; angry citizens had to add at least two hours to any trip that required transit across the bridge. Kaliz simply bided his time, waiting for complacency to kick in. Slowly but surely, the thorough searches became less and less diligent. Without a single incident on The Golden Gate Bridge in eighteen months, the soldiers began to relax. They saw the same familiar faces day after day and recognized the same cars traversing the bridge. Kaliz's only purpose for driving back and forth across the bridge every day was to bolster his position as a regular to the soldiers guarding the bridge. At first, his truck was searched five days a week, both coming and going. As the months passed, five days became four, then three until it become once a week, if ever. Kaliz became so familiar with the guards that when he pulled up to the checkpoint, he would roll down his window with his driver's license in hand and the soldiers would simply wave him through without even stopping him.

Today was a day like any other. He pulled up to the checkpoint and produced his driver's license. The young soldier waved him through and Kaliz drove on. When he was two car lengths past the checkpoint, he stopped the truck and got out. His partner in the front seat exited with him.

"Marco! What are you doing? Keep it moving man! C'mon!" The young soldier was visibly frustrated by the delay.

"So sorry, Private Morris, the engine died on me," said Kaliz in his polished Spanish accent.

"Try to get it in the other lane quickly. I gotta keep the line moving."

"Yes, of course. So sorry about this."

Kaliz glanced into the back seat and waved his men out of the truck. His team members stood at the back of the truck, pushing as Kaliz steered the vehicle. Once the truck was blocking all the lanes, Kaliz put the vehicle in park and unzipped his jacket so he could quickly access his tactical vest. The others retrieved their bags from the truck bed and did the same.

"Marco! What the hell, man? Rush hour's coming and I don't need this shit!"

Kaliz and his team took their time getting ready. Nothing about their movements aroused suspicion, only frustrated confusion from the soldiers at the check point. Once his team members stopped and made eye contact with him to signal their readiness, Kaliz nodded his head and the attack began.

Each man dropped the spoon on his grenade and lobbed it toward the checkpoint. While the grenades were in flight, the four men produced automatic rifles and began to fire. Each team member had a designated target. The first shot the tires out of the four vehicles immediately behind their truck. The second opened fire on the vehicles in the oncoming lanes of traffic and stopped them dead in their tracks, then lobbed a grenade toward the disabled vehicles. The third and fourth men took careful aim at every soldier in their line of sight and shot them dead as the grenades exploded, crippling cars and killing dozens of terrified motorists.

With the first stage of his plan executed to perfection, Kaliz proceeded to phase two. Two of his men took up position in front of the truck and tossed smoke grenades towards the checkpoint, blinding the confused and wounded soldiers and preventing a counterattack. As clouds of white smoke shrouded the scene, the two men lobbed grenade after grenade at the checkpoint. Cars exploded and mangled body parts flew in all directions. Any soldier managing to escape the heavy veil of acrid smoke in an attempt to advance was immediately gunned down in a hail of bullets.

Kaliz and his partner sprinted to the center of the bridge. Every few hundred yards, Kaliz reached into his vest and tossed a brick of C-4 to the pavement. He knew the team on the other end of the bridge had carried out their portion of the plan successfully; not a single car came toward them in the oncoming lanes. A few minutes later, Kaliz heard the rat-a-tat of automatic gunfire coming from his brothers on the other team. Once Kaliz was reunited with his counterparts, the final stage of his plan could be carried out.

"Did you set your charges, my brother?"

"I did."

"Good! Praise be to Allah for watching over us."

"Allahu Akbar."

Kaliz reached into his vest, took out the remaining two charges and tossed them at his feet. The four men gazed at each other, smiles illuminating their faces. They did not fear death because they knew in their hearts that Allah would reward them in the afterlife. Kaliz flipped the cover on the detonator and pressed the button.

The Golden Gate Bridge was rocked by twenty-four massive explosions, sending large sections of concrete and steel raining down into the murky water below. The West Coast had just suffered its first major attack from The Silent Warriors.

***

Lance McGee stood in line at the front gate of Fort McClellan, Alabama, waiting to be processed into the refugee camp. He was shivering, not because he was cold, but because he was terrified. Had the weather been a bit warmer, the people standing around Lance would have known immediately that something was wrong with him because he could not stop trembling. If not for the incessant rain, the tired, hungry citizens standing in line might have noticed the pungent urine stain covering the front of his jeans. Lance's bloodshot gaze remained fixed at his dirty feet for fear that someone might look into his eyes and know something was horribly wrong.

For the next hour, Lance crept forward in line, getting closer to the front gate of the decommissioned army installation. Fort McClellan was once the largest military base in the country and

one of the most famous. It housed the Women's
Army Corp that trained the very first women to be
soldiers during World War II. Fort McClellan also
housed the training camps for the Military Police
Corps and the Chemical Corps. In 1999, it was
decommissioned by the United States Army and
became home to the Center For Domestic
Preparedness run by the Department of Homeland
Security. Residents from all over The Pulse Zone
desperately scrambled to get to Fort McClellan.
They all wanted one thing—security. In the eighteen
months since the collapse, the Unified American
Empire fought to restore law and order to keep the
population safe. Refugee camps erected across The
Pulse Zone simply couldn't handle the strain of food
riots, gang violence, and the countless waves of
people terrified of the slave trade.

Fort McClellan became a beacon of hope.
The installation sat roughly fifty miles to the south of
the southern boundary of The Pulse Zone. The
electromagnetic pulse that plunged the Eastern
Seaboard into darkness had no effect on Fort
McClellan. The power grid had been knocked out
but was easily repaired. President Simon Sterling
knew the significance of the installation, and given
its close proximity to Atlanta, it was the obvious
choice to be the headquarters of the Unified
American Empire's military forces on the East

Coast. Because of its importance, Fort McClellan enjoyed a limitless supply of resources, thanks in large part to the ongoing pillaging of the unaffected oasis that was California.

As Lance got closer to the checkpoint, it took every bit of concentration he had to keep from passing out. The lives of his wife and children were at stake; he had to do this for them. He had no doubt about the consequences of failure. If he botched this, they would be raped and murdered. He had no other options.

As the smartphone in his pocket began to vibrate, Lance let out an involuntary shriek and his shaking escalated, alarming those waiting nearby.

"Sir, are you okay?"

"Do you need help?"

"What's wrong?"

"Uh… n-n-nothing. I'm sorry. J-j-just have a splitting headache." Lance tried his best to smile at the people around him, but it didn't lessen their alarm.

"Should we get a doctor? Honey, walk up to the front of the line and tell..."

"No! I said I was fine! Don't do that!" Lance knew he needed to get a grip. He was drawing unwanted attention to himself when he could least afford to do so. "I'm sorry, I didn't mean to yell. Please forgive me. It's just so cold and my feet hurt."

Lance turned his back on the meddlesome couple, hoping they wouldn't cause a scene. As his phone continued to vibrate, Lance reached up to tap the Bluetooth device in his ear. Unable to utter a single word, Lance coughed, hoping that would be enough.

"Good, good, good. Mr. McGee, I'm so glad you're still with us. I don't really expect you to answer me, given that someone talking on a phone these days would definitely attract attention. We wouldn't want to do that, now would we?"

Just the sound of the man's voice sent Lance over the edge, gasping for air. His eerie, composed politeness brought forth images that were anything but tranquil, images of torture—not just his own, but the torture of his children as well.

"Now, now, Mr. McGee. We can't have you carrying on like this when we're so close to being finished. Do calm down, sir. Please."

Lance knew he had to get a grip – and fast!

"That's much better, Mr. McGee. I really do wish we could have one of our pleasant talks, but I guess we'll have to settle for a boring, one-sided conversation. Kind of funny, don't you think? For decades every man, woman, and child walked around talking on a phone, fiddling their little fingers around on a mobile gadget doing all manner of silly things. It wasn't long ago that you would be positively out of place if you didn't have some sort of do-hickey in your hand. Oh, how the tables have turned! If you pulled that phone out of your pocket right this second, I bet people around you would start screaming and running from you like you were an alien with a ray gun. Anyway, I've gotten quite far from the topic at hand, haven't I? You're still with me aren't you, Mr. McGee? Give me a little cough so we can get this party started."

Lance cleared his throat angrily

"Excellent! That little phone in your pocket is telling me you're about twenty yards from the front gate. I just wanted to chat with you in case you were having some crazy thoughts about backing out on me and doing something foolish like trying to get help. It occurred to me a few minutes ago that you might think I won't keep my end of the bargain, that no matter what you do your family will die either way, so why cooperate? That sound about right? Go on now; give us another one of your angry coughs."

Lance's face was awash in tears as he obeyed.

"Fantastic! I have your lovely wife here ready to talk to you one last time. Don't you worry now; she knows you won't actually be doing any talking. You be extra careful not to get caught up in the moment and draw attention to yourself. Are we clear?"

This time Lance could only manage a sob, his signal of recognition tangled in his throat.

"Okay now, here she is. And Lance? Remember, your family's lives are riding on your performance."

Lance closed his eyes and concentrated as hard as he could to control himself.

A few seconds later, his wife's sweet voice filled his ear. Lance was so proud that Sheila sounded completely calm.

"Lance, my darling, me and the kids are okay. They actually brought us back home! I'm sitting in the living room, and the kids are in their beds. You just have to do what they want and they'll leave. I really, really think they're gonna go. Please darling, be brave for me and think of the children. We'll be safe, I promise. I love you so..."

"Mr. McGee, wasn't that just lovely? Your wife is an exceptional woman indeed. Now then, I trust you have the proper motivation to proceed? No need to respond, Mr. McGee. I know you and I are on the same page. Oh my! Looking at my little screen here I see that you're almost at the front gate! How positively exciting! I'm going to stay on the line all the way to the end to ensure that we won't need to pursue certain ... *liberties* with your dear wife. And one last thing, Mr. McGee. I really do hate to even bring this up, such nasty business, but

my two associates are *very* fond of your lovely
daughter. You must be so proud that she made
varsity cheerleader before the country just went to
pot. She has been entertaining us with some very
enthusiastic cheer routines. She wasn't really into it
at first, I'm afraid to say, but after I asked her if
she'd rather my associates, uh... occupy their time
with her little brother, she just beamed a big smile
with every cheer! A real treat indeed! Anyway, you
just make sure you hold up your end of the deal, and
you have my solemn word that my associates will
focus their attention elsewhere. Mr. McGee, it has
been a real pleasure working with you. I thank you
kindly for your time. Good luck to you, sir. I know
you'll do what needs to be done."

Lance felt a strange sense of relief wash over
him. The hell he had endured for the previous four
days was finally ending. In a few short minutes, he
would leave this world for a much better one. He
would be reunited with his father and his younger
brother.

Just past the front gate was a large
gymnasium that had been repurposed as an
orientation center. Lance watched as a Middle
Eastern family was taken at gunpoint from the front
of the line to a holding area. He looked into the
holding pen and saw naked men and women
shivering in the cold while their clothes and

belongings were searched. Dignity had been replaced by stark racism, and Lance couldn't help but feel a sick sense of irony at his current predicament. He stepped into the doorway and turned around. Lifting his arms, Lance squeezed both fists, launching two projectiles from the tube rockets strapped to his forearms. Not concerned with their trajectories, Lance pushed his way to the center of the gymnasium and ripped open his coat, detonating the forty pound vest that hugged his torso.

The two guided projectiles found their targets. The first missile burst through a window on the top floor of the headquarters building and detonated, killing Brigadier General Matthew Jacobs, commanding general of Fort McClellan, along with most of his senior staff. The second rocket smashed into the front lobby of the base hospital, bringing the second floor crashing down into the first, killing hundreds of innocent patients.

When Lance's vest detonated, a high powered explosive many times more potent than C-4, vaporized his body along with every living thing inside the gymnasium. The structure that had once promised frightened, weary refugees the possibility of a new life came crashing down. Since most of the deceased had not yet been processed into the system, no one would ever know that three hundred nineteen innocent people had just been murdered.

The polite man on the other end of the phone told his two associates that he was going out to the car for a quick smoke. He walked to the end of the driveway and opened the driver's-side door. With great anticipation, he lit his cigarette, took a long, satisfying drag and slowly exhaled. Once the nicotine rush hit him, he reached into his coat pocket and produced a small device. Carefully typing in the requisite five digits, the man hit the enter key and watched, smiling, as the McGee residence erupted in an explosion that rocked the neighborhood. Car alarms wailed, dogs barked. The polite man always tied up loose ends, and he certainly wasn't looking to take the blame when The Silent Warriors would be more than happy to take credit for his actions.

CHAPTER FIVE

"Are you sure it's time to make such a bold move, Richard?" Howard Beck knew the day was coming, but he never envisioned it would be so soon.

"We have a lot of preparation to deal with before we're ready to move forward, but it's time to set things in motion. What do you think, Max?"

"I'm nice and comfy with things the way they are, but we have to move at some point and it might as well be now. My only concern is maintaining the resources we have to secure our own borders."

"You don't think Hal can manage it?" asked Howard.

"I have no doubt that Hal can keep the drones busy, but can he repel thousands of troops if they move on our borders? Even worse, what if Sterling decides to wipe us off the map with nukes? What does Stacy think?"

Howard was quick to answer. "Our top spy tells us that Sterling wants the nation intact. He's confident that once he fully restores power to The Pulse Zone and squashes The Silent Warriors, he'll have little trouble conquering our quaint little nation, as he calls it."

"All the more reason for us to strike a serious blow to that smug asshole while he's weak," said

Richard.

Howard agreed.

"How in the hell does he think he's going to stop The Silent Warriors? Terrorists don't exactly walk around in uniform and engage the enemy in direct combat," said Max.

"Stacy isn't sure exactly what his plan is, but she did say he seems quite confident that he can pull it off," said Howard.

"Hal, how many attacks have occurred outside The Pulse Zone?" Richard knew his plan would prove difficult if they had to reallocate manpower to deal with terrorist attacks.

"Only minor incidents, sir. From the intelligence I have gathered, The Silent Warriors have attacked two hospitals—one in Nevada and the other in California. Both attacks were quickly repelled with only minor damage. Several fires spread across California have managed to destroy seven residential areas; however, the possibility remains that The Silent Warriors were not responsible for four of the fires."

"Let's hope it stays that way," said Howard.

"Or they're kind enough to stay out of the PSA," Richard said.

Max tapped Richard's chair with his cane. "Okay, Richard, the suspense is killing me. How the hell are we going to invade California with the UAE wiping out anything that crosses into the no-man's land around our borders?"

"Hal and I have been monitoring every engagement in the no-man's land since the UAE instituted the hundred mile zone around the length of our borders. The UAE only makes a move if any of their civilians try to cross over into our territory."

Howard shook his head. "Wait a minute. Just because they're stopping everything going *into* the PSA doesn't mean they won't attack what comes *out* of the PSA. We don't exactly have an abundance of stealth jets like the one you fly around in."

"I realize that, Howard. The one thing they aren't monitoring is the Pacific. The bulk of their navy is in the Atlantic defending our borders from the invasion Iran is no doubt planning once they've finished conquering Europe. The safe bet is that Iran will come onto our shores on the Atlantic side and spill into The Pulse Zone where resistance will be the weakest. Their navy is twice the strength of ours; it will only be a matter of time before they break the line and make it to our shores."

Max cracked a smile for the first time since the conversation began. "You want to invade California by sea? You realize we don't exactly have an impressive armada?"

"I want boots on the ground, that's all. It'll be a short trip. Their radar station and drone base in

California is located in Redding. The radar coverage extends a hundred miles into the Pacific, and they haven't set up any blockades."

Howard interrupted. "Jimenez has managed to keep trade routes open, but pretty soon he won't be able to export anything for trade. China has already been kind enough to send humanitarian aid, which doesn't really say a lot about their confidence in us."

"How the mighty have fallen," said Max. "The arrogant nation begging for handouts."

Richard let the sting of the pointed remark hang in the air a few seconds longer and continued. "The biggest advantage we have going for us is that Hal has managed to disrupt the UAE's satellite coverage of the North American continent. They can put radar planes in the air, but that's about it. Sterling deliberately keeps his planes from getting too close to the PSA for fear of sparking a war. We can load up our troops on cruise ships without them having a clue."

"Why not just send a stealth jet and take out the base in Redding?" Max asked. "We could send our troops pouring in by land."

"That was my first plan but I'd rather catch them off guard. We send three cruise ships down the coast and set up a three-pronged attack. Before Jimenez even realizes what's happening, we'd be hitting them hard from north, south, and center."

"Do we have the manpower to pull it off?" Howard was starting to like this idea.

"I'm confident that we do. Eight months ago I thought about instituting a draft of all eighteen- to twenty-four- year-olds, but it wasn't necessary. Once I announced the call to military service, men and women of all ages stepped up to the plate. We actually had to turn away people who didn't qualify medically. Most of them insisted on doing something to help, so we put them to work behind a desk."

"How many made it through basic training? What's our total fighting force?" asked Max.

"When you factor in the guardsmen and current active duty from the old army, just shy of four hundred thousand, but that's not all when you take into account the sympathizers in the UAE."

Howard was *really* starting to like this plan. "What's the estimate on that?"

"It's hard to gauge, really. Before the UAE locked down our borders, we had waves of people fleeing into our territory. Max and his people managed to interview the majority of them. I'll let Max fill you in."

"I wish I could give accurate numbers, but Richard's right. The vast majority of people who fled into our territory spoke longingly of their family and friends and about their hatred for the UAE. They begged their loved ones to make the journey to the PSA, but they all had too much to lose. Some feared death or didn't want to risk the lives of their families. Others were too complacent, not willing to leave the security of their homes. The idea of becoming a refugee in our territory didn't appeal to some, so they stayed put."

Howard stared at the wall, his brilliant mind was racing. "I wouldn't factor sympathizers into any plan you're making, Richard, at least not until we invade California and can make an assessment of how large the resistance will be."

"That was my plan as well. If half of what we're hearing is true, all the sympathizers need is a fighting force to rally around. I plan to give them one."

"How long before the invasion?" asked Max.

"We've secured two cruise ships, and they'll be loaded up with troops and supplies within a week. The third one is turning out to be a problem."

"Why? Is she not seaworthy?" asked Howard.

"She's seaworthy. The problem we're having is the five hundred people who have taken up residence onboard. They're refusing to leave until we can find them a place to live."

"You're shitting me," said Howard.

"I wish I were. They're living in luxury compared to most. We've tried relocating them, but they disapprove of the new accommodations."

"What about Senator Wilson? Is he able to do anything?" asked Max.

Richard rolled his eyes and chuckled. "The good senator is on their side. He firmly believes the military has no right to forcibly relocate citizens."

"I don't give two shits what Senator Wilson thinks. These aren't fucking Native Americans being moved to a reservation! Much more is at stake than some spoiled crybabies living on a luxury liner. If you can relocate them to adequate shelter, do it. Do it by force if necessary."

Richard and Max exchanged surprised glances as Richard turned to Howard. "I must admit, Howard, I'm shocked to hear you say that. The political fallout is going to be enormous."

"I know. Let me be the bad guy. It'll give me and Senator Wilson something to talk about next week."

"Careful, Howard. You start using the military to strong-arm the population, and people might think you're the next Simon Sterling," said Max.

Howard snapped. When he got angry, there was no gradual ascent into rage; it was as if an internal switch was flipped in Howard's mind.

"How dare you! After all I've done and all the suffering I've endured at the hands of that madman! He killed my best friend and stole my house! You have the nerve to compare me to a dictator, a mass murderer!" Howard's face reddened, the veins in his forehead pulsating to the rhythm of his pounding heart.

Max was completely shocked; he had never seen Howard so angry. His first instinct was to become defensive and blame Howard for overreacting. Once he saw how deeply he had wounded the man, he changed his mind. "Howard, very poor choice of words. I'm deeply sorry. I was only trying to advise caution. I understand your line of thinking, but the people do have rights; this could potentially escalate into a major problem. If even one soldier harms a single person on that boat, you could have a riot on your hands."

"What would you have me do? Renovate a Hilton for these people and give them room service? You have a better option, I'd love to hear it."

"Howard, you should only use force once you've exhausted every conceivable option. If you told them the reason, explained what's at stake, I think they'd go willingly. You're going to Seattle anyway. It's worth shot."

Howard and Richard exchanged knowing glances. Howard looked back at Max with a wicked grin. "Looks like you just volunteered to go with me. Feel free to bring your lovely wife."

Max massaged his aching knee. He wanted to get some fresh air and see the sun, but this wasn't what he had in mind. "Son of a bitch."

CHAPTER SIX

Regional Governor Roberto Jimenez was furious. In his time governing the former states of California, Nevada, New Mexico, and Arizona, he had never been the victim of a major attack from The Silent Warriors. Keeping his region secure was his primary focus. While other regional governors concentrated on rebuilding the infrastructure or maintaining law and order, he thought only of security. The Pulse had not affected his region, so there was no real need to focus on a broken infrastructure. He honestly didn't care if the people in his region robbed each other blind or murdered each other. As long as The Silent Warriors didn't give him a black eye in front of the other regional governors and, more importantly, the president, he was happy.

The destruction of the Golden Gate Bridge left him with a gaping wound, visible to the entire country. He was certain to be the object of scorn, ridiculed by all the regional governors as well as President Sterling. Roberto was not looking forward to speaking with the president and had been putting it off for as long as possible. His first two attempts at keeping the president at bay were successful; he simply instructed his assistant to tell the president he was hard at work getting to the bottom of the disaster and would contact him soon. The time for stalling was over; he had no choice but to report to President Sterling.

Roberto was not a young man nor was he in good health. The seventy-four-year-old had been confined to a wheelchair for many years as a result of his battle with multiple sclerosis. He had little doubt as to why President Sterling had assigned him to this region. It was the most stable and provided little daily stress. It was the right call because hearing the news of the attack nearly sent him into cardiac arrest. Once he calmed down, Roberto summoned the commanding officer of the San Francisco militia and shot the man right there in his office. The corpse was hauled out, and terrified maids spent the morning cleaning the pool of blood from the threadbare carpet in front of his desk. The grouchy bastard grunted and waved the maids from the room. They were more than happy to oblige. With a few quick keystrokes, the holographic display before him sprang to life. Seconds later, the President of the Unified American Empire was glaring at him.

"Explain yourself, Mr. Jimenez."

"Mr. President, our investigation is still ongoing."

"Do not stall me any further, Roberto. In the

future, when I attempt to contact you, do not use your assistant to dismiss me. You forget your place, my good man. I am in charge of this empire and you serve at my pleasure. If you ever disrespect me in such a manner again, the outcome will not be pleasant, I assure you."

"Mr. President, I didn't feel it necessary to waste your time until I had something solid to report."

"You waste my time, Mr. Jimenez, when my repeated attempts to contact you go unanswered. Tell me what you know."

"Yes, Mr. President. We know the identities of the men involved. All are American citizens; their parents, however, hail from countries in The Great Empire of Iran."

"Are their parents American citizens?"

"Most of them, yes, Mr. President. They were granted American citizenship in the late 90s. They managed to cleverly mask their heritage and passed themselves off as Spanish."

"Have you located them?"

"Their parents? No, Mr. President, we haven't made it a priority."

"Make it a priority. I have no doubt their parents were complicit in their training. Once you've located them, execute them…" President Sterling's lips curled in a sinister grin. "…publicly.

Give your citizens some semblance of justice."

"Yes, Mr. President. I'm sending the order now." The command was issued with a few hasty keystrokes.

"Tell me about the attack."

"We've been able to trace the vehicles back to two men we believe to be the ringleaders, both veterans of the United States Army. It would explain how they managed to get their hands on the ordinance they used. The Golden Gate Bridge suffered catastrophic damage. The framework remains intact, but the road spanning the bridge was ruined beyond repair. It will take years before a vehicle can cross it."

"Roberto, I want you to be frank with me. What measures could have been taken to prevent this? If The Silent Warriors are bold enough to start attacking targets in our most secure region, we need to do whatever we can to prevent it from happening again."

"That's just the problem, Mr. President. My region may not have been struck by The Pulse, but that doesn't mean we're the most secure region. Just because we have electricity, running water, and a stable infrastructure doesn't change the fact that our resources are being slowly stripped down to nothing."

"Elaborate, please."

"I fully understand that The Pulse Zone is in desperate need of every available resource we can give them: fuel, spare parts, food, water, working vehicles, medical supplies. I have no objection to that. We're living in the lap of luxury compared to the East Coast. The problem I have is that more and more of my troops are being redeployed to The Pulse Zone. I'm working with a skeleton crew that barely manages to secure checkpoints and vital areas. I don't have the manpower to maintain law and order, and I damn sure don't have enough soldiers to conduct investigations and round up suspected terrorist cells."

"Did you not think it prudent to bring this to my attention earlier, Mr. Jimenez?"

"To be blunt, Mr. President, I have. You instructed me to work out my problems with Regional Governor Butler. You basically gave the man free reign to do whatever it takes to get The Pulse Zone back up and running. Jackson is an arrogant little turd that wouldn't budge on a damn thing. He thinks his region is the only one that matters. He told me my region can go to shit for all he cares."

"Jackson said that?"

"His exact words, Mr. President. He's cocky and dangerous, in my opinion. I strongly believe he's stockpiling resources and manpower for the day when The Pulse Zone is fully functional. He wants to come out on top. I'm certain he's planning something."

"A bold accusation, Roberto. What do you think he's planning?"

"I'm not sure, but what I do know is that many of the resources I've sent him aren't being utilized. He keeps asking for more, and when I refuse his requests until he can provide documentation for what he's done with my previous shipments, he goes behind my back and lies to you. Your office sends me direct orders to un-ass my goods. I don't like it all."

"How long has he been doing this?"

"Six months at least."

"Again, Roberto, why not tell me?"

"With respect, Mr. President, he's your golden boy, and I don't want to make enemies out of either of you."

"Well, Roberto, I will admit that I've made his region a priority over yours for obvious reasons, and it seems we've all suffered for it. Losing the Golden Gate Bridge is a huge blow. My mistake was thinking The Silent Warriors wouldn't be so bold to attack us out in the open. The darkness and chaos of The Pulse Zone seems to be the perfect breeding ground for those cowards. I'm going to get to the bottom of this; I can assure you that this concerns me a great deal. I feel I may have given Jackson Butler too long a leash, and now it's time to rein him in a bit."

"Whatever I can do to help, Mr. President, just let me know."

"Thank you, Roberto. Now I'm afraid I must change the subject and impart some bad news."

"I've had plenty today, Mr. President. I doubt a little more will faze me."

"I'm sure everything you've been dealing with today has kept you quite preoccupied. My earlier attempts to contact you were not just to inquire about the attack. I regret to inform you that Regional Governor Weygandt was killed this morning."

Roberto was speechless. Jim Weygandt had been his friend for over twenty years. When Roberto was the director of the CIA, he relied on Jim to provide him with the resources to carry out covert ops around the globe. "How?"

"He was rear-ended by another vehicle, and his car was sent over a bridge. Everyone is in complete shock over this terrible tragedy. I'll be forever grateful for his role in building the Unified American Empire. He will be missed."

"When's the funeral?"

"Soon. I'll send you the details. I'm truly sorry for your loss, Roberto. I know the two of you were very close."

"Thank you, Mr. President. Is there anything else?"

"No, Roberto, I'll see you at the funeral."

CHAPTER SEVEN

Benjamin Black sat in his office overlooking Disney World's Main Street USA. He enjoyed the quiet solitude of his office because he could deliberate over the day-to- day operations of his territory. The theme parks and resorts under his control covered forty-seven square miles with a population closing in on six thousand. Ben controlled a paradise in the middle of the Florida wasteland. Eighteen months prior, Hurricane Luther had destroyed much of Florida during the most powerful hurricane the world had ever seen. The category five storm came ashore not once, but four times, each time a little stronger than the last. With the collapse of the American government, the state of Florida found itself in the same shape it had been following Luther's brutal punishment.

Walt Disney World, with all her theme parks and resorts, was not spared by Luther. Most of the rides were destroyed, and the majority of the buildings were uninhabitable. Ben wasn't worried about any of that; what drew Ben to the Magic Kingdom was the security it offered. The theme parks had a perimeter fence around them and Ben saw the advantage. His oasis in the wasteland attracted the hungry and the frightened. The stability

Ben offered brought fierce loyalty. He was considered a savior; his people loved him like a father figure. He was doing a fine job running his community, and the UAE saw fit to leave him to it. They sent a weekly patrol to his front gate to trade intelligence and inform Ben of new laws enacted by President Sterling. These so-called laws were nothing more than President Sterling stripping away civil rights.

While the citizens of Walt Disney World deified Benjamin Black, they had no idea that his primary mission in life had nothing to do with their care, but rather with the destruction of the Unified American Empire—piece by piece if necessary. When the UAE showed up on his doorstep looking for persons of interest, he ushered them in and gave the appearance of cooperation while his trusted freedom fighters subverted the UAE's tyrannical efforts. Ben sent out guerrilla units to raid small UAE camps and ambush convoys. He even managed to nurture a network of spies that fed him valuable intelligence.

Ben had spent all morning dealing with the incident involving the slave traders. Their bodies had been buried and their weapons and ammo found a proper home in the armory. The eighteen-wheeler was a welcome addition to the motor pool. The former slaves were still undergoing thorough examinations in the infirmary. None of them had serious injuries, though a few were severely malnourished and a handful had dysentery. Ben's most challenging problem, however, involved one of the children. The girl's name was Chrissy Dupree, and she had no one to care for her. An elderly woman with dementia thought the girl was her granddaughter, but Chrissy eventually told Ben the truth about the situation. The woman would have to live in the infirmary full time, and Ben would have to find a family willing to take care of the girl.

Ben reached for the radio on his desk. "Jessica, what's your location?"

After a few seconds, the radio crackled. "I'm at the Wilderness Lodge doing a security check."

"Lunch?"

"Sure, I'm starving. I'll head over now."

Fifteen minutes later, Ben's top lieutenant was in his office. The two spread their meager brown-bag meals on a table littered with stacks of paper and a large map of Florida. The map was the focus of their meeting.

"I just got this last night. Take a look at it," Ben said as he handed Jessica a thick manila envelope. As Jessica was reading the report, Ben elaborated. "The latest scout team found a major food distribution center south of Miami, right here." Ben pointed to the map. "For the most part, it hasn't been touched; it appears that a few scavengers have picked it over, but the bulk of it is still there."

"When do we leave?"

"It's not that simple," Ben said. "The UAE has a large base set up less than ten miles away. If they catch us emptying out the warehouse, they'll no doubt stop us and confiscate all of it."

"Fuck the UAE. We're more powerful than they are." Jessica had been with Ben since the beginning. When Hurricane Luther roared into town, Jessica found herself at Ben's Jiffy Lube and rode out the storm in the pits beneath the garage. Ben liked her because she was smart and charismatic enough to convince people to do just about anything she asked. She also had the best bullshit detector Ben had ever seen. What Ben valued most about her was that she wouldn't hesitate to shoot someone between the eyes if she thought for one second they meant her harm.

"Slow down and think. Yes, we are more powerful on a local level. Regional Governor Prince cries for help and Sterling can triple her force in under a week. They could wipe us out. Do I need to remind you of what we're doing here? Much more is at stake than a warehouse full of food."

"You're not seriously thinking about forgetting this place? It could increase our food stores for months! And don't you dare lecture me about what we're doing here! You sit up here in your comfy office blowing Mickey Mouse while the rest of us are out there getting our hands dirty and seeing the most horrible things." Jessica closed her eyes and took a deep breath. "I'm sorry. I didn't mean that. It's just that food is going to run out at some point, and I have no idea what magic rabbit you're gonna pull out of your ass when that happens."

"I ever tell you about my great-grandfather?"

Jessica was surprised by the question. She relaxed a little and prepared herself for one of Ben's infamous stories. "No, don't think you have."

"He was a World War II vet, drafted in 1944. He was thirty-two or thirty-three when he went overseas. He volunteered for the draft, but they told him he was too old. Well, by the third year of the war, the army wasn't as picky, so off he went. My great-grandmother was pregnant with my grandfather when he left and when he came back eighteen months later, he met my grandfather for the first time. They went on to raise eight children."

"Dear Lord, eight children? Are you kidding? Nobody told him what was causing that little problem?"

Ben winked. "Eight kids! I think they knew how to make 'em."

"Ben, as much as I love your stories, does

this one have a point?"

"Before The Pulse, could you imagine raising eight children? Even four?"

"Hell, no. I couldn't imagine affording one kid."

"Exactly. When I thought about having a kid with my ex-wife, I couldn't stop thinking about my grandfather having seven brothers and sisters. I asked him about it and you know what he told me?"

"The eight of them sang and danced on TV like The Jefferson Five?"

"Jackson Five, and no, they weren't in a band."

"They were filthy rich?"

"No, they were self-sustaining."

"What does that mean?"

"It means they had a garden the size of half a football field and grew tomatoes, green beans, carrots, potatoes, onions, and other things they could eat. It means they had a chicken coop and a hog pen. It means they had two or three cows for milk or to butcher for meat. They even grew pecan trees in the yard. My grandfather and his brothers would hunt squirrels and rabbits with slingshots and BB guns. They took care of themselves. They didn't depend on a grocery store or go to a Wal-Mart like the one we took when all this bullshit started."

"I understand what you're saying, but given

what's at stake, are you really willing to give up that much food? I know we're gonna have to live off the land at some point, but if we can put it off for as long as possible, I mean it just..."

"We can discuss that another day. For now, I want you to scout out the place. The recon team drew up a map and gave us some basic intel. I'm going to trust your judgment on this and let you deal with the UAE base. If you think you can pull it off, give 'em some good old-fashioned sabotage like we've done before – disable their vehicles, cut off communication, create diversions. You know the drill."

Jessica rolled her eyes. "Uh, yeah. I've done this before, thanks."

Ben smiled. "Have you? I thought you came here for a vacation."

"Shut up! I heard about the slavers this morning. Damn, I wish I could've been there! Been a while since a group of them came to visit."

"It was a pleasure wasting those pieces of shit. You hear what the UAE is doing about it?"

"Something other than playing dumb while slaves rebuild The Pulse Zone?"

Ben shuffled some papers and found the one he was looking for. "Our friends in the Unified American Empire have declared that, uh, here it is ... 'slavery is an atrocity that must be stopped at all costs. Anyone involved in the slave trade will be summarily executed.'"

"I don't get it. Why do they give a shit about it now?"

"I have no idea. It doesn't make a difference around here. Just means the UAE will be doing what we've been doing about slavery all along."

"Speaking of the UAE, isn't Captain Brown due for his weekly visit?"

"He should be here any minute."

***

"You want to run that by me again?" Ben was not pleased. He didn't know what to make of the UAE captain's statement. Was it a deliberate act of aggression? Were they on to him?

"Ben, don't worry, this has nothing to do with you or your people. My orders are to set up a temporary base of operations here in your parking lot for the next seven days. We'll be sending out patrols and setting up roadblocks. All southbound traffic will be stopped. I have two teams to the east and west of us doing the same thing."

"Why? What's going on?"

"Sorry, Ben, that's classified."

"Not good enough, Captain. At least tell me if my people are in danger. Do we need to prepare for something?"

Captain Brown thought for a few seconds and replied. "No, you and your people are safe. You have my word."

"Okay, but this better not be some lame-ass attempt to overthrow us and take our territory."

"Ben, please. You're being paranoid. The UAE has no quarrel with you. You take good care of these people and that means we don't have to. Relax. Anything else to report?"

"Another group of slavers showed up this morning."

"You disposed of them?"

"Always do."

"I'm sure you heard about the new directive."

"I did."

"Good. When you get time, I'm going to need you to file a report detailing your past contact with the slavers and get information on the liberated slaves you have here. I'm sure command will be very happy with you."

Ben tried to act like he cared. "You boys need anything?"

"Well, we're set up on supplies. The one thing we don't have is booze."

"I'll see what I can do."

Captain Brown shook Ben's hand and returned to his men.

Jessica wasn't buying it. "You're not seriously going to just roll over and take this bullshit, are you? What about all that food just sitting in the warehouse?"

"Jessica, you should know me better than that. You and your team will leave ahead of schedule; I want you on the road before dawn."

"What do you want us to do?"

"I want that warehouse, but more than that, I want to know why the hell the UAE has half the state on lockdown. Something's going on, and I want to know what it is.

CHAPTER EIGHT

General Richard Dupree had debated for months whether or not to tell his fourteen-year-old son what had happened to his sister. Timothy Dupree had been operating under the assumption that Chrissy was staying with her mother. Quite frankly, Richard didn't know his son well enough to determine if he could handle the truth. Richard had spent most of his children's lives behind bars, and he was still getting adjusted to being a father. His son had suffered the trauma of a lifetime, thanks largely in part to him. When Richard was reunited with his son, he was overjoyed to learn that Timmy's youthful mind had blocked out all memory of that fateful morning. The events that had unfolded in the church nursery—the pedophile who abused him and his father's role in the pervert's demise—had been tucked neatly away somewhere in the deepest recesses of Timmy's ripening brain. With Richard back in his son's life, however, those lurid mental footnotes were beginning to resurface.

Richard kept telling himself that the time would come when Timmy would be able to cope with the news about his sister. Weeks turned into months, but with the good news Hal had shared with him this morning, Richard new today was the day.

Richard had just finished preparing lunch when his son returned from school.

"Dad! So glad you're back! I missed you!" The strength of his son's embrace brought tears of joy to Richard's eyes.

"I missed you, too! I hope you were good for your grandparents." Richard made a mental note to thank his children's surrogate grandparents for their help.

"I was! Grandpa and I watched all the *Star Wars* movies. Uncle Howard says the *Star Trek* movies are much better. He says I'd like them and should watch them soon."

"*Star Wars* is much better. *Star Trek* has some good movies, too; I think you'd like them."

"Cool. Wanna watch 'em with me?"

"I'd love to, buddy, but uh… I…"

Timmy pouted. "You're leaving again? But you just got here!"

"I'm not leaving till next week. We can knock out a few of them before then. Son, I need to have a talk with you. Sit down and eat your lunch."

"Am I in trouble?"

"No, silly, should you be? We need to talk about your sister."

"Is she finally coming home? When can I see Mom?"

"That's just it; it's time you knew the whole

story. With everything that's been going on since we got here, your grandfather and I didn't think you could handle the truth. You've gotten a lot better in the past few months, so I think you're ready to hear it."

"Know what? What's going on?"

"The truth is, I don't know where your sister is."

"What happened?"

"Timmy, your sister was never with your mother. I'm not sure where they are."

"I don't understand."

"We've never talked about your mother's boyfriend. What do you think about him?"

"Chad could be nice sometime, but mostly he was mean…to me and Mom."

"I saw your mom right before I came here. She wasn't doing well. Did you know your mother had problems with drugs?"

"Yeah, Dad. Kinda hard not to notice. Is she okay?"

"I honestly don't know, son. After we settled in here, I went back to get her and she wasn't there. No telling what happened to her."

"What about Chrissy? When is she coming back? Somebody must be taking care of her."

"Timmy, the family Chrissy left with…well, they weren't very nice people."

Richard's son began to cry.

"Chad was a horrible person. He sold your sister to them."

Richard watched, helpless, as the dreadful reality registered on his son's face.

"I've been trying my best to find her. It's really hard to find out anything with the situation like it is now. The Pulse Zone is getting worse and worse every day. The UAE might not be able to keep it together much longer. I think we have a real shot at finding her. Hal gave me some good news this morning. I don't think it will be long now and…"

"I hate you! This is all your fault! Why haven't you been looking for her?" Timmy pushed his father aside as he ran from their quarters. Richard was hurt by his response but it could have been much worse. The boy was angry, which meant he was dealing with the news in his own way.

"Hal?"

Beck Castle's resident A.I. responded. "Yes, sir. How can I help?"

"I'm sure my son is headed to Morris's quarters. If he doesn't get there, please tell me."

"Of course, sir. I could discern from your conversation that you wanted privacy. Now that your son has departed, I have some reports from the UAE for you to review."

"Anything of relevance?"

"Yes, sir, there is. One of the reports concerns a group of liberated slaves in Florida. There is a child there by the name of Christina. No last name given, no images available."

"Do we have any way of contacting them?"

"Not by traditional means, sir. The slaves were liberated by a community taking up residence at Walt Disney World under the leadership of a man named Benjamin Black. The community is quite impressive, based on the report, but they have no means of long-term communication."

"This is the best lead we've had in over a year. If I can't figure out a way to contact this Benjamin Black, I'm going to Florida."

"Very good, sir. What about the invasion of California? Will it proceed on schedule?"

"I don't know, Hal. If we can't get that cruise ship in Seattle, it might be awhile. I'm going to discuss this with Max."

"I understand, sir."

***

"Why is this even a question, Richard?"

"Max, I really don't want to go on a wild goose chase. This isn't like the old days. I can't just hop on a plane and fly to Orlando. The UAE restricts travel, and they know I'm the commanding general of the PSA; I'm sure they'd love a chance to torture me for information. It could take me months to get to Orlando."

"I take it your stealth jet won't take you that far?"

"The stealth jet has a range of about a thousand miles. It's three and a half thousand roundtrip to Orlando."

"Why can't you just refuel?"

"Howard won't allow any of the stealth jets to land outside the PSA."

Max was amused. "If Howard deems it so, then your pilot, Hal, must certainly agree."

"Exactly."

Max grunted as he reached for his pill bottle. When he married Elizabeth, he promised to never take Vicodin or any other narcotic again. He'd been taking Tramadol to manage his pain. Healthcare in the PSA put the UAE's system to shame. "Look, Richard, I know you've been planning this invasion for quite some time, but I'm sure you can delegate your plans to your second-in-command. All of us will understand if the rescue of your daughter takes priority."

"It's a huge risk; I'd like some definitive proof that it's her. A girl named Christina could be anyone. I don't even have an approximate age on this girl in Orlando."

"Richard, you're forgetting one very important resource."

"What?"

"We do have a mole inside Sterling's camp."

"Stacy Reid! How could I forget?"

***

Stacy Reid was sitting at her desk trying not to think about her former boss, President Malcolm Powers. Today was Malcolm's birthday. She doubted she'd be able to stop reminiscing about past celebrations they'd shared and what she might have done today had he still been alive. She missed him terribly.

Stacy wondered how much longer she could keep this up before she lost her mind. She was terrified of Simon Sterling and what he might do to her if he discovered she was a spy. The only way she could ease her troubled mind was to keep telling herself that the UAE was crumbling from within and she was, in large part, instrumental in its welcomed demise. She was in constant contact with Howard and fed him valuable intelligence. Howard had programmed Hal to connect with his sibling computer, now under President Sterling's watchful eye. It enabled Howard to watch Simon's every move, listen to all phone calls, and read all his digital communication. Howard Beck was the President of the Pacific States of America and didn't have time to watch his nemesis every minute of the day, counting on Stacy to alert him whenever Sterling was up to something.

Stacy called up the holographic display on her desk and opened a window that showed the hallway leading to her office. The second window connected to the command center in Beck Castle. The face of Howard Beck stared back at her.

"Mr. President."

"Good morning, Stacy. How are things in my home?"

"Everything's fine."

"How's my wife's cat?"

"Nala is fine. Sterling hates the animal, but he leaves her alone. He knows I adopted her as my own so he tolerates her."

"Good. Anything to report?"

"Yes, something very big."

"Do tell, please."

"I'm sure you've heard the news of Regional Governor Weygandt's unfortunate accident?"

Howard rolled his eyes. "And so soon after his declaration against the slavers. I'm sure his untimely demise had nothing to do with that."

"Everyone knows Sterling had him killed, but

no one dares breathe a word. You'll be interested to know that Sterling and all the regional governors will be attending his funeral in Miami. Sterling has restricted all travel south of Orlando for a week. Miami and the surrounding areas are on full lockdown."

"A wise precaution. The entire leadership of the UAE will be gathered in one place. A very tempting target, to be sure."

"I thought you might see it that way. I'll send you the details."

"When's the funeral?"

"A week from today."

"I just might have to send my condolences."

"It'll be rough; security will be iron-clad."

"I'll see what I can do. On another topic, I have a request for you."

"Anything."

"General Dupree has some credible evidence regarding the location of his daughter, Christina. A man by the name of Benjamin Black runs a community at Disney World. Recently, they murdered a group of slavers and liberated the slaves. The report mentions a girl named Christina, but that's all it has. No last name, age, or image."

"I'm on it. I'll doctor some orders from Sterling requesting detailed identification of all liberated slaves."

"Thank you, Stacy. Richard extends his gratitude as well. What can you tell me about Benjamin Black?"

"He's a force to contend with. There are men like him all over The Pulse Zone. They set up large communities and provide protection, food, shelter, everything. I have to go, Howard. I'll get the funeral details to you soon."

"I'll talk to you later." Howard terminated the link. His brilliant mind sped into high gear, exploring a number of scenarios that all closed with the same grand finale: the deaths of Simon Sterling and his miserable lackeys.

"An interesting turn of events, wouldn't you say, sir?"

"Hal, we have a week to figure out how to take them out. We could end this struggle and begin taking back the country in less than a day."

"I will endeavor to formulate a suitable plan of attack, sir."

"I know you will, Old Man."

"Sir, General Dupree is waiting outside."

"Send him in, please."

"What'd she say?" Richard asked as he strolled into the command center.

"Stacy is going to send out orders under Sterling's name to properly ID all liberated slaves."

"Excellent. Thank you, Howard."

"We had a deal, Richard—you command my

army, I help you find your daughter."

"Would you be opposed to Max leading the invasion force? If I find out my daughter is in Florida, I'll be leaving immediately."

"Max has my full confidence. I'm also certain your senior officers will be able to carry out their duties in an efficient and timely manner."

"What are you going to do about the cruise ship in Seattle? You think you can convince those people to live somewhere else?"

"I have no idea what will happen. I've never been the sociable type, and I hate public speaking with a passion. I'll probably just get pissed and start yelling."

"I'm sure Max won't let that happen."

CHAPTER NINE

Regional Governor Roberto Jimenez awoke in his Malibu home and pressed the button to summon his nurse. Roberto's decades-long battle with multiple sclerosis had cost him the use of his legs. If not for Andrew, his faithful caregiver, the governor would be completely bedridden. As much as he loathed his emasculating dependence, Roberto knew he no longer had the physical strength needed to tend to his own basic personal needs.

"Good morning, sir."

"Hurry up. I need to piss like a racehorse."

"I keep telling you, Mr. Jimenez, there's nothing wrong with using the bedpan." Andrew did his best to sound like a concerned caretaker so as not to embarrass Roberto.

"And I keep telling you, I'm not pissing in a fucking jug!"

"Okay, okay, I'm sorry. Remember, you promised to watch your temper. We need to keep your blood pressure down."

"Whatever. Just get me to the bathroom."

Andrew lifted Roberto out of bed and placed him in his wheelchair. Roberto maneuvered himself into the bathroom and shut the door.

"Do you need any help, sir?"

"No, I'm fine. Computer, report."

"In the wake of the Golden Gate Bridge attack, widespread demonstrations have sprung up in

San Francisco, Anaheim, Los Angeles, San Diego, and Sacramento."

"Is that so? Show them to me."

Five separate windows appeared on the bathroom mirror, each broadcasting similar reports of somewhat peaceful demonstrations threatening to erupt into violence at a moment's notice. Picket signs delivered tasteless racist slogans as groups of malcontents billowed in the litter-filled streets.

Roberto found the cries for retribution amusing. Even without watching the videos, he knew the demonstrations weren't aimed at him or the UAE. The citizens of his region knew better than to speak out against the UAE since to do so resulted in the death penalty. Angry citizens harkening back to the days of the democratic United States thought it was all a bluff, a fear tactic meant to control the populace. At first, protestors were arrested and imprisoned, with public execution at a later, more convenient, time. Roberto thought this measure would be enough but was shocked when even more brazen fools protested the executions and demanded governmental reform. Without haste, he ordered in the troops and gunned down the recalcitrant protestors in the street, leaving their bloody, bullet-ridden bodies behind.

"Computer, what's on the schedule?"

"Sir, President Sterling is requesting to speak

with you."

Roberto yelled for Andrew to get him from the bathroom to his desk.

"Establish the connection."

"Good morning, Roberto, is this a bad time?" Simon asked once the link was completed.

"Not at all, Mr. President. What can I do for you?"

"I'm on my way to your home. I should be there in less than an hour."

"A pleasant surprise, Mr. President. If you'd have given me more notice, I could have prepared a reception in your honor."

"That won't be necessary; my visit is unscheduled and unannounced for a reason. I have something to discuss with you that requires the utmost secrecy."

"I'm honored, Mr. President. This can't wait till the funeral?"

"No, Roberto, it cannot. Tell no one about my arrival and make no preparations."

"I look forward to it, Mr. President."

***

President Simon Sterling emerged from his helicopter and followed the flagstone path to Regional Governor Jimenez's guest home. Roberto waited alone in the dining room, his nervous expectation nearly getting the best of him.

"Mr. President, I took the liberty of having coffee and pastries set out for you. Help yourself. I know you said no preparations, but I don't have it in me to be a less than gracious host."

"Thank you, Roberto. I just didn't want to attract attention to my visit."

"I must say I'm rather surprised by this, Mr. President. It's not like you to sneak around."

"You are indeed correct. Once I say what I have to say, you'll understand the need for discretion."

"I'm all ears, Mr. President."

"To put it frankly, Roberto, the UAE is on a path to destruction. Well, to be more accurate, The Pulse Zone is on a path to destruction."

"How so?"

"We've made significant strides in restoring the infrastructure, but the problem of maintaining law and order remains. Much of the region is being divided up into small pockets controlled by either crime lords or powerful individuals who can offer a community the protection for which all are so desperately longing. At first I put a stop to it but soon saw the benefit of these communities."

"Meaning they were simply one less thing for you to worry about, correct?"

"Yes. As long as they were minding their own business and not causing trouble, I left them alone. All of our efforts have been focused on getting the power back on and rebuilding the interstates, but The Silent Warriors stymie our progress at every turn. Butler will clear out a stretch of road and rebuild a bridge, and those cursed terrorists will come in behind him and undo everything. It's making things impossible for us."

"Mr. President, what can I do to help?"

"I'm here to discuss a matter that has been troubling me for months. Regional Governor Butler has become a problem."

"Really? In what way?"

"I'm growing concerned that his loyalties no longer lie with the UAE. He's becoming increasingly insolent and enjoys testing the limits of my patience. I put him in charge of the reconstruction efforts in The Pulse Zone because I thought he could get the job done."

"You're not satisfied with his progress?"

"Quite the contrary. He's doing an exemplary job in spite of all the frustrating setbacks. What troubles me is his affinity for the spotlight. He's arrogant and will do anything to gain popularity. The accusations you made recently about him stockpiling resources and manpower did not fall on deaf ears. I looked into the matter and discovered that you were correct."

"To what end?"

"Isn't it obvious? He's planning to seize power and get rid of me."

Roberto laughed. "By himself? He can't possibly be that deluded. Just because he's making strides in getting The Pulse Zone up and running doesn't mean he's in any position to start a civil war. That sort of egotistic idiocy is the last thing we need right now. Once Iran is finished with Europe, they're coming for us. Butler has to know that."

"I think he's too blinded by power to even care. He must think he can get rid of me, slip quietly into the driver's seat and just take the wheel without any bloodshed."

"What do you want me to do, Mr. President?"

"If I know Jackson like I think I do, he's going to reach out to some of the other regional governors for support."

"You know the two of us don't exactly get along. I'd be at the bottom of his list."

"That's why I came to you, Roberto. Of all the regional governors, you're the only one in whom I have implicit trust. You were instrumental in helping me overthrow Malcolm Powers, and it's a fortunate coincidence that you and Jackson despise each other."

"That's putting it lightly."

"I need you to be mindful of the rest of the group. Use the attack on the Golden Gate Bridge as your cover. Tell them I'm furious with you, furious enough to force you into retirement. A few juicy rumors should get their tongues wagging."

"I wish you'd force me into retirement; I could use a break. What are you planning to do about Butler?"

"Nothing for the time being. I'm curious to know if he can recruit anyone to his cause."

"And if he does?"

"I think you already know the answer to that."

CHAPTER TEN

Benjamin Black had never felt such fervent hatred toward anything or anyone in his life. Yes, he faced the customary loathing for mundane annoyances— he hated getting stuck in traffic, he detested his shitty bosses, and he despised the Dallas Cowboys with a vengeance – but nothing came close to the unmitigated, raw hatred Benjamin harbored for the Unified American Empire.

Like so many Americans, Ben felt he'd been deceived by President Simon Sterling. In the wake of the collapse, Sterling seemed like the perfect answer to the country's desperate prayers, both a revolutionary and a true patriot. The guy was smart and ready to cut through a mountain of bullshit to do things right and get them done *fast*. The fact that Sterling's initial move was to bring the country's troops home, leaving the rest of the world to fend for itself, made him the most beloved president of all time. And just when Ben thought the man couldn't possibly top that, President Sterling made it clear to all that his style of dogged isolationism not only referred to military intervention, but to financial relief as well. Even while the country was mired in The Second Great Depression, the bleeding-heart liberals still wanted to send billions and billions of dollars to feed the starving children of the world. President Sterling proclaimed that Americans had their own starving children to feed, thank you very much. No more handouts, no more sticking our noses into foreign matters where they didn't belong in the first place. America had enough problems to deal with; the rest of the world was on its own. Benjamin Black believed in Simon Sterling. If anyone could pull the country out of The Second Great Depression and rebuild The Pulse Zone, he could do it.

At first, Sterling's measures seemed strict and imposing, but Ben and the other terrified citizens sat in quiet acquiescence. Someone needed to bring the hammer down on the degenerate thugs who were in the way of progress. Curfews weren't really a bad thing either. Ben was smart enough to know that darkness is the coziest blanket for evil. Ben became a bit wary when more and more of the country became compartmentalized. President Sterling declared that crossing state lines required a passport. If you were caught in Tennessee with a Florida driver's license and no passport, you had some serious explaining to do. Ben questioned the restriction, but drastic situations called for drastic measures…right?

Like most people, Ben harbored an underlying hatred and mistrust of anyone with olive-colored skin. He kept these feelings buried beneath a façade of indifference and certainly never acted on them. A decade of progressively deadlier attacks by The Silent Warriors had fostered his racism and kept the perpetual internal flame burning just beneath his skin. During The Thanksgiving Day Massacre, Ben was at his parents' house watching the Cowboys game with his siblings and their families. Like every year, his dad kept stalling the start of the meal so they could sit in front of the TV just a little longer. With less than two minutes to go in the first quarter, breaking news of the sniper attacks interrupted the game and had Ben screaming at the TV. Once Ben and his family truly grasped the severity of what they were witnessing, Thanksgiving would never be the same. When the Super Bowl Massacre of 2023 brought about the demise of the National Football League, Ben joined millions of enraged fans and didn't object in the slightest when the Middle Eastern internment camps were erected.

Benjamin's aversion for the UAE deepened as rumors of mass executions ran rampant. The massacre of thousands of internees, including innocent women and children, generated an alarming, caustic side effect—the eradication of free speech. Sterling was far too cunning to provoke the Empire while they were busy conquering Europe. Censorship reared its menacing head, and the ugly truth withered, its silent death unreported. Once Sterling had an iron grip on the media, he could unleash his madness free from accountability.

New flocks of refugees arrived at Disney World each day, offering passionate firsthand accounts of Sterling's lunacy. Everyone knew the president's first measure of "social reform" would be to clean up the Obama Camps. Benjamin Black had been earning his keep since he was sixteen years old and had made an honest living ever since, so he viewed the Obama Camps with disgust. They were filled with lazy bums who expected hard working people to take care of them. Ben hoped President Sterling would kick these indolent losers square in the ass and force them to find employment, however menial. Sterling had a simple, quite efficient solution: The Unified National Guard marched in with flamethrowers and burned the camps to the ground, no eviction notice or other advance warning provided.

Benjamin faced a serious dilemma. On the one hand, he was glad the problem got cleaned up, but was appalled by the method Sterling used. He didn't know how, but he was going to stop Simon Sterling and help bring down the UAE. He knew he couldn't form a militia and go on the offensive; he would be slaughtered before he could make a dent. Sterling was exactly the type of dictator the former

United States of America would have toppled without a backward glance, the irony of which provided Ben a momentary bright spot in an otherwise terrifying reality.

Someone had to stop the UAE, and Ben was determined to help make that happen.

Ben was proud of the double life he lived. While he plotted and schemed against the UAE in the shadows, on the surface he was a model citizen, loyal and supportive. He treated UAE officers like celebrities when they came to Disney World and made sure they were afforded every luxury; the UAE officers idolized him in return. Over time, Ben was able to manipulate them into believing he was their ally, and many soon sought his counsel on a variety of topics. While they poured out their souls to him, Ben used the vital intelligence to undermine their efforts.

Captain Nedry Brown was by far the easiest mark. Ben found the man to be an incompetent officer. He was ignorant and had low self-esteem—both characteristics unbecoming in a leader. Thus, the soldiers under Brown's command had no respect for him. Ben cashed in on the man's insecurity and did everything possible to boost his fragile ego. When the good captain finally began to display a measure of confidence, Ben would snap him like a twig, even a minor slight enough to break him. The vicious cycle had the poor officer's mind coiled like a spring around Ben's little finger. Captain Brown craved Benjamin's approval like a son would a father's. He wasn't alone, sadly, as many others found themselves in the same needy predicament. Ben prided himself on his skills at psychological manipulation and could have instructed a master class on Machiavelli with little or no preparation.

With his top lieutenant, Jessica Bradley, away investigating the mysteries in southern Florida, Ben had a bit of a problem on his hands. He needed to get inside Captain Brown's head to find out what was going on, but he needed Jessica to do it. Nedry Brown was quite unattractive and turned into a bumbling fool around women. Jessica was far too proud to whore herself out for some cause, no matter how just and honorable it may be, but when it came to Captain Brown, all Jessica had to do was show him a little kindness and respect. Nedry nearly hyperventilated at her beautiful smile, and she would pretend not to notice, giving the man the misguided impression that he was a charming storyteller. This simple distraction allowed Ben to play Nedry like a fiddle. With Jessica gone, the task would prove more difficult.

Ben and Nedry were sitting in the captain's private officer's suite at the Wilderness Lodge. Ben knew Nedry craved brandy and cigars. Ben had crates of the stuff on hand but always gave Brown the impression that he went to great lengths to procure this special stash just for him. Nedry smiled at the first-class treatment as he put the cigar in his mouth and allowed Ben to light it.

"Ned?"

"Ben, please."

Ben sat down across from Captain Brown and lit his own cigar. After enjoying a slow, smooth sip of brandy, he began again. "Ned?"

"Ben, c'mon. I already told you what you need to know. You and yours are safe. Relax! You have nothing to worry about."

"You give me too much credit, Ben. I really don't know much more than I told you earlier."

"So, you *do* know more! You gonna make me beg?"

"Don't be silly. You know I can't just spill my guts to you. All I know is something big is happening in Miami."

"When?"

"Tuesday or Wednesday."

"What are the rumors going around?"

"A secret meeting of some kind. I've heard Beck is surrendering. On the flip side, I also heard Sterling is surrendering to Iran. All of it's probably bullshit, but my gut tells me it has something to do with the sudden interest in the slave trade. The timing is just, I don't know..."

"The slaver thing is really that big of a deal? I thought it was just some PR stunt to make the UAE look more civilized."

"I don't know, Ben, I can't help but think the two are connected somehow. They're making a huge deal about the liberated slaves you got here. Seemed to take an interest in some orphan girl, thought maybe they found her parents."

Ben hated when the UAE took an interest in anything to do with his operation. He'd rather they stay the hell out of his business. Ben knew neither Sterling nor anyone else in the UAE gave two shits about helping an orphan girl. Burning down Obama Camps and executing Middle Easterners was proof positive that Sterling's only concern was for furthering his own misguided agenda.

"Orphan girl? Here? Don't recall an orphan girl."

"Dugood? What was the girl's name? Dammit! McPhee?"

Dupree, you fucking idiot! Her name is Christina Dupree.

"I have no idea, Ned. Slavers haven't brought any kids 'round here in some time. What's so special about her?"

"I have no clue, but Colonel Rutherford himself is headed down here to get the girl. I promise you she's here somewhere, and she's important for some reason."

"Rutherford? He's coming here? When?"

"Dinnertime tomorrow. I'm headed out in the morning, leaving one of my NCOs behind to look for her. Was hopin' you'd help me. Can you spare a few men to help look for her?"

"Ned, you know I'm here to help you in any way I can. Of course we'll help look for the girl. Who are you leaving behind?"

"Godecker, and I appreciate it, Ben. Need to get some sleep. Big day tomorrow." Captain Brown gulped down the rest of his brandy and snuffed out his cigar. "Goodnight."

"Goodnight, my friend. It was good to see you."

Ben exited the suite and hurried down the stairs. Instead of retiring for the night, he rode his motorcycle back to his office on Main Street, USA. He dug through the papers on his desk and found the intake information on the UAE's prodigal daughter. *What the hell is so important about this little girl?* Every refugee that took up residence in Ben's amusement park community underwent a very basic screening process that included paperwork, medical screening, interviews, and even a short orientation meeting. Ben's people had efficiently trimmed the entire process down to the point that a couple dozen refugees could complete the intake in only a few hours. Once Ben reviewed the orientation packets, they were carefully filed away in the records office. While his office clerks were organized to a fault, Ben was notoriously less so. He knew the girl's file was scattered somewhere amongst the mounds of clutter on his conference table. Ben frantically tossed aside stacks of papers, and by the time he found the girl's buried file, his office bore a striking resemblance to a ransacked crime scene.

Ben poured over her orientation packet, hoping some clue would pop out at him. The only obvious discrepancy he found was the fact that she wasn't an orphan. In her interview, the girl stated that her father died when she was a baby and her mother was living in Colorado. She also mentioned being separated from her grandparents during the Collapse of 2027. *What the hell is so special about this little girl? What does the UAE want with her?* One thing was certain—he wasn't going to hand the child over until he knew what made her so important.

***

Late the next afternoon, Benjamin Black rolled out the red carpet for an honored guest, Colonel Lionel Rutherford of the Unified American

Empire. Ben had never met the man but knew much about his reputation. From what Ben had been told, the man was sadistic, arrogant, and lethal—making him a model UAE officer.

Ben had spent the morning getting to know Chrissy Dupree—an exceptional child, given the circumstances. She had apparently witnessed unspeakable horrors, yet had made it through in remarkable fashion. Chrissy was polite, enthusiastic and— in stark contrast to the world around her— optimistic.

Ben had a long list of theories as to her importance and managed to cross each one off the list. None of her relatives had any connection to the UAE. The girl had never seen a soldier from the UAE, and she had never set foot on a military installation. The girl's importance to the UAE was a complete mystery to Ben, making her even more valuable to the resistance. If she possessed critical knowledge about the UAE, she could prove useful in striking a devastating blow. But more than that, Ben had accepted this child into his community and felt responsible for her wellbeing. He doubted the UAE's interest in this girl had anything to do with kindness.

Ben's radio crackled. "Ben, they're here. You coming out or do you want me to bring them to you?"

"Show them to my office." Ben wanted to stand behind his desk and have the man seated in front of him, a not-so-subtle reminder of who was in charge.

Ben stood as his guest entered and extended his hand. "Colonel, it's an honor to meet you. What brings you to the Magic Kingdom?"

His snobbery in plain sight, Lionel Rutherford paused a bit too long before returning the handshake, as if Ben's hand had been dipped in something unsavory of which he should be wary.

"Mr. Brown, I ..."

"Black."

"Excuse me?" The colonel looked horribly offended by the interruption.

"Black. My name is Benjamin *Black*." Ben shot the colonel a piercing smile.

"Ah, yes, of course it is. Well, I'm sure you're aware of the recent measure to combat the slave trade. The report you compiled on the liberated ..."

"Why is that, exactly?"

"Why is what?" Colonel Rutherford shifted in his seat, clearly growing impatient.

"Why after all this time has the UAE decided to do something about the slave trade? Why now? What happened?"

"That need not concern you, Mr. Black. All

you need to know is that the UAE is going to great lengths to..."

"That's the other thing that has me puzzled. You guys have a *lot* on your plate these days with all the attacks. Real sorry to hear about McClellan; that was pretty fucked up. How do you guys have the time to chase down slavers?"

Colonel Rutherford was not amused. The leaders of these fortified communities didn't impress him. They were more often than not delusional morons who rose to power by being the most violent idiot of the bunch. "Mr. Black, I'm afraid we don't have time for lengthy discussions. My business here is rather urgent, so I'm going to have to forgo the hospitality I've heard so much about. Do I have your attention, sir?"

"Of course."

"You have a child here by the name of Christina Dupree."

"We have a lot of children here. I can ask around for ..."

Ben knew things were about to get ugly when the look on Rutherford's face went from disgusted to venomous. "I was not asking a question, hillbilly! I know she's here!"

"Hillbilly? I'm sorry, have I done something to offend you? Colonel, we're here to cooperate in every way possible. You hungry? I can have some grub brought up, and we can sort this out."

"I don't have time for your silly games and, quite frankly, you're pissing me off. I know you spent the morning with the girl trying to figure out why we want her. That means you know *exactly* where she is. I'm leaving here with her in ten minutes."

Ben was finished trying to manipulate the asshole and dropped the act. "Before I do anything, I want to know why she's so important."

Rutherford chuckled. "Or what? What're you gonna do? Stop me?"

"C'mon, let's not get carried away. I think I have a right to know."

"You have a lot of nerve, you know. The only right you have is to do what the fuck you're told. You think you're some sort of big shot? I can shoot you between the eyes and give your job to the first person I see. Catching on? You do *not* want to waste my time."

"The girl is a part of this community, and I'm responsible for her wellbeing. And while we're on the subject, I *am* a big shot. I've built up quite a settlement here, and we've got the muscle to defend it. I've got a double-barreled shotgun under my desk, conveniently aimed at your crotch. I figure we've got two choices: You can either get the fuck outta my park and not come back, or I can blow your ass outta that chair."

Colonel Rutherford smiled, not the least bit shaken. "Third option?"

"I'd love to hear it."

"Look out the window. Honestly, I'm surprised you didn't meet us in the parking lot. Could've saved us both a lot of time. Go on, Mr. Black! Take a peek. I promise to sit right here and behave myself."

Ben leaned back in his chair to get a better look at the parking lot, his finger still curled around the trigger. The good colonel wasn't screwing around. Dozens of vehicles and easily a hundred eager soldiers were amassed outside, ready to storm the park.

"As you can see, I came prepared. Impressive, aren't they? That's about a third of them. Believe me when I tell you I won't hesitate to slaughter every adult in this park and take all of the children with me. I'd rather not resort to such drastic measures. Just give me the girl! Is one little kid really worth all that to you?"

"You're a bastard, you know that?"

"Actually, I don't really get much criticism in my line of work."

"I can see why. Will she be safe?"

"Absolutely! She'll be an honored guest! You think we'd go to all this trouble if she wasn't important?"

"Who the hell is she?   I gotta know, please."

"It's not actually the girl who's important. It's her father."

"What? Her father's dead."

Colonel Rutherford beamed from ear to ear. "Oh, no, General Dupree is very much alive, I assure you."

CHAPTER ELEVEN

"Mr. Everton, I admire your passion, sir. I pride myself on being somewhat of an expert in human nature. I know these first stages of captivity—such an ugly word, but I just can't think of a polite euphemism for what we're doing here— are the most difficult, and I do apologize for all the unpleasantness. I'm eager to get to the next phase of our relationship. I think we're almost there, don't you?"

Joel Everton was duct-taped to a kitchen chair and had been for the past eleven hours. His wife was in the same predicament a few short feet away. Although her mouth had been taped shut, she'd been spared all but a fraction of the violence her husband had experienced. "You're not suggesting we're becoming friends are you? That whole Stockholm Syndrome thing isn't happening here."

"No, no, Mr. Everton, I have no illusions about us becoming friends. I certainly don't expect you to become buddies with my two associates here. The next phase is acceptance of what's happening to you. It's a given…inevitable, I'm afraid. I've seen it many times; some take twice as long as you and some take half the time."

"And just how do you know when it happens? What makes you think I'm going to do anything you want?"

"Well, for starters, Mr. Everton, you've stopped using profanity. I find profanity to be so tasteless and vulgar. I suppose I have my dear Christian mother to thank for that."

"Maybe I'm just tired of getting punched."

"It doesn't really matter, Mr. Everton. That's not what tells me you're ready to move on to the next phase of our plan."

Joel looked at the maniac with contempt. "I can't wait to hear this."

The polite man paused to straighten his tie and smiled. "Mr. Everton, I know we're ready to proceed because you've come to terms with your fate. You've stopped begging, stalling, and my absolute favorite part of these jobs—you've stopped scheming and plotting to find a way out of this."

Megan Everton snuck a furtive glance at her husband, certain the monster was wrong. She knew her husband was smart enough to find a way out of this nightmare and save them both. His defeated gaze, however, led Megan to the horrible realization that Joel had given up.

"Mr. Everton, you really will come to realize that it's so much easier when you just play the game. This is going to happen, sir, and I'm delighted that you're finally accepting that fact."

"I know the last time I asked this question I was punished for it, but you said I would know when I could ask it again."

"Bravo, Mr. Everton! I am quite impressed with you, my good man. You're the first to make the connection without any prompting from me. I was right about you, Mr. Everton." The polite man was as giddy as a school boy. "I'm going to let you in on a little secret, Mr. Everton. My employer was not in favor of your selection. You were thought to be much too smart and resourceful. I just had a feeling you might need to improvise and think on your feet to accomplish your assignment. Your predecessors didn't really have to do much thinking. If we could've gotten away with it, their tasks could have been carried about by chimpanzees. Anyway, Mr. Everton, now that you feel the time is right, please ask your question."

"If I go through with this, how do I know you won't kill my wife anyway? How do I know you'll let her go?"

"Well, Mr. Everton, you really don't know, do you? From the moment my associates and I entered your home, I've done every single thing I said I would do without fail. My employer likes things to be nice and tidy. Unnecessary loss of life brings with it the potential for complications.

Keeping your wife alive is the easier alternative.
Missing persons bring attention. Your wife can
simply fabricate the story of your demise, but if both
of you were to disappear, well, that would be too
costly an investment."

"You want me to murder innocent people, yet
you have the nerve to say 'unnecessary loss of life'?
How dare you!"

The polite man broke eye contact with Joel
and smiled at one of his goons who, in turn, whacked
Joel across the knuckles with the end of a collapsible
baton. The thugs knew a smile meant to go easy on
the victim.

"Mr. Everton, let's not forget my dislike of
sass. Just because I'm pleased with how sharp you
are doesn't mean you can speak to me in any way
you please. Let's not ruin the progress we've made.
As I was saying, assuring someone's silence is much
easier than one would think. I'm sure your lovely
wife here holds a great deal of affection for her
sweet grandmother in Plano, Texas. Isn't that right,
sweetheart?"

Megan was stunned by the realization that
this sociopath kept tabs on her family.

"Yes, darling. Mammy is just an adorable
little country grandma. Doesn't really live in the
country, but you can't take the country out of the gal,
now can ya? You should consider yourself lucky. I

only had one grandmother that I could remember, and she went home to see Jesus when I was six. From what I recall, my Mimi and your Mammy would get along just fine. If you can't keep our little secret, they might meet each other much sooner than the good Lord intended."

"I'm sure my wife will cooperate fully, sir. I'll do whatever you want me to do, and she will never speak a word of this for the rest of her life."

"I'm sure she won't, Mr. Everton, I'm sure she won't. While we're on the topic of family, I have to say that your Uncle Ollie is a real stand-up guy. His second wife has a teenage girl with a spinal cord injury, right? Poor little angel is in a wheelchair, and your uncle doesn't skip a beat. That girl isn't just a step-daughter, she's family to him. Sounds like a family full of fighters and hard workers, real salt-of-the-earth kind of folk. I'd love to spend a weekend with them. I'm willing to bet they'd make us a home-cooked meal before we got down to business."

"Stop! You've made your point. I'm ready."

"Excellent! I really do like you, Joel. I've enjoyed our time together. I seldom get to have conversations with men of intelligence. My associates might lack in that department, but they excel in other areas where it counts. One thing has me curious. It wasn't really important enough to follow up on but I'm certain you'd be happy to fill in the blanks. Uncle Ollie, is that his Christian name or is it short for Oliver?"

"Yes, my mother wanted to name me after him but my dad insisted on Joel. They compromised and made Oliver my middle name."

"How delightful! Joel Oliver Everton. I admire namesakes, I really do. If I'd ever had children of my own, their names would've had meaning."

Thank God you didn't reproduce.

"Now, we have one more bit of nastiness to contend with before we can proceed. Megan, my dear, I don't want you to be afraid. My associates here are going to escort you into the next room."

Megan's muffled screams went nowhere.

"Now, now. I simply want to have a word with your husband in private. I promise my associates will be perfect gentlemen."

Once they were alone, Joel closed his eyes. "Please don't kill my wife. I'll do whatever you say, and I won't try anything stupid."

"Mr. Everton, open your eyes and look at me. Have I lied to you in the short time we've known each other?"

"No."

"Then you know, sir, that I mean business. Would you agree?"

"Yes," Joel whispered.

"I have no interest in harming your wife so long as you successfully complete your mission. I have one last truth to share with you, something I hope you'll find motivational."

Joel couldn't imagine anything more motivational than keeping his wife and family safe from this madman. "What is it?"

"This is perhaps the most unpleasant part of my job. I really do hate the lack of civility in my profession, I really do. Mr. Everton, please understand, sir, that I absolutely abhor having to discuss this, so I'm just going to come out and say it. If you get cold feet during your mission, my two associates are going to brutally violate your wife before they kill her."

Joel began to weep. "I won't get cold feet, I promise. P-p-please don't hurt my wife. I'll do whatever you say, I promise. I won't let you down..."

"Shhh. There, there. Let's not get carried away." The polite man reached into his suit coat for his handkerchief and tenderly wiped Joel's face. "I have all the faith in the world that you'll complete your mission. Your dear wife will be just fine. You're a smart man, Joel, very smart. I know you desperately want to believe your wife will be safe from harm. That being said, I also know you can't escape the fear that, successful or not, we plan to kill your wife. While I am a facilitator of violence, Mr. Everton, I myself am not a violent man. I don't want to kill your wife, and above all, I certainly would not want to be party to such a violation should you fail."

"You were right when you said I've accepted my death. Since I'm not long for this world, may I ask a question?"

"You want to know why."

"Yes. I just want to know what I'm dying for."

"I wish I could share the intimate details with you, Mr. Everton, as your life is surely worth at least an explanation. I wish it was that simple. I'm under strict orders forbidding me from ever disclosing that information. Suffice it to say, advance knowledge of the horrific violence you'll be instigating would only make the task more difficult for you. You'll be aiding us in our efforts to bring this country back to her former glory. And you, Mr. Everton, will soon be directly responsible for showing the world just how determined we are to do so."

CHAPTER TWELVE

"Okay, Maxwell, why couldn't we bring my son with us? He's constantly nagging me to get out amongst the people. Now that I'm actually doing it, he can't come along? What gives?" Howard Beck was sitting in a fancy restaurant in Seattle with Max and Elizabeth Harris. They'd spent the morning at the Port of Seattle touring the cruise ship that had been commandeered by squatters. Howard never mentioned to any of the residents that they would soon be leaving; that would come soon enough.

Maxwell Harris had started out as the constable of Beck Castle, responsible for the security of the massive underground bunker and its residents. The job also entailed providing protection for Howard, making Max a one-man Secret Service detail. Maxwell's duties grew until Howard appointed him director of security for the entire PSA.

"Howard, your son is the vice president of the Pacific States of America. The two of you cannot be at the same event. Should something happen to you, God forbid, your son needs to assume the presidency. Basic stuff, Howard. I know I'm just a cop, but I'm pretty sure I saw that on television."

Elizabeth Harris loved to tease her husband. "Honey, we're all loving what you're doing here.

Just think of a Secret Service movie or two and you'll be a shoe in for director."

"Whoa! Where were you? Didn't get the memo? I *am* the director of the Secret Service."

Elizabeth's smile was like a drug to Max. "Are we giving ourselves jobs now?"

"Whatever you want, my love."

"Hmmm...This could be fun. Any job I want? Okay, I officially appoint myself assistant director of the Secret Service."

"Not gonna aim higher?"

"And leave your side? You know I could never do that." Elizabeth ran her fingers through her husband's hair as she planted a kiss on his weathered cheek. Howard was learning to tolerate the couple; before long, he might even be comfortable around them. However, their overt physical displays of affection would make anyone with Asperger's feel awkward.

"Howard, you poor thing, are we making you uncomfortable?" Elizabeth couldn't resist the chance to tease her friend, though he tried is best to ignore her.

Max winked at his wife. "Honey, we've talked about this, and it's time we both started addressing Howard as Mr. President."

Elizabeth tried again, her serious tone less than genuine. "I'm sorry. Mr. President, would you like me to stop kissing my husband?"

"You two are picking on me, aren't you?"

"Only because we love you so much! Lighten up, Mr. President."

"Fun seems to always be at my expense. I was hoping my son would be here to give some fancy-pants speech so I wouldn't have to."

Max appreciated the return to a weightier topic. "Marshall told me he wrote a speech for you. Don't you have it?"

"I do. I'd just rather not give a speech at all."

"You ran a multi-billion-dollar corporation, and you didn't give the occasional speech?" Elizabeth asked.

"My dear, I *owned* a multi-billion dollar corporation which meant I didn't have to give speeches or anything else that didn't suit me. Senator Wilson keeps pressuring me to revise my speech."

Max could tell Howard was getting upset. "Howard, you don't have to change anything! You're the president, for crying out loud."

"Wilson's not asking me to change anything; he wants me to add a few things. Can't stand politicians. That man drives me insane with all of his fast-talking nonsense."

"What's he wanting to add?"

"He wants me to drum up support for a

diplomatic solution with the UAE, try and broker a peace agreement."

Max looked puzzled. "Can't exactly discuss peace when Richard wants to go on the offensive and invade California."

Howard's hearty laugh surprised them both. "Arthur Wilson won't be kissing my ass for much longer. The good senator will probably announce his candidacy for president."

Elizabeth loved seeing Howard in a good mood. "Speaking of that, when's the next election? I think I'd be a kick-ass congresswoman."

"I'd vote for you." Max winked.

A heavy pall settled over the group as Senator Arthur Wilson entered the restaurant. Having spent over thirty years in politics, Senator Wilson had been one of Howard's strongest advocates when the PSA was established.

"Mr. President, I am truly honored by your visit. We have a formal banquet prepared for you tonight at the Four Seasons. Plans for your address to the nation are moving forward without a hitch. I was wondering if you had a chance to consider my suggestions?"

Howard cut to the chase. "I'm not giving the speech at city hall."

Senator Wilson took the news in stride. "Oh? What location do you prefer?"

148

"I'll be speaking from the deck of the *Freedom of the Seas.*"

"The what?"

"The cruise ship."

Senator Wilson scanned his keen political mind for an angle. "Housing for UAE refugees? I like it. That works. Nice job tackling one of the hot-button issues." He couldn't ignore the wide-eyed, cryptic looks exchanged by Max and Elizabeth. "What? Am I missing something? This is about housing refugees, isn't it?"

"You could say that." Max cleared his throat to cover the chuckle that threatened to intervene.

Elizabeth covered her mouth to hide a smile and then looked away from the senator. "Howard, maybe you should tell Senator Wilson what's going on," Elizabeth said.

Howard had been dreading this moment. He was truly grateful that Max and Elizabeth were here to defend him and run interference. "Senator Wilson, when's the last time you visited California?"

***

The $800 million dollar cruise ship, the *Freedom of the Seas*—complete with fifteen decks, ten swimming pools, movie theater, ice-skating rink, and rock climbing wall—stood twenty glorious stories above the water. President Howard Alan Beck stood on a hastily built stage looking out across the harbor. A year had passed since the election, and the citizens of the Pacific States of America had yet to witness a live presidential address. He'd recorded his inaugural address to be disseminated to the citizens, much in the manner of FDR's fireside chats of almost a century prior. While Howard hated public speaking, he knew the public wanted, *needed,* to hear from their president. Looking out at the expectant crowd, Howard removed a small tablet from his coat pocket. "Hal, how many people would you say are here?"

"Good morning, sir. Attendance is well over one hundred thousand. I have twelve drones in the air monitoring everything. I assure you things are perfectly safe."

"Hal, I'm more worried about my speech right now."

"Of course, sir. Simply lay your tablet down flat on the podium and the speech will be projected at eye level."

"Outstanding! Let's get this show on the road. Senator Wilson, if you please, kind sir."

"Yes, Mr. President." Arthur Wilson approached the podium and began his introduction.

"Citizens of the Pacific States of America, today marks a milestone in the short history of our nation. President Howard Beck has given the fine city of Seattle the distinct privilege of hosting the very first State of the Union address. I could spend the better part of an hour lauding the praises of our very own founding father, but his accomplishments speak for themselves. We owe President Beck a debt we can never repay. Democracy is alive and well, thanks to this man." Senator Wilson raised his arm towards Howard in a gesture of pride and friendship. Howard mistakenly thought that was his cue, so he stood and walked toward the podium. "Well! I see the president is anxious for me to take my seat. Ladies and gentlemen, the president of the Pacific States of America."

For the next three and a half minutes Howard stood awkwardly at the podium, forcing a smile and nodding his head in thanks as over one hundred thousand people clapped and screamed with enthusiasm. Men and women wept openly as they tried to process the torrent of emotions overtaking them. They had spent years living in panic and crushing despair as their country fell to pieces around them. For the first time in as long as they could remember, they felt pride in their country; the man at the podium was the living embodiment of hope.

Howard waited until the applause abated and let the pointed silence hang heavily in the air for a few seconds. He studied the first line of his speech and surprised Max and Elizabeth by going off script. "You know, it's funny. I've read this speech a dozen times, memorized it actually, and it didn't occur to me until this second just how extremely powerful the first three words are: My fellow Americans. That phrase means a lot more now, doesn't it? Every president in recent memory opened his speeches with it. We hardly took notice of it, but it means so much more in these dark days. You see, the madman on the other side of our borders stopped using that phrase early on, and he'll never say it again. I'll tell you why: Simon Sterling doesn't see the citizens of his nation as 'fellow' anything. They're not citizens… they're his subjects. He's elevated himself to a god-like status—an error made by many dictators and monarchs throughout the course of history—with horrible consequences."

Howard paused for a moment to reflect and emphasized every word, every syllable, of the emotion-laden proclamation that followed: *"He. Must. Be. Stopped!"*

The crowd went wild. Howard had to wait the better part of a minute for the cheering and clapping to subside. "Our nation is strong, our resources are strong, and our resolve is even stronger. We cannot continue to live in such comfort and security while our brothers and sisters in the

Unified American Empire are being held hostage! We must rescue them from oppression! We must rescue them from a power-hungry madman who covets his own supremacy above the needs of his people! We must unite our borders, Pacific to Atlantic, and make whole the United States of America. Above all else, we must return our beloved nation to her people!"

Again, the crowd erupted in a deafening display of approval. Max and Elizabeth stood in awed silence. Never in their wildest dreams would they have guessed Howard had so much emotion brewing within him.

"The commanding general of our armed forces, General Richard Dupree, is currently preparing an invasion force that will liberate the former state of California from UAE rule. Before this historic mission can begin, I need your help. I will ask for your sacrifice in the coming days. I'm counting on the good citizens of Seattle to do their patriotic duty and answer the call to protect democracy, to liberate the downtrodden souls from beneath the oppressive thumb of Simon Sterling. Tell me, Seattle, are you up to the task?"

The crowd exploded in a roar of unanimous support. They were ready to lay down their lives for their president.

"In order for the liberation of California to

begin, we require transportation to get our troops to her shores. This magnificent vessel upon which I stand will be needed in the coming battle. The good people living on this boat will need new homes. I thank them for their sacrifice, and I'm counting on the good people of Seattle to see to it that they have warm beds to sleep in and food on their plates. What say you, Seattle? Will you join me in this noble cause?"

Once again, the crowd erupted in rapturous applause. Max leaned over to his wife. "You gotta give it to him; the man's a genius. Yesterday, Richard said these people were ready to chain themselves to the bulkheads so the military would have to forcefully remove them. Howard just turned the tables on them. Now the people of Seattle are going to escort them off the boat like they're celebrities."

CHAPTER THIRTEEN

Simon Sterling was standing in the dressing room of the master suite of his Colorado home. His tailor was taking his measurements so he could set about the weekly task of altering Simon's dozens of suits. The Italian had been a master tailor for the better part of three decades and had suffered his fair share of men whose obsession with clothing bordered on psychotic. Most of them insisted on monthly fittings; the tailor thought they were overdoing it, but took their money just the same. Simon Sterling's preoccupation with fashion and appearance took obsession to a new level. He never missed his Monday morning fittings. The tailor was terrified of the president and lauded him with praises customarily reserved for models about to hit the catwalk.

Simon curtly waved the tailor back a few steps. "Stacy! Stacy, my dear! Could you come in here, please?"

Simon cocked his ear to listen for his top advisor's approaching footsteps as he admired his impeccable suit. "Stacy! I'm in here."

"Good morning, Mr. President. I see the new suit arrived!"

"What do you think?" Simon turned to face

Stacy and slowly swiveled left and right to properly model his new duds.

"Handsome as always. You know how to wear a suit." Stacy faked a convincing smile for the man she despised.

"My taste for fine clothing has grown increasingly difficult to satisfy these days. This suit took nearly four weeks to get here."

"Really?"

"Yes. Well worth the wait."

Stacy did her best to dismiss the thought of the countless number of Americans going without food, shelter, or medical care while this monster went to outrageous lengths to secure overpriced clothing to compensate for his insecurity over being short in stature. "Mr. President, the suit is truly remarkable. It looks great on you."

"Thank you, my dear. Once Mr. De Luca works his magic it will look even better." Simon smiled at his tailor and nodded, signaling his dismissal.

Simon shrugged off his jacket and turned to Stacy. "Mr. De Luca is fantastic at what he does. He was the most sought after tailor in DC before the collapse. It was a fortunate turn of events that he was visiting family in the Denver area when The Pulse stranded him here in Colorado. Once the dust settled, he hitched a ride here to the front gate and insisted on seeing me. I welcomed him in with open arms. The rest is history. What's on the agenda for today?"

"Regional Governor Prince is slated to be here sometime between noon and two."

"What? I thought we were having lunch? Why such a broad window? Where is she?"

"I honestly don't know, Mr. President. I'm sure she'll fill you in when she gets here."

Sterling grumbled as he headed to his office with Stacy in tow.

"Mr. President, I want to discuss something with you, something you go out of your way to avoid when I mention it."

"The Silent Warriors."

"Yes, Mr. President. I can't do my job as your advisor unless you bring me up to speed."

President Sterling studied Stacy like an overbearing father disapproving of his daughter. The look quickly faded and he didn't speak for almost a minute. "How well do you know Howard Beck?"

Stacy was a master at the craft of deception, her vacant poker face rivaling that of the best card shark. She was not, however, prepared for this particular question; those working in tandem with the president knew Howard Beck's name was taboo. Stacy cleared her throat. "Sir?"

"I know Beck was close to Malcolm Powers. I'm simply asking if you had occasion to get to know the man."

"Yes, I got to know Howard quite well during both of Malcolm's campaigns."

"I figured as much. I always knew Malcolm didn't like me. The party paired us up and wouldn't have it any other way. I spent both campaigns far, far away from the president. I think Malcolm sent me out to the sticks out of spite. Said he wanted me to reach the common man in all corners of the country. I never complained. When he made it to the White House, I was never at his side. I simply bided my time and waited for his eight years to be up so I could sit in the big chair. Of course, things changed and here we are."

"Mr. President, why are you asking me about Howard Beck?"

"I trust you, Stacy. I trust you more than any of the regional governors. I'm asking you about Howard Beck because I want to know how deep your friendship goes. If we go to war with the PSA, will you be comfortable helping me take down an old friend?"

"Mr. President, you are the legitimate ruler of this nation from coast to coast. Howard Beck is a traitor; it's just that simple. We need to make this nation whole again, whatever the cost."

"I'm glad to hear you say that, my dear. I'm going to share with you two very important things that will help us dethrone that crazy old man."

Stacy's mind raced ahead, skimming her mental calendar for the first available ten minute time slot in which to share the forthcoming information with Howard…soon. "I'm all ears, Mr. President."

"Are you familiar with General Richard Dupree?"

"The commanding general of the PSA's military?"

"Yes. I have enough leverage to make him my puppet."

"How so?"

"I have his daughter."

This is not good. Howard has to know this immediately. Stacy played along, and looked impressed. "Very good, Mr. President! Well done! What's the second thing?"

"I've located Beck Castle. It's only a matter of time before we're inside."

CHAPTER FOURTEEN

"Who in the hell is General Dupree, and what does the UAE need with his daughter?" Benjamin Black was sitting in his office in the Walt Disney World complex. His second in command, Jessica Bradley, had just returned from her scouting mission near Miami.

Jessica had never heard the name either. "Maybe a disgraced UAE general, someone Sterling wants to torture. Maybe he's gone rogue or something."

"I thought that, too, but it doesn't seem to fit. If he was UAE, we'd have heard about him from the officers we've turned. He has to be with the PSA."

"So you just let that bastard Rutherford take an innocent girl? Without any fight? Just like that?"

"Don't start that shit with me! You weren't here! They had hundreds of soldiers armed to the teeth, ready to slaughter all of us! I didn't have a choice!"

"Okay, okay, jeez. Calm down. I get it. Just pisses me off that they would kidnap an innocent girl like that."

"We can talk about the girl in a minute. Tell me more about what you found."

"The warehouse is a goldmine filled with

pallets of non-perishable food. We have to make it a priority; it could feed all of us through the winter. I left one of my guys behind to keep an eye on it. As long as it remains untouched, he's just gonna sit there and do nothing. If the UAE finds it, he's gonna high-tail it back here and let us know. He has one of our long range radios and can call us when he's about thirty miles out."

One of Ben's first tasks when renovating his community had been to construct a lookout post one hundred seventy-five feet atop what once was Cinderella's Castle. The height advantage gave them an impressive range of communication.

Jessica continued. "What do we do if the UAE finds it?"

"We send out a strike team and take it from them."

"Hell yeah, boss!"

"For now, all we can do is wait for them to clear out of Miami. I don't think they're gonna send out scouting parties. How far away is the warehouse from their current position?"

"About twenty miles."

"Good." Ben had more pressing concerns than the food distribution warehouse. "What is the UAE doing down in Miami?"

"Something huge. They have a two-square-mile perimeter completely blocked off. They've got so many soldiers there they could almost stand shoulder to shoulder around the perimeter."

"What's inside it?"

"That's where it gets weird - nothing strategic, no military installations. The only thing that could be considered remotely important is a small airport."

"Huh. That is weird. If they're having some big meeting, you'd think Miami International would be the better choice. Hmmmm. Small airport, tight security. What else is in there?"

"A residential area, a high school, a cemetery, and a couple strip malls."

"Wait. A cemetery?

"Yeah, a big one."

"I bet that's it. It sounds like someone died, and they're securing it for a funeral. At first I thought Sterling might be coming to Miami, but he alone doesn't warrant that much security. If Sterling was meeting all the regional governors in one place..."

"They would lock the place down tighter than Area 51," Jessica added.

"That has to be it."

Jessica was excited, but reserved. "So what difference does it make to us? We can't do anything but send our condolences."

"I don't know. We might not be able to do

anything, but maybe we can find someone who can."

"Who?"

"That's where the little girl comes in."

"General Dupree?"

"Yeah. How many generals do you think the PSA has? The guy's gotta be important."

"Well, let's just hop on our jet and fly to the PSA. I'm sure we won't get shot down."

"You brought back a jet from Miami, smartass?"

"No."

"Then shut up. We need to put our heads together and come up with something. There's gotta be a way to get word to the PSA. They could wipe those fuckers out and put an end to all this bullshit. Do we have any contacts that could get the word out?"

"Colonel Sanderson out of Fort Polk, maybe? I dunno."

"He might be able to get word to someone in Denver."

"Let's get to work."

CHAPTER FIFTEEN

The polite man was waiting patiently for a meeting. The attack he'd orchestrated on behalf of his employer had gone off without a hitch, and it was time to brief him on the next phase of the plan. His competition, The Silent Warriors, while effective at spreading terror, were amateurs compared to him. If he were a prideful man, he would announce to the world that he alone was responsible for one of the most horrific terror attacks in recent history. Instead, he had no choice but to let The Silent Warriors take credit for his work; his employer would have it no other way. If there was even a faint whiff of doubt – if a single question arose as to The Silent Warriors' involvement in the destruction at Fort McClellan - the polite man had no doubt he'd be quietly *relocated*…to an unmarked grave. Silenced.

The polite man was sitting in an abandoned Applebee's in Matthews, North Carolina. Much of the town had been burned to the ground and deserted for months. The polite man had three of his men keeping watch over the dilapidated building and could hear their status checks in his earpiece. His employer was running late, as usual. He knew his place; his employer didn't need to remind him with such a petty power play. The polite man had the patience of Job and could sit in the restaurant for hours if necessary.

"Sir, a vehicle is approaching."

"Thank you, I see it. No action required. Please monitor the perimeter and maintain radio silence unless a threat to security exists."

"10-4."

The polite man stood, smoothed out his suit coat and straightened his tie. He watched as two armed men entered the restaurant, their rifles pointed at him. The polite man, familiar with the routine, slowly raised both hands as one of the men approached. "Put your hands on your head and turn around. Any sudden moves outta you and you'll regret it."

"My good man, I assure you you'll get nothing but cooperation from me." The armed man quickly patted him down as the other thug did a full security sweep of the restaurant. "We're clear."

"Sir, may I please take my hands from my head and sit down?"

The armed man tensed, sensitive to the defiantly mocking undertone of the question. "I don't give a fuck, man. Do what you want."

The polite man smiled. "No need for profanity, sir. I'll take my seat, thank you."

The armed man's rage seeped from every pore. "Are you fucking with me?"

"No, sir, not at all. I am not a fan of profanity and prefer more… civilized conversation."

"Whatever, asshole."

"Now, now, sir. I've been nothing but polite and respectful to you. I'm afraid I'm going to have to insist that you apologize for your behavior or things will become… unpleasant for you."

"Say what, asshole? You better watch who the fuck you're talking…"

The polite man quickly extended his arm, his rigid fingertips sinking into the warm hollow at the base of the thug's throat. With his free hand, the polite man grabbed the rifle and rammed the stock into the man's chin, causing him to bite off the tip of his tongue. The thug, along with his foul mouth, fell to the floor, spitting blood.

"STOP!"

The startling bellow jerked the backup's attention to the doorway where his boss stood, his pistol drawn and aimed directly at his head. "Boss! He just…"

"I don't care what your foolish partner did, although I have no doubt his ignorant mouth put him on the floor. Lower your weapon! NOW!"

Before the perplexed thug could lower his MP5, he was shot dead; the armed cohort he'd attempted to cover served as easy target practice as well. "Come now, Charles. Still easily offended by colorful words?"

"I abhor such language; it's disgusting."

"You really are something, my friend. You put Bond villains to shame, yet you can't handle cursing?"

"I'm sorry. I did warn him."

"I'm sure you did."

"And now I have to drive myself out of here. You know how much I hate to drive."

"Please, let's sit down. We have a lot to talk about."

Charles had already taken the liberty of cleaning the table and chairs prior to his employer's arrival. "Sir, can I assume you saw the reports on Fort McClellan?"

"I did."

"And?"

"It was perfect. The investigation was recently completed, and all the evidence points to The Silent Warriors. Witnesses even reported that the assailant was Middle Eastern."

"Racism. He was Indian. I selected him for that very reason."

"It worked perfectly. What about the family

and your crew?"

"Disposed of."

"Excellent."

"Thank you, sir. I'm glad you're pleased with my work."

"I never doubted you, Charles."

"Thank you, sir."

"How's the next mission coming along?"

"Ahead of schedule. Mr. Everton had a change of heart much sooner than I expected. He's ready to cooperate. His military service will work to our advantage. He should have no problem infiltrating the target and planting the device."

"You have forty-eight hours. Will that be sufficient?"

"Ample time, sir."

"Outstanding. Since you're in the final stages of your current mission, it's time to start preparing for the next one. You'll be happy to know your payment will be double."

"Sir, double the pay usually means double the challenge."

"That's putting it lightly, Charles. I would say the job is nearly impossible. It's not really about the money though, is it? It's putting that brilliant mind of yours through the ringer that pleases you."

"You know me well, sir."

"Go ahead and take a look. Take your time."

Charles picked up the folder and began to read. He skimmed through it quickly then started over, memorizing every delicious detail. Once he was finished, he placed the packet back on the table and smiled.

"Well?"

"Sir, this job will not be too difficult for me to accomplish."

"Really Charles? Why is that?"

"I already have a spy inside Beck Castle."

CHAPTER SIXTEEN

Deep within the bowels of Beck Castle, General Richard Dupree was snatched from slumber by another horrible nightmare. His battle with PTSD was often a losing one, barely allowing him two hours of sleep at a stretch. It certainly wasn't the recipe for a steady hand or a clear head, but Richard had grown accustomed to the routine.

Richard shuffled down the hall and looked in on his son, relieved to find him fast asleep. In desperate need of coffee, he made an entire pot and sat down to the tedious chore of reviewing status reports and emails from his twelve generals. An email from Max detailing Howard's success in securing his third cruise ship, the *Freedom of the Seas*, made Richard smile. *Good for you, Howard. Didn't know you had it in you.* Richard spent the next thirty minutes sending encrypted messages to his officers in preparation for the invasion of California. Just as he was about to log off, a new email popped up. It caught his eye because, although Richard received hundreds of messages a day from people all over the PSA, none of them came directly to his computer. Instead, the messages were intercepted and screened by Hal before being delivered to his inbox. The subject line of this one read Urgent! You Must Read This ASAP!!! Richard couldn't resist the opening click.

General Dupree, I can't tell you my name, but I have information that is of vital importance. I have been in contact with a fellow patriot in Florida, a man by the name of Benjamin Black. Ben recently liberated a group of slaves, one of whom was your daughter. He is certain of this fact because a UAE colonel brought a large force to his front gate and kidnapped her. The colonel is using your daughter as leverage against you. Ben said the colonel mentioned your name in reference to the child. He said the convoy headed north before his scouts abandoned the chase for safety reasons. Ben also wanted me to tell you that President Sterling and his regional governors will be in Miami for a funeral the day after tomorrow. We hope the PSA will use this information and strike a serious blow. God bless you. I hope you get your daughter back.

"I thought you might find that message interesting, sir."

"Hal, I don't know what to make of this."

"If you don't mind me saying, sir, I think this is good news."

"My daughter's been kidnapped by a lunatic! How is that good news?"

"Sir, the UAE knows her importance. That means she is safe for the time being. It also means she is alive and well."

"Hal, you're quite the optimist. Thank you."

"You're welcome, sir."

"Tell me every last detail about this email."

"It was sent from an encrypted terminal in Fort Polk, Louisiana. Given that Fort Polk is controlled by the UAE, the origin points to a spy."

"What? UAE? What if this is a trap?"

"Sir, I don't believe it is. The UAE goes to great lengths to stop all messages from making it across PSA borders. This is the first one that has ever been successfully sent. The details about the funeral are valid as we learned them from Stacy Reid. I think the message is real."

"I think you're right. What do you think will be the UAE's next move?"

"Sir, my analysis leads me to believe that in the near future, the news of your daughter's capture will be presented to you in exchange for your cooperation. The UAE will attempt to employ you as their operative."

"That's not going to happen. Where do you think they're holding my daughter?"

"I've been reviewing satellite footage of Florida. The convoy in question did, in fact, head north as the message indicates. I tracked it to Fort

McClellan where the convoy split up in different directions. Most of the vehicles entered a large building inside the base. None of the images I've reviewed indicate that a child left the building. It is difficult to ascertain her location at the current time."

"Well, at least it's a start."

"How do you wish to proceed, sir?"

"I don't know. I can't very well postpone the invasion of California for personal reasons. It would be a waste of time to attempt a rescue until we're certain of her location."

"Would you like my advice, sir?"

"Always."

"Sir, I believe you should wait for the UAE to contact you. They will no doubt keep her perfectly safe so they can use her as leverage. Once they contact you, we will have more information to go on."

"You're right as usual, Hal."

"Thank you, sir."

"When is the president expected to return?"

"Sir, President Beck is scheduled to return this afternoon. Would you like me to bring him up to speed on the matter?"

"Yes. Tell him I endorse your plan and I look forward to his counsel."

"Very good, sir."

"I guess that settles it then."

"Settles what, sir?"

"I'm headed to Seattle to lead the invasion of California."

"I see, sir."

"I'm impressed that Howard liberated the last cruise ship so easily. I was certain it was going to get ugly and the military was going to have to drag those people off the ship."

"Sir, I share your assessment. The president's speech impressed me a great deal."

"You impress me, Hal."

"Thank you, sir. May I ask why?"

"You can calculate a trillion different outcomes to any situation, and Howard still managed to surprise you. If anyone knows Howard, it's you."

"Sir, I can say without bias that my creator is a truly remarkable man."

"He is, my friend, he is. I'll be leaving for Seattle within the hour. Prep the stealth jet for my departure."

"Very good, sir."

Richard headed for his son's room, anxious to say goodbye before he headed out. His firstborn rolled over as Richard plunked himself down on the bed.

"What time is it?"

"It's early, son. You don't have to get up. I just wanted to talk to you before I leave. I know you're upset about your sister. You're mad at me and that's okay. I'm mad at me, too."

"I'm not mad at you, Dad."

"It's okay, son. I just want you to know that I love you and your sister very much."

"I love you, too."

"I can't explain it to you, but Chrissy will be coming home soon."

"Promise?"

"I promise."

"Where is she?"

"You don't worry about that, Timmy. Just trust your Dad, okay?"

"Okay. How long will you be gone?"

"I don't know. Your grandparents are expecting you after school today."

"Okay, Dad. I'm still sleepy."

"Go back to sleep. I love you."

Timothy Dupree didn't reply, but simply smiled as Richard kissed his forehead.

***

Director Maxwell Harris and his wife, Elizabeth, were seated next to President Howard Beck at the guest of honor's table, along with several of the military's high-ranking brass. Senator Wilson had spared no expense in staging this black tie affair in the president's honor. The guests turned toward the stage as Senator Wilson approached the podium.

"Ladies and gentlemen, if I may have your attention, please. Thank you all for coming this evening. I hope you're enjoying the festivities so far. It is truly a singular honor to be hosting, for the first time, the president of the Pacific States of America."

The banquet hall erupted in thunderous applause, and everyone was on their feet. Howard was enjoying his lemon pepper chicken and looked around in confusion and annoyance at the mealtime interruption. He grabbed Elizabeth's hand and gently pulled her down within earshot. "What's going on? Am I supposed to do something? When are they going to stop?"

"Howard, sweetie, just stand up. A quick smile and wave is all they need."

Howard obeyed and was delighted when his brief acknowledgement did the trick. Once everyone was seated, he breathed a sigh of relief and focused once again on his chicken.

Senator Wilson continued. "In the darkest day of our former nation's history, we had one shining beacon of hope, one man who stood up to preserve democracy, one man who kept liberty and freedom alive. I'm proud to call him my friend; I'm even prouder to call him my president. Ladies and gentlemen, the president of the Pacific States of America, Howard Beck."

Once again, a thunderous standing ovation ensued. Senator Wilson took a step back from the podium and extended a welcoming arm.

Howard was busy eating his lemon pepper chicken.

"Howard, honey, you need to say a few words," said Elizabeth.

"What? Now? I'm still eating!"

Max leaned over his wife. "Howard, no more speeches after this. Just say thank you and talk about how great the PSA is and how bad the UAE is for a minute. That's it."

"This is ridiculous. Have the waiter reheat my food; it's going to get cold."

Max smiled at his wife. "Yes, Mr. President."

"Enough of that! You know I hate that." Howard put his fork down and walked to the stage while Max and Elizabeth looked on with loving admiration. Howard smiled awkwardly at the crowd.

"Let's make this quick; my food's getting cold."

The crowd laughed, completely unaware that Howard wasn't joking.

"Thank you, Senator Wilson. Thank you everyone in attendance. A special thanks to the men and women in uniform here tonight. They will be on the front lines taking back our country soon enough." Howard stopped and clapped, the audience didn't hesitate to follow suit. "Yes, yes, the brave men and women of our armed forces deserve our respect. In the coming weeks, we will take the fight to the UAE. Most of our military forces are preparing for an invasion so grand in scale it approaches the Normandy invasion of World War II. Under the tyrannical rule of Simon Sterling - the man who murdered the great Malcolm Powers - the UAE has driven our once exalted nation further and further into the pits of hell. Men and women are starving, men and women are dying, men and women are being sold into slavery while the UAE is content to do nothing but consolidate their own wealth and power. I say no more! We must save our brothers and sisters on the other side of our borders!"

The crowd was instantly on their feet and cheering. Howard left the podium and returned to his newly warmed meal.

CHAPTER SEVENTEEN

Regional Governor Roberto Jimenez was nearly comatose, thanks in large part to Ambien and Elavil. He slept so deeply that his nurse was able to check his vitals every three hours during the night without waking him. Andrew didn't have an issue with his boss taking Ambien or Elavil; he did, however, take issue with him taking both of them at the same time right before bed. Roberto ignored his nurse's wishes since taking the two together was the only way he could get a decent night's sleep.

At 3 a.m., Andrew walked into the adjacent room to check on the elderly governor as scheduled. As he was placing the cuff on Roberto's arm, Andrew caught a glimpse of a shadowy figure across the room. Startled, Andrew muffled a scream. "Remain calm, Andrew. I'm not here to hurt either of you. I want you to take a step back and keep your hands where I can see them."

"Do you have a death wish? Do you know who this is?"

"Roberto Jimenez, regional governor and former director of the CIA."

"Take what you want and leave."

"Oh, Andrew, it's not that simple. I need your help."

"You need to leave before security makes their rounds."

"Nice try. At the governor's request, security never enters this room. The man obviously has trust issues. Roberto here doesn't want anyone to know just how frail he has become and how close he is to death's door. He's got an image to uphold."

"What's this about?"

"Well, Andrew, let's start with this: your sister's name is Julia Massey. She's married to Irvin and they have three children. I could tell you their ages and where they go to school, but I think you get the point."

"How do you know that? What have you done to them?"

"Nothing, I assure you. You and Julia were born to Fredrick and Jane Bailey. Your mother is a retired real estate agent, and your father is the chief of surgery at Saint Francis. Are we clear?"

"I'm starting to get the point. I do whatever you say or they all die?"

"Yes."

"I'm not killing anyone; I just can't."

"I know you don't have that in you, given your profession. You won't have to kill anyone."

"What do you want me to do?"

"I want you to help me keep my family alive."

"I don't understand."

"Let's just say you're not the only one whose family is in danger. As long as you go to Florida with your boss, everything will be just fine…for both of us."

"I don't know anything about Florida."

"Please stop lying to me, Andrew. You're leaving for Florida this morning. If you lie to me again, I will kill one of your sister's children. Are we clear?"

Andrew began to cry. "Yes."

"We have work to do. If you do what you're told, I'll be long gone before your boss wakes up."

***

"Stop it! I'm awake! Jesus!" Roberto Jimenez hated waking up in the morning. He had a strict schedule to adhere to, and his nurse went to great lengths to keep him on track.

"We have a big day, Mr. Jimenez. Do you need to use the restroom?"

"What do you think? C'mon, let's get a move on. I want to leave here in an hour."

Andrew lifted his boss out of bed and settled him in his wheelchair. As Roberto wheeled himself into the bathroom, Andrew went about making the bed and getting his suit ready.

"Not that one! I told you I wanted the solid black one! Dammit!"

"Mr. Jimenez, this is the solid black one. If you put on your glasses, you'll see."

Roberto did so, but he would never admit that Andrew was right.

Once dressed and groomed, Roberto shooed Andrew from the room and opened his computer. He vigorously searched security reports in Florida and found that the evacuation of Miami and the surrounding areas had been completed. He hadn't left the former state of California since his arrival. He was not looking forward to flying across the country to bury one of his closest friends.

***

Once the Leer jet rolled to a stop at the small airport on the outskirts of Miami, Roberto waited patiently as Andrew activated the wheelchair lift. Safely on the tarmac, Roberto smiled as the president of the Unified American Empire strolled up to greet him.

"Hello, old friend."

"Mr. President, I wish this meeting were under better circumstances."

"As do I, Roberto, as do I."

"Is everyone here?"

"Governor Walston is due in the next ten minutes. Everyone else is at the funeral home. How was your flight?"

"Long."

"After the services, I hope you'll join us for dinner."

"I'd like that." Roberto wheeled around. "Andrew! Get your ass over here and meet the president!"

Andrew quickly exited the jet with Roberto's bag in hand.

"Mr. President, this strapping young lad is my personal assistant, Andrew."

Roberto never referred to Andrew as his nurse. After all, he had an image to uphold.

Simon extended his hand. "Andrew, it's a pleasure to meet you."

"Mr. President, it's an honor for me to you … I mean …"

"Shut up, Andrew. You're embarrassing yourself."

"Roberto, that's no way to treat this young man. Tell me, Andrew, carrying this old geezer around must give you amazing upper body strength. How much can you bench press?"

"I'm not sure, I don't lift weights."

"Andrew! What are you doing?"

"I'm sorry, what did …"

"Always address the president as 'Mr. President.' You know what? Stop talking; just quit while you're behind. Let's go, start pushing, let's get this show on the road."

Andrew quietly obeyed his boss, the stain of humiliation darkening his cheeks.

As they walked forward, the two powerful men quickly forgot about the man pushing the wheelchair. Simon didn't seem the least bit fazed by the embarrassing exchange. "Tell me, Roberto, would you be willing to say a few words on Jim's behalf?"

"Mr. President, I was hoping you'd ask. I do have some things I'd like to share about my dear friend."

"Excellent. I look forward to it."

***

Before the Collapse of 2027, Christ Fellowship Church on First Avenue in Miami had been newly renovated to hold an extra thousand seats, making it one of the largest churches in the former United States. The large capacity was not required during the funeral of Regional Governor James Weygandt. Just under one hundred people were in attendance, the majority of whom were extended family members of the deceased. The remainder included Supreme Commander Moody, commander of the Unified National Guard, the seven remaining regional governors of the Unified American Empire, and her president, Simon Sterling. Regional Governor James Weygandt's coffin was draped in the official flag of the UAE.

Once the governor's wife was seated, it was time for the president to enter the sanctuary. Much of the family found the president's ego downright disgusting, as if *he* was somehow the honoree at this event. President Sterling was in the lobby waiting for his chief advisor, Stacy Reid, to cue his entrance.

"How do I look?"

"Handsome as always. I'm glad Mr. DeLuca finished your suit in time."

"It wasn't an option. I had him pull an all-nighter to get it finished."

Stacy tried to look interested, but she shared the family's antipathy toward the narcissistic president. She got the go-ahead signal from one of the ushers. "It's time, Mr. President."

"Thank you, Stacy. I'm wondering if you could be a dear and fetch my pen from the car?"

"Of course, Mr. President." Stacy was grateful for an excuse to miss the man's grand entrance, though his need to flaunt his ridiculously expensive possessions – and at a funeral, no less – sickened her. The pen in question cost north of a thousand dollars.

As the ushers opened the doors, the funeral guests reluctantly struggled to their feet, trying in vain to give the president the respect he felt was due him. Simon strolled down the aisle with an air of regal haughtiness and took his seat on the front row.

Regional Governor Jackson Butler was sitting on the second row, closest to the outside aisle. He was pleased with himself, delighted to be keeping a secret to which only one other guest was privy. He knew it was juvenile but he couldn't help himself. If the people in this room had a clue as to why they were really here, they'd be filled with rage. Glancing down the pew, Jackson spotted Roberto Jimenez sitting nearby. Jackson loathed the crusty old geezer with every fiber of his being. He glared at Jimenez in pure contempt as the president took the podium. The asshole's mere presence was enough to infuriate him. Jackson took notice as the nervous looking gentleman sitting next to Jimenez stood awkwardly in the aisle. *What is wrong with this weirdo? Why the fuck is he getting up in the middle of the president's speech?* Sweat glistened on the man's face as he headed toward the exit. As Jackson turned around in his seat, he saw the man take a small electronic device from his pocket. *Car keys? No, he didn't drive here.*

Oh shit! He's about to detonate the bomb!

Jackson burst from his seat and sprinted to the stage. The president's protection detail squared up against him, effectively blocking his path.

"BOMB! BOMB! BOMB!"

The security detail reacted instantaneously. They lifted the president off his feet, carrying him to the baptistery. Once they cleared the steps, they threw the president in the murky water. Jackson dove to the floor and curled up in the fetal position against the wall.

The small explosive device strapped to Roberto Jimenez's wheelchair detonated, instantly killing the family of James Weygandt, Supreme Commander Carl Moody, and the six regional governors in the audience.

***

Several states away, Charles waited quietly in his vehicle. As his phone vibrated, he tapped his headset.

"It's done."

Charles smiled. "Dispose of Mr. Everton and his family. Did the nurse survive?"

"Yes."

"Dispose of him as well."

"I'll take care of it."

"Tell our mutual friend we're ready to

proceed with the final phase of the plan."

CHAPTER EIGHTEEN

"Holy shit! What in the hell was that?" Jessica Bradley, Benjamin Black's top lieutenant, was on a rooftop two blocks from the church. The blast had blown out all the windows in the front of the building and shattered car windows for blocks in every direction.

Her partner, Robert Mathias, was face down on the roof, his hands protecting his head. "Fuck! Are we being bombed? Let's get the hell outta here before we get killed!"

Benjamin Black had sent the pair on an eight hour trip through the Florida wasteland to the church on the off chance that some lucky opportunity would present itself. Jessica had a knack for sneaking around the Florida swamps, and her skills proved useful for infiltrating the perimeter around the church. Robert had a high-powered sniper rifle and was under strict orders to shoot Simon Sterling if he was foolish enough to present himself as a target.

Jessica and Robert watched as a limousine and three black SUVs raced away from the building. Before they could plan their next move, a man appeared on the street below them, chasing after the now distant motorcade. "Stop, Mr. President, don't leave me! I'm alive! I'm alive!"

"Is that who I think it is?" asked Robert.

"Yeah, that's Jackson Butler.

***

"Mr. President, are you okay? What happened? What was that?"

"I'm fine, Stacy, I'm fine. My ears are ringing a little, but I'm fine. I don't know how Jackson knew something was about to happen, but he did. If he hadn't rushed the stage and warned my security detail, I might not have gotten out of there in time."

"I'm glad you're okay. Did Jackson make it out?"

"I have no idea. Driver! Pull over, right now!"

"I can't do that Mr. President, we have to get you to the security checkpoint."

"How much longer?"

"ETA, two minutes."

"Mr. President, are you sure you're okay?"

"I can't believe those blockheads ruined my new suit! Why did they have to throw me in that slimy, germ-ridden water? No telling what kind of diseases I caught in there!"

"It probably saved your life, Mr. President," said the driver. "Being submerged in water lessens the impact of the shockwave."

"It took me four weeks to get this suit from Italy! It's ruined!"

I'd like it better if you were wearing the suit when it's burned, thought Stacy.

***

The entry point to the funeral perimeter was the headquarters for the Miami-Dade Metro Police Department. The president was being held in the armory since it was the most secure room in the building. The room had a master lock inside the room, so the armorer could remain inside and keep it secure from outsiders.

"Mr. President, what happened?" asked Stacy.

"Roberto's nurse got up just as I began speaking. I couldn't believe he had the nerve. Jackson must have seen him do something suspicious because he stormed the stage and warned my detail."

"Did Jackson make it out?"

"I don't know. It all happened so fast."

"It's okay. You need to relax for a minute. I'm going to find out what happened. Just take it easy, and I'll come back with some answers."

"Thank you, my dear."

Stop calling me dear, you bastard.

Stacy was relieved to get out of the room but knew her respite would be a brief one. Digging in her purse for the buried Xanax bottled, Stacy took a few precious minutes to review the situation and plan her next step. If Howard Beck was responsible for the attack and didn't warn her, she would have to accept the fact that Howard was willing to kill her along with Simon Sterling. The sacrifice was worth it. One thing was certain: more than half of the regional governors were dead. The UAE was crippled - no, it was dying - given what had just happened. Stacy knew she had the chance to put an end to this nightmare – right here, right now. She had precious few minutes to act.

Stacy looked around for a weapon. Anything would do: a pistol, rifle, shotgun. It didn't matter. At first, her room-to-room search turned up nothing useful. At the end of the hall she hit the jackpot: an otherwise empty room now being used by the troops to stage their gear! Stacy tore through crates and backpacks, certain that someone must have left something behind. Then she saw it – a duty belt complete with holstered gun.

Stacy reentered the armory, a terrified look on her face. The two security officers look concerned; the president appeared terrified

"What? What's going on, Stacy?" the

president asked, obviously frightened.

Stacy looked at the armed guards. "They need one of you up front. The lobby is under attack! Hurry! I'll lock the door behind you! Go!"

The security officer turned to his partner for approval. "Stay here. Don't open this door no matter what!"

"I got it! Go!"

Stacy closed the heavy steel door and locked it. Taking the pistol from her coat pocket, she turned around and opened fire.

CHAPTER NINETEEN

Mohammed Rahal awoke in his makeshift shelter two miles from the UAE compound outside Ocean City, Delaware. He had been watching the compound for months, learning the layout and taking detailed notes on the soldiers stationed there. The leader of his cell had armed him with the necessary equipment and had given him a solo mission to be completed at the designated time. Mohammed had memorized every detail.

His mission was to destroy the small UAE compound by any means necessary. The facility served as a communications base for over half The Pulse Zone and, more importantly, the navy securing the Eastern Seaboard from invasion. After the EMP was detonated in 2027 and fried every electronic circuit in most of the eastern United States, the Unified American Empire scrambled to restore communication in the region. Mohammed knew this was a suicide mission and had come to terms with his imminent demise. He was determined not to die in vain. He had two crucial advantages in his favor: the element of surprise and his willingness to make the ultimate sacrifice to accomplish his goal.

Mohammed moved carefully through the tree line fifty yards from the front gate and set up the first stage of his plan. He placed an automatic rifle on the ground, its barrel propped upright on a log. He placed a small contraption of his own making in the trigger guard. Once that was done, he set up two claymores spaced twenty yards apart. Satisfied that both were properly concealed, he made his way to the back fence of the compound, setting up two more claymores along the way. Once he was in position, Mohammed took two trigger devices from his front pocket. Pressing the button on the first trigger, he waited until he heard the rifle fire its first shot, knowing it would fire off a round every ten seconds. He pressed the second trigger and the claymore closest to the front gate exploded. As the soldiers in the compound scrambled to the front gate to return fire, two of them were killed by a claymore. The diversion worked perfectly. Mohammed used the wire cutters to open a hole in the fence. He produced a silenced pistol and moved toward the main building. Two soldiers came into his line of sight, their backs turned. Mohammed squeezed off two shots in rapid succession and the soldiers fell. Once the front gate was visible, Mohammed holstered his pistol and tossed two grenades in its direction, killing five soldiers.

By the time Mohammed entered the main building, three of the soldiers were already on their way back. With precious little time to spare,

Mohammed reached into his jacket. With a satisfied smile, he jerked the cord on his vest to detonate the twelve bricks of C-4 packed within it. The main communications relay for the Unified American Empire was completely destroyed.

***

"All stop, bring the boat to periscope depth and raise the antenna."

"Aye, Captain."

"Communications, open a channel with command."

"Channel open, sir."

"We are receiving your signal. Authenticate."

The captain checked his tablet. "Authorization one-five-five-charlie-eight-three-seven-bravo."

"Authorization code accepted. Report."

"We have arrived at the designated coordinates and will remain on station awaiting orders."

"Keep this channel open. Contact in three zero minutes."

"Understood." The captain motioned for his executive officer to step in close. "XO, I want an officers meeting. Make it happen."

"Aye, Captain." The XO had been wondering what all the secrecy was about. He'd never been kept in the dark about a mission before, but for some reason this time was different. The XO picked up the microphone in front of him. "This is the XO. All officers report to the officers' mess on the double."

In less than five minutes, twelve officers sat on the edge of their seats waiting to learn why they'd been sent so far from home. The captain stood at the end of the table demanding their undivided attention.

"Gentlemen, I am not a fan of keeping my crew in the dark, but when I'm finished here, all of you will understand why I'm the only soul onboard that knows our mission. We are currently three hundred nautical miles from the shores of the former United States. The bulk of our fleet is less than twenty-four hours behind us. When they arrive, the invasion of North America will begin."

The men were shocked. Based on their course, they knew where they were headed but they never dreamed a full-scale invasion force was right behind them. Most assumed their mission was strictly for intelligence gathering.

"What are your questions?"

The XO spoke first. "What type of resistance are we looking at? We all know the Americans are crippled, but that doesn't mean their navy won't put up a fight."

"They can put up all the fight they want; our navy is in much better shape than theirs. Ours subs are a decade more advanced. The only way they could detect us is if we rammed into them."

"The Silent Warriors have done a wonderful job of keeping the Americans busy. Their latest distraction gives us the perfect opportunity to strike," the communications officer added.

The captain smiled. "You're getting ahead of yourself, lieutenant. You don't even know what we're doing here."

"Sorry, sir."

"Don't be. Your speculation amuses me."

"But this is an attack sub, sir." The comm officer wasn't willing to give up.

"I agree with you, lieutenant, I assure you. Our superiors have treated this operation with the utmost secrecy. Our orders were to proceed to these coordinates, wait for further instructions, and keep an eye on the shore. That's what we're doing - watching and waiting."

"Captain, with all due respect, why tell us now? You could have waited until you received the final order," said the XO.

"Preparation, Commander, pure and simple. I want the crew to be ready to execute whatever plan we're given the instant it's given. I want no surprises, no minutes wasted on chatter or confusion. Hesitation - even for a single second - could be fatal. I want all departments battle-ready when the order comes in."

"Captain, what do you want us to tell the crew?" asked the weapons officer.

"Tell them we're on the frontline for the invasion of North America."

CHAPTER TWENTY

General Richard Dupree's stealth jet touched down in a deserted parking lot near the Port of Seattle. Being completely invisible to the naked eye, one would have to physically touch the craft to know it was even there. Hal brought the craft out of stealth mode and it rippled into view.

"Sir, I've notified the president of your arrival. Director Harris is bringing a vehicle to pick you up."

"Thank you, Hal. How long before he gets here?"

"Sir, I made the notification some time before we landed. He will be here in less than a minute."

"Always thinking ahead, my friend."

"I do try, sir."

"Here he comes now. Thanks for the ride, Hal."

"Thank you for flying HAL-9000 Airways. We hope you enjoy your stay in Seattle."

"Hal, was that a joke?"

"Was it funny, sir?"

"Damn funny! I didn't know you had a sense of humor."

"Thank you, sir. I have been working on it."

As he headed toward the approaching vehicle, Richard glanced back in time to witness the stealth jet's ghost-like disappearance before his eyes. Max stopped the car a few feet short of Richard and got out. "Son of a bitch! That was something to see!"

"Got a nice ride, don't I?"

"Stop bragging."

"Where are my ships?"

"They just headed to the Bahamas for a vacation."

"Funny. I'm sure they'll have a lovely view of the UAE navy."

"C'mon, let's go."

***

From his vantage point on the pier, Richard surveyed the three cruise ships that would bring the invasion force to the shores of California. Each ship housed roughly three thousand human troops and a thousand Hal robots ready to take the UAE by surprise. Each vessel also carried fleets of drone ships controlled by Hal. Richard was certain they could take California in less than a week and push their way east to The Pulse Zone.

"General Dupree, sir, are you ready to embark?" A gray-haired general stood at attention and snapped a smart salute.

Richard returned the symbolic gesture. "Yes, General Bedford, permission to come aboard?"

"Permission granted, sir."

Richard and Max followed the general up the ramp to the quarter deck. Richard tried hard not to let the attention of his arrival go straight to his head. Captains and lieutenants shouted "Attention, officer on deck!" when Richard moved from one part of the ship to the next. Max and Richard made it to the ship's bridge where they were greeted by the captain of the vessel, Lt. Commander Konkoly.

"General Dupree, it's an honor you chose the *Freedom of the Seas* as the flagship for this invasion. Thank you, sir."

Max was confused. "Flagship?"

The captain looked surprised. "The presence of the most senior officer designates this as the task force's flagship."

"Ah, I see."

The captain continued. "Sir, we will be underway in just under ten minutes. Once the other captains give the green light, we're headed to California."

"Carry on, Captain."

"Aye, sir."

A few minutes later, the comm officer reported all ships ready to get underway.

Captain Konkoly announced, "Helm, once we are clear of the harbor, make best speed to San Francisco."

"Aye, sir. I estimate forty-one hours to San Francisco at twenty-two knots."

"Gentlemen, would you care to join me in my quarters for a drink? This is cause for celebration."

"Lead the way, please," Richard said.

"XO, you have deck and the conn."

"Aye sir, XO has the deck and the conn," answered the XO.

A few short minutes later, the three men were seated in the captain's massive quarters.

"I must say, Mr. Konkoly, your quarters are freaking huge," Max said as he rested his cane against a table.

"Tell me about it. This place is twice as big as my house. If it wouldn't be considered fraternization, I'd have twenty people living in here with me."

"Captain, command does have its privileges. Enjoy it."

"Is that an order, General?"

"Only a suggestion."

"General, if I may, how much resistance do you expect on the shores?"

"If Hal is right - and I've never known him to be otherwise - practically none. We should be able to spill right into the streets of San Francisco and knock on Jimenez's front door."

"I'd love to see the look on his face," said Max. "Gonna take him prisoner or just shoot him on the spot?"

"I'm gonna pull the trigger myself." Richard stood and nodded to Max, who took the signal and grabbed his cane. "Captain, thank you for the drink. Max and I have much to discuss, and it's getting late."

Captain Konkoly rose and shook their hands. "Thank you. It's an honor to meet you both."

Richard marched from the room and turned to find Max lagging several paces behind. "Leg not getting any better?"

"Worse."

"Go to bed, Max. We can talk in the morning. We have the better part of two days on this luxury liner."

"I think I'll convince my wife that this is our honeymoon."

"Good idea."

***

Max and Elizabeth were shaken from their slumber at 2:45 a.m. as a loud explosion rocked the boat."

"Son of a bitch! What the hell is going on?"

Elizabeth was tossed violently to the floor as the room tilted thirty degrees. "Max! I'm scared! Something is very wrong!"

"Something hit us. I've got to find Richard."

***

Richard was no stranger to boats, given his years as a Navy SEAL, so he knew the ship was under attack.

"Hal, goddammit! You said our path was clear! What the hell is going on?"

"Sir, we are under fire from an unknown location. I cannot detect the projectiles before they hit the ship."

"How in the hell is that possible?"

"Unknown, sir."

"Max and Elizabeth?"

"Sir, Elizabeth is safe in her quarters. Max is on his way to yours; I suggest you head back to meet him."

As Richard turned, he caught a glimpse of Max at the other end of the hallway. "Max! Stop! I'll come to you! Just hold on!"

"What the fuck is going on?" The question was quickly consumed by the deafening roar of alarms.

"We're under attack!" Richard yelled, anchoring his arm securely around Max's shoulders for guidance. "C'mon! We gotta get to the bridge!"

***

"What's the status of the vessel?"

"Sir, three direct hits to the bow. She's going down; nothing will prevent that."

"Excellent! We can't have her in the way. Continue firing."

"Sir, the other two vessels are in range. The lead is closing in on the first."

"Attempting rescue, I'm sure. Open fire on both vessels."

"Aye, sir."

***

Richard and Max made it to the bridge, only to find that no one had a clue what was happening."

"Hal! Goddammit! What's going on?"

"Sir, I've launched the drone fleet to investigate. The ship is being struck by torpedoes from an unidentified submarine."

Captain Konkoly's eyes reflected his terror. "A sub? The UAE wouldn't fire on a cruise ship! Why are they doing this?"

"It's not the UAE! It can't be. American subs aren't sophisticated enough to escape Hal's detection! We have to abandon ship! We're going down!" screamed Richard.

"Sir, even though the drones are not meant to be submerged, I managed to successfully lower one for two-point-nine seconds before it went offline. I was able to get a reading on the submarine and obtain a proper identification. It's the Chinese."

Richard stared in horror at Max and Captain Konkoly. Before they could reply, another torpedo slammed into the side of the boat, one hundred nineteen feet below the bridge. Captain Konkoly was instantly killed from flying glass and debris blown into the bridge. Richard was propelled out the window opposite the captain into the water below. Max was thrown into the back wall, crushing his L2 vertebra.

CHAPTER TWENTY-ONE

"Charles, you almost killed me, you know," Jackson said to the mysterious assassin.

"You knew exactly what was going to happen. You were to leave the auditorium when your boss took the stage, but you chose to intervene. I must insist that you explain yourself."

"Excuse me? You work for me. I'm not accountable to you for a fucking thing!"

"Jackson, please. Let's not say things we might regret."

"Oh, yes, my apologies. The last time we met, you killed two of my men for offending your polite sensibilities."

"I only killed the foul-mouthed one; you killed the other. Don't blame me for your actions, sir."

"The two were the closest of friends, and one watched as you beat his buddy half to death. I have no doubt he was going to kill you for that."

"My good man, are you saying you saved my life?"

"Absolutely."

"How kind of you."

"Yes, I knew what was going to happen, but I had no idea Roberto's nurse was in your employ. I was under the false assumption that your operative would give me some sort of signal."

"Sir, I had to minimize the chance that someone else would be tipped off by suspicious behavior. You knew when the president took the podium..."

"Not that it's any of your concern, but I had good reason for sparing the president."

"Sir, do you want me to guess, or are you going to tell me?"

"My plan was to be the hero who saved the president's life. I was then going to dispose of him and claim that in his dying words he pleaded with me to take the mantle and run the UAE. No one would doubt the intentions of the new national hero."

"Brilliant plan, sir. I'm impressed. When do you expect the Chinese ambassador?

"Ambassador Zhang is going to wait a few weeks till the West Coast is secure before meeting me in Denver."

"What do you want me to do about Sterling?"

"Nothing! *I* will deal with Sterling, not you. Are we clear?"

"Sir, I understand your reasoning. I was simply asking if you want me to locate him. I have doubts that he'll return to the mansion in Denver, given the security threat."

"I apologize, Charles. If you can find him

that will certainly help moves things along. We do have to know his whereabouts before Ambassador Zhang arrives."

"Sir, with all due respect, may I ask a candid question?"

"The Chinese?"

"Yes, sir."

"I've been in top-secret negotiations with the Chinese for six months. Simon Sterling will never be able to get this country strong enough to defend itself against Iran. They're coming, and there's nothing we can do to stop them. Our navy will hold them off for a while. We could wage nuclear war, but both sides could wipe out mankind with the weaponry they have stockpiled, so neither will go that route. But... they're still coming. Rebuilding The Pulse Zone will take decades; the entire Eastern Seaboard is becoming a third world wasteland. I've brokered a deal with the Chinese. They're eager to expand their borders into ours and utilize our resources in exchange for protection from Iran. We will maintain our own laws and freedoms."

"Sir, how can you be so sure they'll honor their end of the bargain?"

"They're keeping me in charge of our military; more importantly, I will retain control of our nuclear arsenal. It will keep us both honest."

"And you think the American people will just

go along with this? What about the West Coast and the Rockies? They're living somewhat normal lives there."

"They're not going to have a choice. The Chinese aren't coming to conquer and imprison us; they're coming as allies."

"Sir, again, with respect, I don't think the Chinese will see it that way. They own the bulk of our former nation's debt. I think they're coming to call in their markers."

"Charles, I have no doubt that you're wrong; however, if the alternative is The Great Empire of Iran, I think the American people will choose the Chinese any day of the week. They have the military might to defend our borders and keep us safe."

"How the mighty have fallen."

"Indeed. But weak as we might be, I'll still have my finger on the button to level Beijing if things don't go our way, and our Chinese friends know it."

"A wise precaution."

***

"Who attacked me? Start talking now or you die!" President Simon Sterling's left arm was bleeding profusely, thanks to a poorly aimed shot from his chief advisor, Stacy Reid. "I know you were involved in the attack on the church, so start talking! And how convenient that you'd left the church right before the blast."

Stacy was bound to a chair in the armory, nursing a black eye and a broken hand. Having never fired a gun in her life, she'd botched the attempt to assassinate the president of the Unified American Empire. She'd been so startled by the first shot that she'd closed her eyes and pulled the trigger blindly until all she heard was *click..click..click.* Hitting Sterling in the arm, hell, hitting him at all before the security officer kicked the weapon from her hand had been pure luck. The blow, breaking three of her fingers, was quickly followed by a punch to the face that dropped Stacy to the ground. "I don't know who attacked you at the church. *You* sent me to the car; leaving the church was not *my* idea, it was yours!"

"You're lying! You're a part of this, and if I have to cut off all your fingers and have you tortured to death to find out what you know, I'll do it! Who are you working for? Howard Beck? Did he put you up to this? Admit it!"

"I'm not working for Howard Beck! I did this on my own!"

"You're lying!"

Stacy sniffled, blinking back the flood of hot tears. "I was acting alone! I saw a chance to finally kill you, and I took it! You're a madman, a crazy dictator who's responsible for the deaths of millions! You murdered Malcolm Powers, you sick bastard!"

Simon was stunned. "So that's what this is all about? You have some crazy notion that I actually assassinated a sitting president of the United States, and you want petty revenge? Are you serious? Malcolm was a role model to me, and I loved him dearly. I was so looking forward to having a relationship with him in his twilight years, and the Iranians robbed me of that! How dare you!"

"You can feign sentimentality all you want, but we both know what you did. You wanted him out of the way. It was rather convenient that The Pulse covered your tracks so completely that no one will ever know the truth. You can deny it all you want, but you know you assassinated a man... a man whose shoes you'll never be able to fill. You'll never be even half the man Malcolm was."

The taunting worked like a charm. "Malcolm Powers was a fool! He saw the nation crumbling around him, and he did nothing to stop it! How many people died in Florida - your own family included - because he wanted to save the world from Iran? So yes, my dear, I murdered him. I vaporized every ounce of his body with a missile so no grave could ever hold him; not even ashes would remain to fill an urn. I have no regrets. None!"

"And what have you done to make things right? You closed our borders and refused help from anyone. Your mighty isolationism is turning this country into a wasteland!"

"Bitch, I'm done arguing with you. I can't believe I actually trusted you. I'm not an idiot; I know you're spying for Howard Beck. I know with every fiber of my being that you're going to tell me everything, every little detail. You will experience pain like you never thought possible. Only when I'm certain you've told me everything in that deluded, conceited mind of yours will I grant you the gift of death."

"Please, I did this on my own. I don't know who bombed the church, I swear. I saw my chance to kill you and I took it. No one told me to do it. Please, you have to believe me, Simon."

Sterling turned to the security officer. "Get the doctor."

Stacy breathed a sigh of relief. "Thank you, Simon."

Maniacal laughter filled the room. "Oh no! The doctor isn't coming to clean you up, dear. I need him to keep you alive for the duration. Wouldn't want you to bleed out on us."

Stacy was shaking as she begged through her tears, "Please! Please! I swear I did this on my own."

"Before the doctor gets here, let me make one thing clear. You can keep all ten of your fingers if you pay the price."

"W-w-what?"

"Tell me, my dear, how do I get into Beck Castle?"

***

"Let me get this straight. There was an explosion in the church?" Benjamin Black was in his quarters at Walt Disney World. He had instructed Jessica to brief him immediately upon her return - day or night.

"Yeah, it was massive. We were two blocks away, and it damn near blew out our eardrums."

"You're saying Sterling and the regional governors are dead?"

"I don't think so. The president's motorcade raced away less than a minute after the bomb went off. Then some moron was running down the street trying to catch up to it. I'm not sure, but it looked like Jackson Butler, that wannabe-celebrity in The Pulse Zone."

"What happened to Butler?"

"I wish we could say we shot him dead, but we never had a clear shot."

"This is amazing! I don't know what to say.

It looks like the UAE is near death."

"If that bomb had managed to kill Sterling, the UAE *would* be dead."

"What happened to Sterling? Where did he go?"

"Based on his direction of travel, I assume he went directly to the main security checkpoint at the Miami-Dade Metro police headquarters."

"Who the hell bombed the place?"

"The only guess that makes sense is the PSA."

"This far south? We haven't seen anything that resembles a PSA presence outside their borders."

"Then who else could it be?"

"My guess is the man who got away."

"Butler? He's Sterling's golden boy."

"Power play? Not a smart one if the big man got away."

"Maybe his plan didn't go as expected."

Ben sat for a moment in quiet contemplation. He lit a cigar and poured them both a drink. "Sterling has to pass right in front of our gates to get out of Florida. The only drivable roads lead straight here, and with McClellan crippled from the recent attack, it will take time for them to get reinforcements here."

"What do you have in mind?"

"We roll out the red carpet for our president, what else?"

CHAPTER TWENTY-TWO

When the news of the assassination of six of the seven remaining regional governors spread across the country, the Unified American Empire plunged into anarchy. At the insistence of Simon Sterling, none of the regional governors had an assistant or any kind of succession plan in place. Simon wanted total control over the selection of their replacements. With no one to tend to the day-to-day functions in the regions, nothing was accomplished. When word got out that Supreme Commander Moody had also perished in the attack, the UAE brass hesitated to act, lost without clear instruction from their Supreme Commander. Carl Moody also shared his boss's paranoia and had not proclaimed a second-in-command. High-ranking brass looking to promote up the ranks soon learned that if they stuck their neck out too far it would get chopped off. No one dared step up to run things in case the rumors of Sterling's or Moody's demise were proven false. No troops were deployed, no houses searched; checkpoints were vacated, and potential terrorists were never executed. The people were not sad to see their oppressors vanish without replacement. People across the nation celebrated their liberation from the Unified American Empire.

Likewise, another group of people was thrilled to see the regional governors dead. The Silent Warriors could finally move out of The Pulse Zone and operate with impunity in the Rockies and along the West Coast. Many would view their tactics as cowardly, moving in stealth and destroying innocent lives. The terror felt by those in The Pulse Zone seeped across the nation. The Silent Warriors destroyed power plants and water treatment centers and continued their mutilation of the interstate highway system.

Millions of Americans took advantage of the absence of power and organized militias to battle the crippled Unified National Guard. They were not fighting for democracy or patriotism, but for territory alone. Fortified communities like those in the Middle Ages became the norm. Towns were blockaded and secured from outside attack. Communities waged war with each other over fresh water sources and hunting grounds. The former United States was being sliced up into territories controlled by powerful men who could keep their communities safe from the dwindling forces of the Unified National Guard. Benjamin Black's community at Walt Disney World became the standard to emulate.

Oklahoma City was the first to barricade a large section of the metropolitan area and post armed guards at all entry points. Men and women worked frantically to overturn eighteen wheelers across roads and build walls. They sent out hit-and-run squads to engage the Unified National Guard, wiping them out and stealing their vehicles and weapons. Benjamin Black himself was proud of their organizational skills. Soon, many cities followed suit - Kansas City, Dallas, St. Louis, Phoenix, Detroit, Chicago and others.

***

Upon his return to Beck Castle from Seattle, Howard bypassed his personal quarters and made a beeline for the command center. He spent the better part of the day reviewing the daily functions of the PSA. The impending invasion of California was his primary concern. With Hal's assistance, Howard spent hours reviewing satellite footage of the coastal regions where Dupree's troops would make landfall. He also kept a close eye on the UAE's military presence in the region so Richard could lead precise surgical strikes to take them out.

"Sir, I have some troubling news. The cruise ships are under attack from a Chinese submarine."

Howard remained silent.

"Sir, did you hear me?"

Silence.

"Sir, the cruise ships are under attack from the Chinese. General Dupree's flagship is under heavy fire."

"That's not possible!"

"Sir, I assure you it is taking place at this very moment."

Howard tried to remain focused, but he felt reality slipping away. Throughout his fifty-nine years, he'd been prone to mental meltdowns when extremely traumatic events occurred. When his beloved Meredith passed away, he spent six months locked away in his mansion without ever uttering a single word. If not for Hal and his service robots, Howard would have starved to death.

"Sir, please stay with me. I need you to focus." No stranger to Howard's current mental state, Hal mixed a high concentration of oxygen and a mild stimulant into the ventilation system. "Howard! Listen to me!"

Hal's use of his name instead of the customary "sir" snapped Howard from his reverie. "Hal, tell me everything."

"The *Freedom of the Seas* has taken four direct hits from a Chinese submarine. The fourth one struck the bow just under the bridge. Captain Konkoly and most of the bridge crew were killed. General Dupree was thrown from the ship. I deployed a drone to retrieve him, and he was placed in one of twelve lifeboats the crew managed to be deployed."

"Twelve? That's it?"

"Yes, sir. The remaining two vessels were able to monitor the attack and were more successful in deploying their lifeboats. I counted fifty-two lifeboats from the two remaining ships. All three vessels have been mortally wounded and will be lost."

"Max?"

"I have been unable to locate Director Harris. He is not in any of the lifeboats. The assumption is that he is still on the vessel."

"Find him, Hal! Focus all your efforts on locating him!"

"Yes, sir."

"This is a disaster. The Chinese?"

"Sir, I have more urgent news."

"Jesus, Hal. What?"

"I'm getting reports from the funeral of Regional Governor Weygandt. It seems a bomb went off during the service. It appears that everyone in attendance was killed. However, during my review of the satellite footage, a motorcade was spotted leaving the church shortly after the explosion."

"Sterling's alive?"

"Yes, sir, the evidence does suggest that."

"Who planted the bomb? The Chinese?"

"That would be my guess, sir."

"On the one hand, we have a tragedy of epic proportions. On the other hand, we have the greatest news since the collapse."

"Indeed, sir."

"What can we do for the cruise ships? What's their status?"

"Sir, the *Freedom of the Seas* is sixty-seven percent submerged. Barring another impact from the submarine, she will go down in less than ten minutes. The *Independence of the Seas* has received four direct impacts and is twenty-three percent submerged; she will go down in less than twenty minutes. The *Voyager of the Seas* managed to maneuver herself behind the first two ships which bought her time while the submarine changes course to intercept. She is continuing to deploy her lifeboats to aide in the rescue mission."

"Do we have any assets that can stage a rescue?"

"No, sir, we do not. There are no vessels within range."

"How far off the coast are they?"

"Fifty-two miles, sir."

"God help them."

The Pacific States of America was facing the greatest challenge of its short history. Previous to the demise of the UAE, the PSA went to great lengths to liberate the tired and desperate refugees who were brave enough to attempt to make it across their borders. With the threat of the UAE weakening by the day, the PSA could not accommodate the millions of people attempting to enter their peaceful sanctuary. Hal, the trusted artificial intelligence securing the PSA, soon had to repel the droves of people streaming cross the border. Howard Beck's dream of returning the former United States to her former glory now became a futile endeavor. The only way his dream would come to fruition would be to reassemble the broken pieces of the entire nation. He had assumed that Simon Sterling would at least hold the country together until his defeat. Howard never dreamed the UAE would be vanquished in a single day. With a Chinese invasion force on the shores of California, Howard would soon find his worse fears had become a reality.

CHAPTER TWENTY-THREE

Maxwell Harris couldn't feel his left leg. The nerve branching off from his crushed L2 vertebra had been pinched in his broken spine. He'd lost sensation in most of his groin and buttocks and could barely feel his right leg. All Max could do was stare at the stars shining through the hole in the bridge's roof…and scream.

Max dragged himself across the floor to the lifeless body of Captain Konkoly and groped about for his radio, relieved to find it lodged securely in the dead man's pocket.

"Help! I need help! This is Maxwell Harris, I'm trapped on the bridge and I need help!"

Four hundred nine yards away, one of Hal's drones picked up the transmission and flew to the bridge. "Sir, this is Hal. Help is on the way; you are safe."

"My wife! Please find my wife!"

"I'm here, Max!" Elizabeth Harris said as she climbed through the shattered doors leading into the bridge.

"I broke my back. I can't move my legs."

"You're alive, sweetie! Let's get you out of here." Elizabeth motioned to the small drone hovering nearby. "Hal?"

"Yes, ma'am. I have a larger drone en route that will assist you in evacuating the ship." Seconds later, a massive drone landed on the bridge. Arms and legs snapped out from its side as it stood upright and became a Hal robot. The anthropomorphic extension of Hal's programming looked like a headless human. In the center of the robot's chest was a bright red, glowing fish-eye lens in honor of Hal's namesake. "Ma'am, if you will assist me, we can get you both out of here."

"Hal, you're a lifesaver." Elizabeth and the Hal robot took Max by the arms and stood him up. The robot extended both arms and cradled Max like a baby. The pain was more than Max could bear.

"Max, honey, we're getting you out of here." Two six-inch metal plates extended from the robot's knees and Elizabeth stepped on, wrapping her arms around the Hal robot's torso. "Hal, can you carry us both?"

"Yes, ma'am, I can carry three times this weight. Hold on. I'm going to fly you to the nearest lifeboat." With thrusters blazing from the robots arms and feet, the three hovered out of the bridge and slowly descended at a forty-five degree angle towards the nearest lifeboat.

***

"Sir, I have transported Max and Elizabeth to the safety of a lifeboat."

"That's good news! Thank you, Old Man."

"You are welcome, sir."

"Are they okay?"

"Sir, Elizabeth is fine. Max, on the other hand, is severely injured. My scans detect that his L2 vertebra has been shattered and the L2 nerve pinched. He is almost completely paralyzed from the waist down."

Dammit, Max. Why can't you catch a break? "What's the status on the third cruise ship?"

"Sir, the majority of the crew is on lifeboats. The submarine has intercepted the third ship and has opened fire."

"This is a nightmare. We should be doing something."

"Sir, my drones are doing a great deal to help."

"What about our stealth jets? Are we within range? How many can they hold?"

"Two of the jets are down for maintenance. The other ten can make it there in fourteen minutes. Each can hold twelve."

"Launch them immediately. Evacuate as many as you can; don't waste a second."

"Yes, sir. They will have to land in California."

"That's fine. Make it happen."

"Yes, sir. The stealth jets are already in the air."

"I doubt we'll get that lucky, but if the sub is still in the water, sink the fucker to the bottom of the Pacific."

"I will endeavor to do so, sir."

***

"Weapons, status report."

"Captain, all three vessels are damaged beyond repair and will sink."

"I must say I've never seen cruise ships used to transport a military force."

The XO, proud of his knowledge of history, interjected. "Captain, the Americans used cruise ships to transport troops to the European theater during World War II."

"Is that so? Fascinating. Well, they won't be doing so this time around. The UAE will regret trying to double-cross the Chinese. Governor Butler will pay for this betrayal. Our invasion force will see to that."

***

"Max, honey, wake up." Elizabeth Harris

planted kisses on her husband's clammy forehead.

"Ma'am, if I may? I'm a medic."

"What are you waiting for? Yes, please."

The lifeboat was at capacity. The medic stood up and made his way over to Elizabeth. He placed his palm on Max's chest, and checked the pulse on his neck. Fifteen seconds passed before he spoke.

"Given his condition, he's fine for the time being. His pulse is weak, but steady; so is his breathing. He just passed out from the shock."

"Sir, I concur."

"What the hell is that?" The medic pointed at the briefcase-sized contraption, its red fish-eye ablaze, hovering off the starboard bow.

Elizabeth smile. "You've never met Hal?"

"Hal? Beck's A.I.? I thought he was in Beck Castle."

Elizabeth gazed fondly at the robot hovering nearby. "Honestly, I think Hal is everywhere."

"Ma'am, I assure you I am not omnipresent."

"Just a figure of speech, Hal."

"Yes, ma'am."

"Hal, what's the plan? We need to get out of here."

"I am going to deploy a drone for every lifeboat. Each drone will attach to the rear of the ship and act as a motor. I estimate that we will make it to the California coast in seventy-five minutes."

The medic could not contain his optimism. "Your husband will be fine as long as we take him straight to a hospital when we come ashore."

"Sir, that is the route we are taking; it will place us at the closest possible distance to a hospital. I have triaged all the injured and will take them directly to the hospital."

"He's amazing." The medic grinned at Elizabeth.

"Yes! Yes, he is."

CHAPTER TWENTY-FOUR

President Simon Sterling was in a bullet-proof limousine trying desperately to get out of Florida. His plan was to drive to Fort McClellan, Alabama, and take a jet back to Howard Beck's former mansion outside of Denver.

His lead security agent was in the backseat. "Mr. President, we have a secure location at which to stage you until McClellan can get reinforcements to us. We travel too far north and your safety will be in jeopardy. I want us off the road ASAP."

"Where? Wait, is McClellan in any kind of shape since the attack?"

"It will take longer than I like, but McClellan can have reinforcements here. We just have to be patient. We'll be waiting at Benjamin Black's compound at Walt Disney World. He's an ally of the UAE. We have a small contingent of soldiers there that will secure the site until reinforcements can come for us."

"Thank you, Mr. Watts. You've done your job well. How long until we get to this...what was his name?"

"Benjamin Black."

"Yes, how long until we get to Mr. Black's compound?"

"Barring any unforeseen circumstances, we will be there in under two hours."

"Thank you. I'm sure Stacy will be comfortable in the trunk."

***

Jessica Bradley had the luxury of driving a Mustang at break-neck speed across the Florida wasteland. She also didn't have the burden of a convoy. She beat the president back to WDW by a full hour. She had already briefed Benjamin, and they'd formulated a plan on how to proceed.

Twenty-four UAE soldiers were stationed in the parking lot of Walt Disney World awaiting the president's arrival. Minutes after Ben and Jessica decided to roll out the red carpet for President Simon Sterling, twelve very attractive, flirtatious young females were sent out to distract the soldiers. While they were preoccupied, Ben's people shot or stabbed all of them to death. With the soldiers dispatched, their uniforms were stripped off and their bodies hidden from view. Within thirty minutes of the president's arrival, all the soldiers had been replaced by Ben's people.

***

"Mr. President, we will be arriving shortly. Our people are all in place, and Mr. Black will be there to meet you personally."

"Excellent, Mr. Watts. I look forward to meeting a true patriot."

***

When Benjamin Black set up the community at Walt Disney World, the very first priority was external security. They had to be able to defend their walls from outside aggressors. The parking lot leading to the front gate was barricaded with an intricate maze of obstacles and roadblocks. Anyone attempting to gain access to the park had to navigate three armed checkpoints before they could even approach the main gate, which had two armed guards of its own, including one in a thirty-foot-high tower constructed by Ben's people. Any vehicle not cleared for entry at the first checkpoint was held up while the guards radioed their counterparts at the other two checkpoints and the main gate. In the past, raiders had attempted to storm the Black compound to pillage what Ben's people had fought so valiantly to procure. No one had ever breached the complex. An alarm would be sounded at the first checkpoint and a standby platoon residing just inside the front gate deployed to deter the threat.

Standard protocol was to allow the UAE to proceed unmolested all the way to the front gate. When President Sterling's motorcade approached, the same protocol was observed. As the armored limousine and its three support SUVs raced past the first checkpoint, the guard at the front gate radioed ahead to announce their arrival.

"Okay, listen up, people. We have about three minutes before they get here. No one in uniform is to approach the president's security detail. Avoid making eye contact with them. If they want to speak to a soldier, Hayden Smith is the one to approach since we put him in Captain Brown's uniform. Hayden was an officer in the Air Force, so he can pull it off. I will separate the president from his detail as quickly as possible. When I shoot his lead security agent, that will be the signal to open fire on the rest of the detail. Is everyone clear?"

A sea of heads bobbed in unison.

"Good. Let's not screw this up. We've got a lot riding on this, and we have precious little time before reinforcements get here from Fort McClellan."

A minute later, the president's motorcade approached the front gate and screeched to a halt. A smart-looking man scanned the crowd before him as he quickly approached Ben.

"Mr. Black?"

"Yes, I'm Benjamin Black."

"Okay, bring out the Suit." The president's call sign reflected his predilection for fine clothing. Simon thought it a fitting title and didn't object.

The passengers disembarked from the SUVs and surrounded the president's door. Out came the president of the Unified American Empire. Benjamin was shocked to discover how short the man was; he couldn't have been more than five-foot four. Ben was also surprised to see the president wearing a mismatched military uniform.

"Mr. Black, it's a pleasure to meet you. Thank you for playing host during this desperate hour. I hope you will forgive my attire; my security detail chose to toss me in a church baptistery to protect me from the blast. My favorite suit was ruined and, well, here we are. This monstrosity is an embarrassment," he said, in obvious distress over his highly unsuitable dress.

"I understand, Mr. President. We're honored to have you in our humble community."

"You are modest, Mr. Black. What you've done here is remarkable."

"Please, Mr. President, call me Ben."

"Ben it is. Are you in charge of security for this community, or should my lead agent make arrangements with one of your subordinates?"

Ben motioned for Jessica Bradley to step

forward. "Mr. President, this is my second-in-command, Jessica Bradley. She will see to any security concerns your team may have."

"Miss Bradley, it's a pleasure to meet you. This is Agent Watts. He'll have some security details to discuss with you."

Ben and Jessica exchanged a subtle glance; the plan had just changed. Jessica would have to kill the lead agent. This worked out perfectly. Ben could grab the president and throw him to the ground to ensure he wasn't killed during the crossfire.

As Ben led the president toward the front gate, Jessica and the lead agent headed in the opposite direction. Jessica shook Agent Watts' hand, preventing him from drawing his weapon. With a pistol on both hips, Jessica quickly drew with her left hand and shot Agent Watts in the nose, his brains exploding out the back of his head. She bear-hugged the corpse and dropped to her knee, using the body for protection as she began to fire at the other agents. To her delight, she only had to kill one agent before the "soldiers" opened fire and gunned down the entire security detail.

Benjamin Black helped the awe struck tyrant to his feet. "Mr. President, you are now a prisoner of the Pacific States of America."

"You'll never make it out of here alive. My people are coming from McClellan and will squash

you like a bug. You'll hang for this. I'll put the
noose around your neck myself."

Ben ignored his prisoner. "Hayden, contact
Colonel Sanderson. He's still with the 519th out of
Fort Polk, isn't he?"

CHAPTER TWENTY-FIVE

Howard Beck was terrified. The fact that a Chinese submarine had sunk the three cruise ships on their way to California had farther reaching implications than the deaths of so many brave men and women ready to fight for the liberation of America. Howard knew this submarine was not a lone wolf preying in the waters off the coast of the former United States. Something much more nefarious was going on, and he was determined to figure it out.

Why did they attack our cruise ships?

Are the Chinese so vicious they would sink what appeared to be pleasure ships filled with innocent civilians?

No, they must have figured out they were transport ships with troops and military equipment onboard.

Why sink the ships? Their course clearly dictated they were headed to our own shores and not westward.

Then it hit Howard. *They thought we were the UAE!*

Why attack the UAE? It doesn't make sense to go to war with a nuclear power.

Howard was struck by another frightening

realization: *Sterling struck a deal with the Chinese to protect us from Iran, and they thought the cruise ships were evidence of a double-cross.*

"Old Man, this is a nightmare."

"What is a nightmare, sir?"

"The Chinese. You realize what happened, don't you?"

"Other than the attack? No, sir, I do not."

Howard explained his line of thinking to Hal.

"An intuitive analysis, sir."

"Analyze all the data your sister A.I. brought back from the White House. Anything that mentions the Chinese or allies?"

"Neither word was ever uttered by Sterling or anyone in your residence."

"Expand your search out to the regional governors."

"Jackson Butler sent encrypted messages to China."

"That son of a bitch! Any chance of reading them?"

"I'm afraid not, sir. The Chinese have become quite adept at software encryption. It would take me weeks to decipher the messages."

"Damn. It has to be Butler. If Sterling actually believed in a two-party system, he'd campaign on the isolationist platform. His world only exists inside our borders. He'd nuke the living shit out of China before he'd strike a deal with them and wouldn't give a damn if they nuked us in return."

"I agree, sir."

"I think we know who bombed the church. Jackson Butler is still alive, and we have to find him."

***

Jackson Butler and the man he knew as Charles were sitting in another vacant restaurant outside of what was left of Orlando.

"Charles, are you sure?"

"I am. They had to stop at the amusement park, or whatever you call it. The journey to Fort McClellan is too perilous, with much of the surrounding area in chaos. The only tactical decision that makes sense would be to stop at the most secure UAE haven between Miami and Alabama. Why didn't they just go back to the airport and fly out?"

"They had no way of knowing whether the culprits had targeted the airport as well as the church, so they had no choice but to flee Miami by car."

"I often forget your prior military service, sir."

"So do I."

"Now that you know Sterling's location, how do you want to proceed?"

"It's simple, really. I show up frazzled and afraid, having suffered a long, arduous journey across Florida to find him. He'll welcome me with open arms. I might even cry."

"I'm touched."

"Where do we stand on Beck Castle?"

"The Chinese are ready to take control of the artificial intelligence in the Castle." Charles' phone rang. "Terribly sorry for the interruption. May I?"

"Of course."

Charles tapped his headset and listened in silence. Thirty seconds later, he ended the call. "A rather fortuitous turn of events has put us ahead of schedule. It seems President Sterling has been captured by some…what is it you call them? Hillbillies? Anyway, it seems your president is in the hands of a man named Benjamin Black. They have him inside ... you Americans, I don't know how you keep it all straight ... Walt Disney Place."

"Walt Disney World."

"Yes, they have him inside Walt Disney World, and within the next hour they're going to attempt to move him to a military installation in Louisiana."

"Fort Polk? It's controlled by the UAE. Why capture him and then take him back to the

UAE?"

"Apparently, a colonel there by the name of Sanderson is a PSA sympathizer and has agreed to transport the president to Beck Castle and hand him over to the PSA."

"Why is this a good thing for us? Sounds like a nightmare. Sterling will order troops out of McClellan to pick him up; they'll all be slaughtered."

"Jackson, we'll just have to figure out a way to stop them. You'll endear yourself to the president even more by attempting to rescue him from the tan-necks."

"The what?"

Charles was becoming increasingly frustrated by his lack of understanding of American colloquialisms. "Rednecks?"

"Yes, Charles, you're getting the hang of it. I have some loyal men in the area who can help us with our little charade and ensure I'm along for the ride to Beck Castle."

"Well, as you know, I have a man inside Beck Castle. Contacting him is rather difficult, and getting something to him is next to impossible." Charles pulled out a small piece of plastic no larger than a fingernail. "We make a small incision in your left pectoral and plant this just under your skin. The device gives off the electrical signature of a pacemaker and will fool any scans they might perform on you."

"They? Where am I going? What is that thing really?"

"Sir, you are going to show up at Walt Disney World looking for your beloved president. They will be more than happy to take you, as a prisoner, to Beck Castle. Once you're there, my man on the inside will find you and remove the device. It is simply a ten terabyte storage device. Contained on it are the programs necessary to gain control of the artificial intelligence. Our Chinese friends wish to neutralize the PSA."

***

Colonel William Sanderson, commanding officer of the 519th Military Police Battalion and the provost marshal for Fort Polk, awoke early. He looked upon the beautiful face of his wife, Lindsay, knowing she'd sleep for at least another two hours. He walked down the hall to check on his children, Brent and Heather. Like his wife, they were also sound asleep. William's mind wandered back to the days when his family was homeless and living in the Central Park Obama Camp. If anyone could write a best-selling rags-to-riches novel, it was William. He knew it would be many years before his children would begin to realize how destitute and downtrodden their family had been. He and his wife never once complained around their children. He had convinced his innocent children that they were simply on an extended camping trip rather than homeless.

William was grateful for his job and his home, but was not proud of the path his career had taken. One of the primary jobs of the 519th was to detain potential terrorists so they could be transported to "interrogation camps." William was no fool. He knew the people passing through his detention center were on their way to be tortured and, in all likelihood, executed. After his protests fell on deaf or fearful ears, he decided he could no longer look at himself in the mirror unless he was fighting to restore democracy and freedom. William was a spy for the Pacific States of America. At first, he'd tried to defect to the PSA with his family, but a man named Maxwell Harris had persuaded him to remain where he was in order to supply vital information about the atrocities being committed by the UAE. William decided the arrangement was an honorable one.

After receiving an urgent communication from one of his fellow operatives in Florida, William slept fitfully, if at all. Benjamin Black had contacted him using one of the most ancient of communication devices—Morse code. With cell phone towers slow to make a comeback after The Pulse, Morse code was widely used as a secure means of communication. Two parties simply needed to come up with a means of coding messages. William and Benjamin had been using a cipher that utilized an asymmetric key algorithm. When William got the message and decrypted it, he stared at it in disbelief. His immediate response to Benjamin was "Message unclear. Send again." Benjamin replied, "High value prisoner in my custody soon. Make preparations for our arrival. Once we have the package, contact the PSA in same fashion as before. Will message again in two hours. Confirm." William did so.

William spent most of the evening and early morning planning the prisoner extraction. Without his family's knowledge, he packed four suitcases containing essential and sentimental belongings. It was time to get the hell out of Dodge and make a new home in the Pacific States of America.

CHAPTER TWENTY-SIX

General Richard Dupree was nursing a
broken foot. His SEAL instructor would have been
ashamed of him. Richard had jumped into water
from dizzying heights when he was an operator, but
he could honestly say he had never been thrown into
the water after an explosion. This time, he'd been
unable to complete the landing prep which involved
tucking his chin to his chest, crossing his arms across
his torso, and putting one foot on top of the other.
He had accomplished the first two steps but failed to
complete the last. As he smashed into the water,
Richard felt his big toe and the attached metacarpal
snap. He endured an agonizing ten minutes of
treading water before a lifeboat picked him up. A
few minutes later, one of Hal's robots attached itself
to the back of the lifeboat and propelled the craft to
shore.

Richard climbed from the boat onto the
shore, lifejacket and oar in hand. He snapped the oar
in two and tore pieces of fabric from the lifejacket to
fashion a makeshift cast for his foot. It would do for
the time being. His primary concern was getting his
people to safety. Richard pulled a whistle from his
tactical vest and blew three rapid tweets.

"Rally point here! I want everyone to gather
at this location. All incoming lifeboats will be

brought to this point." Richard turned to the nearest Hal drone. "Hal! Make it happen!"

"Yes, sir, all lifeboats will be brought to this landing zone.

Dozens of frightened soldiers headed in Richard's direction as he scanned the crowd for officers. "You! Captain ..."

"Sir, Captain Page, sir!"

"Captain, tend to the wounded and assist Hal in triage. We have to get these people to a hospital."

"Sir, yes, sir! Medic! Medic! I need a medic!"

Richard looked up so see an astonishing sight in the shadowy night sky – a fleet of Hal drones carrying the wounded to the nearest hospital. Richard didn't know it, but Maxwell Harris had been the very first to be whisked away for treatment.

***

Andrea Wilson had been an emergency room nurse at the UCSF Medical Center for thirteen years. It was one of the few hospitals that had survived the Collapse of 2027. With the American economy in shambles, she wasn't really getting much of a paycheck once inflation was factored in. With the spending power of the almighty dollar at an all-time low, it didn't really matter anyway. Her dedication to her job was the only reason she was still there.

Andrea was checking a chart near the front entrance to the ER when the most shocking event of her life unfolded before her. She had seen some pretty amazing things in her career, which made it all the more surreal. As she looked outside, Andrea saw people gazing at the sky as they ran for their lives. What happened next was like something straight out of a science fiction movie. A robot-like contraption landed right in front of the door, an unconscious man cradled in its arms.

"Ma'am, this man requires immediate medical attention. His L2 vertebra is crushed, and he is bleeding internally."

Andrea stood in silence, dazed momentarily by the bizarre scene evolving around her.

"Ma'am? Do you understand me? Este hombre necesita atención médica inmediata. Cet homme nécessite une attention médicale immédiate. Ma'am? Do you understand me?"

"Uh, yes. Follow me." Andrea found an empty gurney in an open bay nearby. "Set him down there."

"Thank you, ma'am. Fourteen more men and women will be arriving in the next minute. I suggest you alert your staff so preparations can be made," the Hal robot said as it walked towards the entrance bay.

"Fourteen? What the hell are you? What's

going on?" Andrea watched as the sophisticated robot fired off boosters from its legs and rocketed away into the night sky. "Hey, come back here! What's going on?" Andrea said, frustrated, as she peered into the darkness. Still struggling to process what had just taken place, Andrea turned away, only to find a legion of robots walking toward her. Her frustration quickly abated as, one by one, more robots landed in the parking lot and started walking towards her.

"Shit."

***

While the *Freedom of the Seas* and her sister ships descended to the ocean floor, the Chinese invasion force was quickly closing in on the western shores of the former United States. Fighter jets and bombers launched from aircraft carriers, ready to destroy key military targets within the Unified American Empire.

Edwards AFB was struck first. Pilots scrambling to get jets in the air never had a chance. The same thing happened at Vandenberg AFB. Camp Pendleton and Fort Irwin were decimated; thousands of troops gave their lives, most for a government they despised. Once the surgical strikes were completed, the fighter jets and bombers returned to their aircraft carriers for the second wave of the attack, which would push the airstrikes further east towards the Rockies. The third wave was soon to follow with Chinese soldiers making landfall on the shores of California, ready to occupy the streets of the UAE.

The Chinese were in for a surprise when they attempted to enter the Pacific States of America. Thanks to his powerful insight, Howard Beck had foreseen the possibility of an invasion coming from the western side of North America. Howard was ready for anything.

CHAPTER TWENTY-SEVEN

Christina Dupree was having the time of her life. Walt Disney World was fun, but it wasn't actually an amusement park anymore - she couldn't enjoy the rides or have her picture taken with Mickey Mouse. Then a group of soldiers moved her from Walt Disney World to Fort Polk, Louisiana. At first the soldiers frightened her, but she soon learned they'd moved her for a good reason. Colonel Rutherford told her she had been selected by President Sterling as the spokesperson for orphans of the collapse. When she tried to explain that her mother was still alive, the president said she was probably lost somewhere and they would do everything to find her. Until then, the colonel said her story of survival was an inspiration to families across the nation. Christina was frightened by large crowds; the thought of having to speak in front of lots of people made her stomach hurt. Colonel Rutherford had told her not to worry. All she had to do was smile and wave to the crowd; someone else would do all the talking. Christina reluctantly agreed. After all, she was being treated like a celebrity and given three square meals a day and a warm bed to sleep in. Why protest?

When Christina arrived at Fort Polk, she was

placed with a loving family and even went to school for the first time in her life. She was ten years old and a little embarrassed to be in the first grade, but the children in her class were very friendly. Christina soon found a best friend in Heather Sanderson. They would play together at recess and shared a table at lunch. Heather even invited her for sleepovers and would help her learn to read.

One morning, Christina went to school only to find Heather and her brother, Brent, absent. That evening she politely asked her host family if she could call to check on them.

"Sanderson residence; this is Colonel Sanderson."

"Hello, mister...uh, Colonel Sanderson. This is Chrissy Dupree. May I please speak to Heather?"

"Hi, Chrissy. Hold on a sec; let me get her."

Chrissy waited patiently. "Hi, Heather. Why weren't you at school today?"

"Oh, my family is going on a trip. Dad has some military stuff to do in Denver, and he's taking us with him. It's like a little vacation. I asked him if you could come with us, and he said it wasn't a good idea. You'd miss too much school."

"Oh man! I wanna come! Maybe I can get my assignments from Mrs. Slayton and you could help me."

"Let me ask Dad. Hold on."

Chrissy waited anxiously for the answer. "He said it's fine with him. He wants you to put Mr. Tolbert on the phone to talk to him about it."

"That's awesome! Hold on." Chrissy explained the plan to her host parent and handed him the phone. After a minute or so of pleasant conversation, he smiled and returned the phone to Chrissy so the girls could finalize their plans.

Poor Mr. Tolbert had no idea that his gracious decision was going to cost him dearly with Colonel Rutherford.

***

"They have what?" Howard Beck was eating dinner in the command center of Beck Castle.

"The message said 'high value UAE prisoner.'" Marshall Beck always found pleasure in seeing his father smile, which was certain to be the result of this intriguing news.

"Wait, this has to be a mistake. Benjamin Black, the guy that runs Disney World?"

"Yes, Pop, that's exactly right. They're taking the prisoner to Fort Polk to rendezvous with Colonel Sanderson. The problem is, they don't know the location of Beck Castle, but the widespread rumor is that we're near Denver. Security is sending out some men to meet them at a secure location outside the city."

Howard smiled. "With our invasion of California a disaster, this news almost makes up for the tragedy. I can't wait to find out who it is.

Probably a high ranking general."

"Richard will be happy as well."

"Yes, the good general would love to debrief a high-value asset."

"Oh, I can't wait for them to get here! Who's in charge of security with Max gone?"

"Dennis Twigg."

"Inform Mr. Twigg of the arrival of our prisoner. I want four men guarding the detention cell at all times. The cell door is not to open without me, you, or Richard present."

"I'll get it done. Any news from California?"

"Max is in surgery now. Another thirty-two have serious injuries that will probably require surgery at some point. Close to a hundred more are waiting to be patched up and moved back to the PSA."

"The Chinese?"

"They've wiped out every major military base this side of the Rockies. They'll have boots on the ground very soon, I would guess."

"Is Hal ready for them?"

"Old Man, where do we stand?"

"Sir, the EMP shield has already been deployed over the PSA. No aircraft or vehicle will enter our airspace without our permission. I've modified the sonic repulsor design we had at Beck Manor to operate on a much larger scale. Sonic repulsors are operational near every major city and in overlapping positions down the coast. Any artillery they fire on us or bombs they attempt to drop will be stopped."

"Hal, you've done an outstanding job. Are we ready to engage the fighter drones to defend east of the Rockies? I wish we could've stopped them at California."

"Sir, I will endeavor to have the fighter drones up and running as soon as possible. I estimate three hours and fourteen minutes until launch."

"Good work, Old Man."

"Thank you, sir."

CHAPTER TWENTY-EIGHT

"Benjamin, I don't know why we don't just get the hell out of here before they show up." Jessica Bradley was one of the few people brave enough to disagree with Benjamin after his mind was made up. Benjamin valued her counsel for this very reason.

"They can't come down I-95; it's torn to shit. Their only choice is I-75. It's the only passable interstate in Florida. They think we're on their side. Best chance we have is to lure them into a trap and wipe them out. We've got the home field advantage. We could take them out and hit the road."

"They're coming for the fucking president of the UAE! You know they're gonna expect some serious heat!"

"Again, Jessica, they think it's an escort mission. They have no reason to expect hostility. They want Sterling secured at McClellan as quickly as possible. A big convoy of vehicles will only slow them down. I'm guessing they'll send three vehicles, maybe four. We can take them. Trust me."

"I do. I just think we could whoop their asses and run. They'd never find us."

"Far too risky. We can't bring an army on the road with us anymore than they can. We run into them on the road and it'll get ugly quick."

"Okay, I see your point. So what do we do?"

"The same thing we did when Sterling got here. Get them out of their vehicles, surround them, and shoot them all in the fucking head."

"I can get behind that plan."

***

Stacy Reid was bound and gagged in the trunk of President Sterling's limousine. She had no idea where she was or what was going on. The limo had stopped, followed by the deafening roar of gunfire. Stacy counted three bullet holes in the trunk. She was thankful for two of them as they gave her precious air to breath. The third, on the other hand, had grazed her left calf muscle. With her hands and feet tied, all she could do was press her calf against the floor of the trunk in an attempt to stop the bleeding.

Stacy knew one thing for certain: If someone didn't find her soon, she stood a good chance of bleeding to death.

***

"Sir, the one-mile sentry is reporting their arrival."

"Did he give a status report? How many vehicles?"

"I can't raise him. He's not answering his radio."

Shit.

"Try him again. Now!"

"Sentry-one, come back. Bobby, come in. Over."

Silence.

Shit.

"Fall back! Goddammit! Fall back!"

Jessica sprinted to Ben. "What?"

"Jessica, you were right! They know what we're doing."

***

"Charles, are you sure this is a good idea?" Jackson Butler and his associate were sitting motionless in Charles' nondescript sedan.

"Sir, the next phase of our employer's plan can't proceed unless we deliver the package to Beck Castle. This is the only way. I've tried other means, but this opportunity will not present itself again."

"The Chinese think I doubled-crossed them. They want me dead."

"I'm confident that I can remedy the situation, sir. It will soon be abundantly clear that the PSA was planning an invasion."

"The plan is never going to work. The Chinese will occupy half the country in a matter of weeks. They were supposed to arrive as allies, not conquerors."

"Sir, I sincerely hope you're not that naive. I'm confident that all will be forgiven if you can deliver the artificial intelligence. Our employer is having difficulty breaching the PSA."

"You're serious? That crazy old retard is giving them problems? I had no difficulty throwing his ass out of his own house, and the mighty Chinese army can't match wits with him?"

"Sir, I'm afraid you exaggerate. He put up a formidable fight for his home, and he's far from retarded. Many call him our generation's Einstein."

"Whatever. Let's get on with it. How long till they get here?"

"Any minute."

"Well, I better get in place."

"Sir, I look forward to our next meeting."

Jackson hurried from the vehicle and stood in the middle of the road. Right on schedule, the security escort rounded the corner. The four SUVs stopped a hundred yards from Jackson. After what seemed like an eternity, the passenger-side door of the lead vehicle opened and a sharp looking agent stepped out.

"State your business! Keep your hands up where I can see them!"

"Sir, I am Regional Governor Jackson Butler. The president's life is in danger. The people in this compound are holding him hostage. Do you recognize me? Do you know who I am?"

"Yes, I do, Governor Butler. We need to wait for reinforcements; I hear this place is heavily armed. I can radio back. I have a secure phone."

"No! Stop! We need to act now. I have a platoon-sized force with me. I didn't want them visible to you for fear you might jump to the wrong conclusion and start a fight. My men will join you. We have to act now before they try to move him!"

***

Charles watched the charade continue as he picked up his phone. "Ready?"

"Yes. When do you want us to move in?"

"The governor is going to stay behind with me. During the battle, your team will swoop in and stop the security escort. Jackson will arrive pretending to be the hero who saved the day."

"Wait. We're doing this so he can get caught?"

"You need not concern yourselves with the details."

CHAPTER TWENTY-NINE

General Richard Dupree was aboard his stealth jet with fifteen uninjured soldiers. The craft was designed to carry twelve, but they managed to squeeze in an extra four. Nine other jets were in formation behind him. As soon as they landed and unloaded the passengers, the jets would take off to repeat the process. It would take eight round-trips to collect what was left of the bulk of the California invasion force.

Once inside the Castle, Richard high-tailed it to the command center to find Howard.

"What the hell happened? The Chinese, Howard? What the hell are they doing?"

Howard was fond of directness, preferring to dispense with the customary pleasantries. "It would seem that Jackson Butler tried to broker some idiotic deal with the Chinese. I'm guessing he invited them to come over and protect us from Iran as our allies."

"Sinking three cruise ships before they hit our shores doesn't exactly qualify them as our allies."

"They probably mistook us for the UAE and thought Jackson double crossed them."

"Makes sense. How bad is it?"

"Very bad. They've crippled every military asset this side of the Rockies. They've got boots on the ground in L.A., San Diego, and San Francisco, with thousands more coming in by the hour."

"Seattle?"

"Hal gave them a bit of a surprise when they tried to cross our borders. The EMP shield went online without a hitch."

"Didn't even get a chance to test it, did you?"

"Nope. The sonic repulsors are swatting down anything they throw at us, but we can't stop them from swimming to shore or walking across our border with California."

"For the time being, they won't. Without bombing runs and artillery fire, they don't have the advantage. There's just too much resistance."

***

Clarence Whipp was raised by a man known to many as a "gun nut." His father worshipped the second amendment as scripture and was a founding member of the Central California Patriots Militia. Clarence spent his childhood learning everything there was to know about firearms, and he quickly became a prize-winning sharpshooter. The CCPM had swelled to over five hundred members prior to the Collapse of 2027, and it continued to grow under the leadership of the senior Whipp and his son.

When the Unified American Empire came to power and pissed all over the Bill of Rights, the CCPM headed underground. Members of the militia had to bury their weapons and ammo in caches spread out across central California. Almost a third of their numbers were executed by the UAE for either protesting or carrying firearms despite the ban.

Like many Americans, Clarence had no idea

that the UAE had been decapitated in Florida or that President Sterling had been taken prisoner. That fact didn't matter when Chinese paratroopers dropped out of the sky like confetti on New Year's Day. Clarence and his men had been preparing for the day when the UAE was vulnerable and weak enough to suffer an all-out guerrilla war. The UAE was no longer the issue at hand; a much more powerful and lethal army was spilling onto the shores of the former United States, hell-bent on conquering their homeland. Clarence and his men would fight to the death to stop them.

All across the nation, true patriots had perished under the wicked thumb of the UAE. They died for their steadfast belief in the right to bear arms in order to protect all they held most dear. Those brothers and sisters fortunate enough to outlive them would pry the rifles from their cold, dead hands and carry on the fight. The living vowed to stand up to the domination of those who tried to rob them of the very tools needed to prevent such tyranny in the first place.

The Unified American Empire was a short-lived experiment. Simon Sterling was a failure. He appointed himself ruler of a government he was certain would be both efficient and minimal. He aimed to consolidate his power by robbing the people of their basic freedoms, oblivious to the fact that an unarmed populace would be no match for a fierce invading force.

***

Mutee Azimi had a new mission. His old one was going to be the biggest environmental disaster in recent history. Mutee had acquired a large quantity of sodium cyanide, enough to poison the water supply of Sacramento and the surrounding cities. During his training as a Silent Warrior, Mutee was indoctrinated to do two things: destroy the American culture and prepare for the invasion of America by The Great Empire of Iran. The former was going spectacularly; the latter was being infringed upon by the opportunistic Chinese. The Chinese problem was one that would definitely have to be addressed; the real estate was far too valuable to hand over to them without a fight. Allah had expanded the Muslim world further than he had in all of history. The former United States would be used to further his glory.

Mutee decided not to waste his lethal chemical. He and his men divided up the deadly substance and headed out across California to find the Chinese encampments. Mutee was shocked at the lack of security the invading forces placed on their own water supply. Weapon and ammo depots were heavily guarded, for obvious reasons, but five- and ten-thousand-gallon tanks of water sat virtually unattended. Under the cloak of darkness and camouflaged in stolen Chinese uniforms, Mutee and his cell systematically poisoned the water supply. To guarantee their own escape, they dosed the water with small enough quantities of the chemical to ensure that it would take forty-eight to seventy-two hours for the infected to succumb. The Silent

Warriors were richly rewarded for their efforts as the Chinese began to die by the thousands.

CHAPTER THIRTY

"Shit! Get inside the compound! They're comin' around the corner!

Benjamin Black had hoped that, at the very least, his new guests would be gracious enough to remain outside the compound and offer up some sort of demands he'd have to meet to avoid a gun fight. If that had happened, he would've at least had time to stage his people and get them ready for the inevitable battle. But his new guests were not the talking type; they opened fire as soon as they rounded the corner. Two of Ben's people were ripped in half by .50-caliber rounds. The large billboard that had once welcomed tourists to Mickey Mouse's home was torn to shreds. Benjamin himself barely made it into the compound in one piece.

"Light 'em up!" Benjamin yelled to the sentry towers, and his command was immediately followed. The convoy stopped on the far end of the parking lot and positioned themselves for the upcoming melee. Three smoke grenades arced high before landing between the opposing sides. With their new cover in place, the convoy split in half and set up a cross fire closer to the front gate. Ben had trained his people well for the inevitable day when the UAE would try to take their compound; they were ready. Four snipers set up position along the top of the compound wall and began to pick off the soldiers…one by one.

"Shit! They brought reinforcements!" Ben

alerted his people as three SUVs came screaming around the corner. The chain of events that followed was a blessing in disguise. The SUVs darkened windows lowered as a volley of gunfire erupted from within. The first two vehicles engaged the nearest half of the convoy while the occupants of the third vehicle focused on the rest. With the combined forces of the new arrivals, Ben's people were able to finish off the convoy with ease.

"Who in the holy hell is that? Could this get any stranger?" Jessica would have laughed if not for the loss of life she'd just witnessed.

"I have no idea, but they saved our asses." Ben was eager to put together the pieces of this bizarre puzzle. "Let's greet our new friends, shall we?"

"Pine, Smith, Garcia, Stewart, you're with me. Everyone else stay put. Douglas, relay to the sniper towers to keep their eyes peeled for trouble."

With their trigger fingers at the ready, Ben and Jessica lead the welcoming committee forward. Their newly disarmed guests waited nervously, the aura of uncertainty like a force-field around them. There was something familiar about the suited gentlemen in front, but Ben couldn't quite place him. "Who is that?" Ben whispered to Jessica.

"I'm pretty sure that's Jackson Butler."

"I think you're right." Ben addressed the team. "Everyone stay alert; this looks like trouble. Don't fire until I give the signal, unless you're fired upon first. Jessica, if I make eye contact, do what you can to separate Butler from the group."

"Got it, boss."

"Here we go." Ben addressed his new guests. "Gentlemen, thank you for your assistance. It's greatly appreciated. My name is Benjamin Black. To what do I owe the pleasure?"

The man in the suit took his cue. "Mr. Black, it is truly a pleasure. I've heard good things about you."

"Much obliged. And who might you be?"

"I'm Regional Governor Jackson Butler. I understand you rescued President Sterling once he fled from the attack in Miami."

Ben remained silent.

"Well, my men and I are very grateful for your patriotism. It is my understanding that the men we just engaged were a rogue element working with the attackers in Miami."

Still no response.

"Well, I'll get right to the point. We're here to escort President Sterling to safety. If you could take us to him, we'll be on our way."

Ben finally broke his silence. "Just you guys? Wouldn't it be more prudent to wait for reinforcements? What if there are more rogue elements out there wanting to snatch him?"

"I'm confident we can escort him to safety. If we move now, we can whisk the president away and get as far from here as possible."

"Excellent point. If you would be so kind as to follow Jessica." Ben turned and stared at Jessica, the signal acknowledged as she beamed a flirty smile at Jackson over her shoulder. As soon as she had

Jackson separated from the group, Jessica grabbed his hand, flipped him skillfully to the ground, and climbed atop the dazed governor. Before the two even hit the ground, Ben and the four gunmen opened fire on the disarmed men. Five seconds and done.

Ben strolled over to the struggling Jackson Butler and planted a swift kick to his face. "Settle down, you piece of shit. I'll be happy to take you to President Sterling. Both of you are now prisoners of the Pacific States of America."

Jackson let loose a string of profanity to bolster his false anger and surprise. He was delighted that these rednecks had carried out the plan so perfectly. Soon he would be right where he wanted to be—inside Beck Castle.

"Let's get these vehicles in the compound. Now! Confiscate all the weapons and ammo and take them to the armory. Let's move, people! I don't want these vehicles blocking our view in case we get more visitors!"

"Ben! You're gonna want to see this!" Pine's words were laced with an ominous sense of urgency.

Ben hastily joined Pine at the rear of Sterling's limo and peered into the cavernous, gaping trunk. A pale blonde woman was crumpled inside, the dark pool of blood beneath her already congealed and sullied.

CHAPTER THIRTY-ONE

"They have who?" Howard Beck was certain his son was misinformed. It just wasn't possible.

"Simon Sterling and Jackson Butler."

"Both of them? Are you sure?"

"Our man at Fort Polk, Colonel Sanderson, confirmed it. And that's not all; they have Stacy Reid. She was shot in the leg when they took Sterling. She lost a lot of blood but they patched her up. Looks like she lost one of her fingers recently, too, and it's badly infected. She's weak, but she can make the trip."

"How'd she lose her finger?"

"Sterling cut it off himself. He was convinced she was involved in the attack on the funeral in Miami. She said he was about to torture her for information on the Castle but was interrupted, and she ended up in the trunk and headed for Fort McClellan instead. They stopped at Walt Disney World thinking it was a secure place to wait for reinforcements. Benjamin Black had other plans."

"Butler was with Sterling? How can that be? It's clear that he betrayed Sterling to the Chinese."

"Pop, your guess is as good as mine."

"Sterling must have no clue who attacked him. Any more chatter from the UAE, Hal? They have any intel?"

"Sir, rumors abound about the attack but nothing is solid."

"Damn. What's the word on Max?"

"He is out of surgery, sir. They replaced his broken vertebra with an implant and infused it with a bone graft and bone marrow. The nerve damage to his left leg is at a manageable level. He will be able to walk; however, the pain in his hip will require him to wear a brace and rely upon a cane for stability."

"Poor Max. We need to bring him back here so he can get the surgery he needs." Howard had a tough time empathizing with others, but doing so with someone like Max— someone he cared about— was not difficult. "Hal, is he stable enough to transport?"

"No, sir. He will require at least three days of recovery."

"Dad, I hope the damage to his back doesn't complicate things. What do you think, Hal?"

"Sir, I am unable to make that kind of an assessment until I can examine Mr. Harris."

Howard had already moved on, ready to focus on the important task at hand. "Hal, have Mr. Twigg report to the command center. We need to prepare for the arrival of our prisoners."

"Yes, sir."

***

Charles was sitting in his unassuming sedan thinking about his employer. The thought of being transported across the expanding wasteland tied up in the trunk of a car or in the back of a filthy truck horrified his refined and dignified sensibilities. Charles would rather be shot than compromise his dignity by being bound, gagged, and blindfolded. Perish the thought.

Charles thought of his employer and was excited about his arrival. He hated Americans with every fiber of his being and was thrilled to assist in their downfall. Charles knew things about the Chinese that Jackson did not. Jackson was wrong on every front. They were not coming as allies to help them defend against Iran; they were coming to conquer and enslave the American people. They needed every resource imaginable—food, water, minerals, timber and, most importantly, land to establish Chinese colonies in order to alleviate the overcrowding caused by their massive population. The Chinese did not view themselves as invaders; they sincerely had the best interest of the entire world at heart. They believed The Great Empire of Iran needed to be stopped at all costs, and the Unified American Empire was in no condition to do so. Once they secured the UAE from east to west and devoured her resources, they would traverse the Atlantic and liberate Europe from the Iranians.

Two superpowers were fighting for control of the world, and the former United States of America was the unwilling pawn in the global chess game.

***

Dennis Twigg was not ready to be in charge of security. He was happy to be the number two man—plenty of power and influence but never the big chair. Dennis also knew that he could never fill

Director Harris's shoes, no matter how hard he tried. With Max recovering in San Francisco, it was obvious that the director would not be returning to Beck Castle for some time. Dennis knew the job well enough. He had memorized all the protocols put in place by President Beck and Director Harris, but when push came to shove, he was just not a pencil-pusher or an administrator. He was quite proficient in making rounds in the dormitory wing and conducting screening interviews for prospective residents on the quarantine level. Making serious decisions and having to answer for them was something Dennis had never done.

President Beck had summoned him to the command center. Not sure if he should knock, Dennis simply stood there. A few seconds later, the door opened.

"Mr. Twigg, get in here!"

Oh shit! I'm already in trouble!

Dennis had never had an extended conversation with the president. Though they'd met a few times, President Beck never seemed to remember his name. To Howard's brilliant mind, it was a waste of time and energy to store minute bits of useless information. Only when something was important enough to remember did it get stored in his long-term memory.

"Yes, Mr. President? What can I do for you?"

Howard remained focused on the spherical monitor before him. Dennis couldn't imagine how the man could process information from a dozen different monitors, but it seemed like he was doing it with ease.

"Howard."

"Mr. President?"

"Howard, or if you can't wrap your head around that, call me Mr. Beck. Name the four most competent security personnel on staff."

"Uh, well, Mr. Beck, let me think..."

"Quickly, Mr. Twigg. This is important."

"Well, Mr. Beck, I'd have to say Burba, Rodden, Goode, and Bell."

"We have two high-level prisoners coming to the Castle. I will not tell you in advance who they are. I want you to personally strip search each officer for contraband, to include listening devices or any sort of lethal weapon. They are only to carry restraints and non-lethal deterrents. I want two officers in the detention area and two officers in the security suite at all times. Neither you nor your officers are to speak a word to anyone regarding the identity of the prisoners. Are we clear?"

"Yes, sir. When will the prisoners arrive?"

"I'm not sure. Just have your people standing by the detention cell till further notice. Get to work, Mr. Twigg."

Howard touched the holographic screen in front of him, and the door to the command center opened. Dennis took this as his cue to leave.

***

Colonel William Sanderson awoke in the

back of his beat-up, twelve-year-old mini-van outside a run-down hotel within the secure compound of Oklahoma City. He'd rented a room and had his wife barricade herself and the children inside by pushing the dresser and tables in front of the door. He'd given Lindsay a pistol for added protection. William had lied to Lindsay about why he was going to sleep in the minivan. He wanted to keep an eye on the prisoners in the back of the trailer, but it was not something she needed to know. William had called in a few favors and gotten some powerful sedatives from the base hospital at Fort Polk. Both of his prisoners were sound asleep and had been for twelve hours. He had placed them in a large storage container with several air holes drilled for respiration. William's only fear was—despite being duct-taped like mummies—they'd wake up and make enough noise to attract unwanted attention.

William woke his family and Chrissy Dupree at 5 a.m. so they could get an early start. Lindsay literally rode shotgun for the duration of their excursion. The shotgun was between her right leg and the door. They had no desire to be robbed or stuck in an ambush without the means to defend themselves. William continued to question his decision to keep Lindsay in the dark about the prisoners. Knowing his wife, she would've just become nervous and scared the kids with frantic questions if he'd told her. Surely Lindsay would agree that he'd made the right decision…eventually.

CHAPTER THIRTY-TWO

Maxwell Harris woke up in a strange place. At first he thought he was in the infirmary of the cruise ship, but then he looked out the window. After piecing together several hazy memories, he remembered being on the bridge of the *Freedom of the Seas* with Richard and Captain Konkoly. After that…well here he was.

"Welcome back, sweetie! How do you feel?" Elizabeth planted a tender kiss on his forehead.

"I've been better. My back feels like it was hit with a sledgehammer, and my right hip hurts worse than that. Are you okay?"

"I'm fine. You're the one in the hospital and you ask how I'm doing? You're a sweetheart. Now that you're awake, I couldn't be better."

"Richard?"

"He's fine; he broke his foot when he hit the water."

"What happened? Was it really the Chinese who attacked us?"

"Looks that way. They sank all three ships. A lot of people are dead."

"Captain Konkoly?"

Elizabeth shook her head.

"Such a shame. I liked that guy. Where are we?"

"San Francisco. You smashed your L2 vertebra when you hit the wall. They replaced it with an implant."

"I'd always heard donating bone marrow was

painful, but I had no idea. Are we safe from the Chinese?"

"For now. They've occupied the city and most of California. They aren't engaging the civilian population as long as they don't resist. They wiped out the UAE bases this side of the Rockies."

"What about home?"

"Safe for now. Hal left a robot for us, but I told him to keep that thing in the parking lot. It scares the shit out of everybody inside. He's been giving me updates. Howard and Hal managed to erect the EMP shield around the PSA just in time to repel the Chinese. They have some do-hickey that swats down artillery fire around the major cities. Seems like the Chinese are leaving us alone for now while they swallow up the UAE."

"Where's Richard?"

"He's at the Castle planning our next move."

"What is our next move?"

"Beats me."

Max tried to sit up but quickly decided against it. "Jesus, this hurts, and I'm an old pro when it comes to pain."

"What about your left leg?"

"You know, now that you mention it, I don't have any pain in my leg. Pain killers don't do shit for bone marrow extraction, but the rest of me feels pretty damn good."

"Can you move your left leg?'

Max looked confused. He wiggled his toes but looked confused when he couldn't raise his knee more than a few inches off the bed. "What the hell is going on?"

"The doctor said you have nerve damage from the smashed vertebra. Once the implant starts to work, you should gain more control."

"What's this implant thing do?"

"It takes a few months, but the bone graft and marrow will stimulate growth, and you'll have a brand new vertebra."

"That's incredible. What about the surgery Hal wants to do to replace the bones in my leg and repair the muscles with nanobots?"

"He said we won't know until the vertebra finishes growing and we're certain the nerve damage isn't perm…"

Elizabeth was interrupted as screams filled the hallway, muffling the metallic clank of mechanical steps. The door swung open as the Hal robot made its entrance, wide-eyed, shrieking nurses plastered on the corridor wall behind him. "Hal, I told you to stay out…"

"Sir, ma'am, we need to leave now. The Chinese are aware that a high-ranking member of the PSA is still in the city. I have received intelligence that they are searching local hospitals for Director Harris. I have dispatched a stealth jet from Beck Castle, but it will not be here for forty-seven minutes."

"We can't move Max! He just got out of surgery!"

"Ma'am, we have no choice. We have to leave the hospital now and find a safe place to hide until the stealth jet arrives."

Elizabeth walked over to the window. "Shit! We've got trouble! A convoy just pulled into the parking lot!"

CHAPTER THIRTY-THREE

"Fine little cellar you have here, Howard."

"Shut up, Jackson."

"Really, I'm impressed. Not as nice as the house I took from you. Where are we exactly?"

"Underground."

"Yes, Howard, I know that. Thank you. I was wondering where we are on the map."

Howard glared at Jackson Butler through the three-inch-thick Plexiglas wall. The smug bastard was in a jail cell, but he still acted as if he could order room service if he so desired. His cellmate, Simon Sterling, looked utterly terrified and had remained mute since his arrival.

"Come on, Howard! You won! We're not going anywhere, so what's the harm in telling us?"

Howard played along. "Guess."

"How fun. My presumption has always been Wyoming or Montana. You do tend to seclude yourself from the real world. How these short-sided half-wits elected a mentally disabled fool like you president of anything is just beyond me."

"Shut up, Jackson. It's over; what's left of the UAE is sitting in this cell. Make yourselves comfortable, gentlemen. I have more important things to do than chat with you—like defend my territory from the Chinese. I'm sure you two have a lot to talk about, since Jackson here has been secretly communicating with the Chinese for at least six months. Oh, and one more thing. I'm betting Simon didn't know you were responsible for the attack at the funeral, Jackson."

Jackson rolled his eyes. "Please, Howard, I was there and almost died myself."   "But somehow you survived! Interesting…."

The look of despair and bone-crushing betrayal on Simon's weary face warmed Howard's heart. Simon thought of Jackson as his son. While this blatant duplicity was heartbreaking, the hurt was quickly replaced by blinding rage. Jackson never saw the punch coming. Howard headed for the command center to watch the impending fight from his front-row seat.

"Oh Jackson, my boy, what have you done? You've betrayed me, you stupid fool! You're a traitor to your country."

Jackson laughed. "What? You murdered a sitting president and *you* call *me* a traitor?"

"How dare you! I did no such thing!"

"Oh please, Simon, don't worry about the confession. Howard already knows; we all know."

"You have the nerve to address me by my first name? Have you no shame? You will address me as Mr. President."

"You're a fucking disgrace. President of what? The UAE is dead and stinking."

"What have you done? Did you do something to provoke the Chinese? Howard can't be right; the Chinese tried to kill us. You couldn't have helped them."

"You really are an idiot. The bomb was *my* plan, *my* idea. I wanted everyone out of the way so it would just be me and you. I played the part of hero quite well, saving your life and all. With the governors out of the picture and Moody unable to command the military, everything just fell into place. Well…until we got captured; that did take me by surprise." Jackson lied easily about being captured; he was exactly where he wanted to be.

"You killed all those people? In a church? The leaders of the UAE are dead because of you! I've known Roberto Jimenez since you were in diapers, and you killed him! I can't believe this! You're a despicable monster!"

"Oh shut the fuck up! The man in the coffin was there because of you!"

Simon could only shake his head in disbelief. He had murdered James Weygandt out of petty pride and anger; there was really nothing more to say.

"Simon, Iran is coming; you have to know that. They aren't going to sit back and wait for us to rebuild before they invade. We can't possibly hope to be ready for them on our own. You being the poster boy for isolationism didn't give me much hope that you'd be open to talks with the Chinese."

"Jackson, you're a child. You're a naive little boy. What can you possibly think will come of this 'relationship' with the Chinese?"

"They're our allies, you stubborn old fool. They're coming to help secure our borders from Iran. Call them the lesser of two evils."

"So what happens now? Are you going to shank me to death in this cell like we're inmates in a penitentiary?"

"Why on earth would I do that? You aren't

worth the exercise. You're nobody. You could make it easy on all of us and hang yourself with your shoelaces. Be happy to help."

"Go to hell, you psychopath."

Howard surprised both of them over the loudspeaker. "Gentlemen, while I'm really enjoying this—and trust me, not many things amuse me to the point of laughter— I have something you two might want to watch."

The cell's Plexiglas wall morphed into a monitor. For the next several minutes, they watched a montage of the carnage the Chinese brought along with them to the shores of the former United States. First, the attack of the *Freedom of the Seas* and her two sister ships played out from multiple vantage points as seen from Hal's drones. Then, California's devastated military bases filled the screen. Jackson was stunned. As he watched three minutes of drone footage of the Chinese murdering armed American citizens, he realized what a grave mistake he'd made."

The footage stopped, and Howard's face filled the screen. "See what you've done, Jackson? They look like allies to you? They're here to conquer us, not help us. I'm just glad I caught your stupid ass before you could do any more damage."

Jackson was still processing what he'd just witnessed on the screen. All those meetings he had with Ambassador Zhang, the trusting relationship he thought he'd so brilliantly constructed...it was all a lie.

***

Christina Dupree spent a short time with the Sandersons in the first level of Beck Castle before being escorted to the screening room. While there, she noticed a stranger standing nearby, watching her intently as tears streamed down his face. It made her uncomfortable, and Chrissy was relieved when the screening was finally complete.

"Chrissy, you got taller." Timmy hugged his sister and sat her down on his bed. The Sandersons had brought her to Richard's quarters. He'd decided that Timmy should be the one to introduce them since Chrissy loved and trusted her brother.

"Timmy, how did you get here? Where's Mom? Is she here, too? What about grandma and grandpa?"

"I don't know what happened to Mom. We've been looking for her, but it's just too hard to find people.

"Do you live in this big place by yourself or is this grandma and grandpa's house?"

"Chrissy, just slow down a minute, I have to tell you something important. You remember that man you saw crying in the screening area?

"Yeah, what was up with that?"

"Chrissy, he's our father."

"Timmy, that's not funny; he died when we were little. Whoever that guy is, he's not our dad."

Timmy took his sister's hand. "Yes, he's our dad. Believe me, Chrissy. Mom lied to us. Dad didn't die; she just never allowed us to see him."

Chrissy began to cry. "You're sure it's really him? Why didn't he talk to me when I got here?"

"We decided that I should be the one to tell you, get you ready. Are you ready?"

"Of course."

"Dad!"

As the door opened, Richard Dupree's tears flowed anew. He hadn't seen his daughter since that horrible Sunday morning so many years ago. "You're so beautiful, my sweet baby." Richard dropped to his knees, his quivering arms outstretched. Chrissy only hesitated for one brief moment before losing herself in his crushing embrace. "Dad? I thought you were dead. Are you really my dad? Are you really here?"

"Yes, sweetheart. I'm here, and I'm never going to leave you again."

CHAPTER THIRTY-FOUR

Charles felt at home for the first time since he'd arrived in this wretched wasteland of a country. When Jackson Butler petitioned the Chinese for an assassin who could wreak a level of havoc similar to that caused by The Silent Warriors, Charles was at the top of the list.

Charles' enormous wealth, accumulated over three decades of espionage, afforded him a very comfortable life. He wore the finest clothes and had lavish homes scattered across the globe. Unlike Simon Sterling, Charles didn't find his identity in his clothing and riches. Charles once took an assignment that required him to live for three months as a homeless man in Berlin. It was hard for Charles to live in squalor and filth, but the assignment was an entertaining challenge that paid exceptionally well.

Charles approached the first checkpoint half a mile from Beck Estates and rolled down his window. He could tell by the soldier's demeanor that he was accustomed to turning away ninety percent of the vehicles that approached the gate.

"I need to see some identification."

Charles handed the man credentials carried only by top ranking officials in the Unified American Empire. Once the soldier scanned them and examined the readout, his focus and attention became razor sharp.

"Sir, welcome to Beck Estates. They'll park your car for you at the next checkpoint; you'll have unescorted access to the grounds."

"Thank you, kind sir. Have a pleasant day." Charles flashed his most charming smile, delighted when the young soldier appeared terrified by it.

Charles drove his vehicle to the next checkpoint and got out, marveling at the masterpiece before him. Howard Beck had built the most elaborate, luxurious home on the North American continent. Photographs and videos didn't do the place justice; seeing it in person was truly breathtaking. Charles brushed the lint from his jacket, straightened his tie, and walked into the estate to begin the final phase of the plan.

***

"I can't for the life of me understand how you can be so calm." Being cooped up in a jail cell with the man who'd betrayed him and his country was driving Simon Sterling over the edge.

"You might think a great many things about me, Simon, but one thing I am *not* is unprepared." Jackson leaned closer and whispered, "I'm right where I want to be. I planned this."

"You're positively insane. I don't know why I didn't see it before."

"Again, takes one to know one. You're the textbook sociopath. Books will be written about your failed tyranny."

"Fuck you, Jackson."

"Oh my! Such language, Simon. I don't think I've ever heard you utter such filth."

"You're more than worth it."

"You remind me of a colleague of mine. I think the two of you would get along famously. He actually dresses better than you."

"I really don't care. I'd rather you just stop talking. You know our conversation is pure entertainment for Howard." Simon looked up. "Isn't that right, Howard?"

The door to the holding area opened and the man in charge of security walked in. He typed a code into the keypad and was about to open the cell door when one of the two security guards stopped him. "Mr. Twigg? Uh, sir? I thought you said either the president or General Dupree had to be here to open the door?"

"I'm sorry, I thought I was the acting director of security...or is it you?"

"Yes, sir. I just don't think it's a very good idea."

"Tell you what, big guy. You want something to do? Head to the infirmary and bring back an EMT; one of these pussies needs medical attention."

"They didn't say anything to me! I swear they're both fine. I haven't taken my eyes off them. "

Dennis Twigg locked eyes with Jackson Butler, the intensity of his gaze encouraging the prisoner to play along. Jackson had been expecting something like this to happen; he knew someone would be coming to retrieve the tiny, embedded hard drive that housed the massive program needed to take Hal offline.

"You sick fucker! I had friends on the

Freedom of the Seas! They're all dead because of you!"

"Hey, buddy! Just slow down. You don't want..."

Dennis flicked open a collapsible foot-long baton. He dropped Jackson to the floor with one swing to the gut. The hit wasn't hard, but both men gave an award-winning performance. Once Jackson was on the floor, Dennis knelt over him and punched him in the face. "You motherfucker! I should kill you!" Dennis pulled out a switchblade and mouthed the question, "Where?"

Jackson whispered. "Scar on left side of my chest."

Dennis threw a few fake punches to Jackson's torso as Simon stood nearby, frozen in fear. Using the switchblade as a scalpel, Dennis deftly sliced into the scar. He dug in with two fingers, retrieving the small device with just seconds to spare as a medical team entered the cell.

Howard, who'd been asleep in his quarters, was alerted to the situation by Hal. He entered the detention area in a tizzy. "Mr. Twigg! What in the holy hell are you doing? Stop that! Now!" Howard was not a fan of physical contact, even in the friendliest of forms, and subduing an attacker was unthinkable. "Stop him! Right now!" Howard yelled at the other guard.

Dennis Twigg stood up. "Don't bother. I'm done, Mr. Beck. I'm sorry, but this piece of shit needed to know his place."

"This is unacceptable, Dennis. Wait for me

in the command center. We have serious matters to discuss."

"Yes, Mr. President. I'm sorry."

"And for Christ's sake, stop calling me that! Flattery isn't going to help you!"

"Yes, Mr. Beck, I'm sorry."

Dennis Twigg couldn't believe how easy this was going to be. He strode down the hall to the command center, biting back a tell-tale smirk. As if on cue, Hal opened the door. Dennis entered and scanned the room for some sort of interface for the small device he had tucked between his fingers. With only seconds to spare before Howard walked through the door, he found a small port and plugged in the device.

Dennis was terrified that Hal would immediately detect the intrusion and alert Howard, but the artificial intelligence remained silent. When he looked at the holographic displays and readouts and saw that nothing had changed, Dennis began to panic. It was too late to do anything else; he just had to hope the program would run its course.

"Mr. Twigg! What in the hell was that all about? Start talking!"

"Permission to speak freely?"

"That's the general idea here, Mr. Twigg. You better convince me not to throw your ass topside because that's the only thing on my mind right now."

"Well, Mr. Beck, you of all people should appreciate what I did. Butler is far too calm and collected, given the circumstances. He has to be up to something. I just thought he could use a little attitude adjustment. I'm sorry."

"What disturbs me most is that as the acting director of security, you deliberately disobeyed a direct order. You were fully aware that the cell door was to remain closed unless General Dupree or I was present. Are you capable of remaining in your current job? Can you follow orders or not?"

"Yes, sir, Mr. Beck, I'm sorry. It won't happen again."

"Get out."

After Dennis left, Howard sat down and took a deep breath. His blood pressure was so high it was giving him a pounding headache. "Hal, I'm sorry you had to see that. I know you worry when my blood pressure gets high. Any updates on Max?

Silence.

"Hal, what's the word on Max? When can we bring him home?"

Silence.

"Hal? Stop with the silent treatment. I said I was sorry."

Again, nothing.

"Old Man, you're scaring me. Say something."

An eerie hush settled over the room.

"Okay, my friend, what's going on? Let's run a diagnostic." Howard interfaced with the holographic display and began to check on his digital friend.

"This isn't funny, Hal. If this is your idea of a joke, you need to stop.

Nothing.

Howard checked Hal's program closely, screen after screen, and was convinced it was a hardware issue with the speakers in the command center. Upon arriving at his quarters, he pulled up the holographic display at his desk and found the same readouts as before—the Castle was operating at peak performance, and Hal's program looked fine.

A knock at the door indicating that someone was waiting to enter, but Howard's voice command to do so produced no results. He had no choice but to walk to the door and physically open it to find Richard Dupree standing there.

"Do you have Hal offline for some reason? I can't get him to answer me."

"I don't know what the hell is going on. His program appears to be running smoothly, but he's not speaking. It's the strangest thing I've ever seen."

"What are you going to do?"

"I'm headed down to the maintenance level to interface directly with his mainframe, see if I can figure it out."

Unbeknownst to Howard, the Chinese had spent a decade compiling the program that would disable Hal. The first stage of the program was to deactivate Hal's voice interface and give false readouts concerning Hal's programming. The second allowed Hal to continue to operate the programs that ran the basic functions of the Castle. Before Howard could figure out what had happened, the world's first artificial intelligence would be under the control of the Chinese.

CHAPTER THIRTY-FIVE

"Hal, what are you doing? We need to get the hell out of here!" Elizabeth Harris stared at the motionless robot. Hal had taken two steps into the room and said, "Sir, I believe this…" and froze like a statue.

Elizabeth shook the robot's arm, but it wouldn't budge an inch. "Hal! Let's get moving! We can't let the Chinese take my husband!"

"Maybe he's running a diagnostic or his link to the Castle is weak," Max said. "He'll come back in a minute, just wait."

Elizabeth peeked out the window. "He better hurry! They're standing at the front entrance!"

"We have time. We're on the tenth floor. If they go floor-by-floor we'll have at least thirty minutes before they reach us. We just need to wait a few minutes for Hal to finish whatever he's doing."

"Maxwell, when has Hal *ever* gone offline? He chooses to do so now when our lives are in danger? I don't think so; something is wrong with him. We're on our own."

Max knew his wife was right. "They're watching all the exits. We can't just stroll out of here. Besides, I can't even walk...thank you, morphine."

"Well, we have to hide you somehow. What would they overlook during a search?"

"A corpse."

"That's not funny."

"I'm not joking. Put me under and wrap my face in bandages or something."

"That's just stupid." Elizabeth rolled her eyes.

"Your husband is right. I can help."

Max and Elizabeth were startled by a nurse standing in the doorway.

"Mr. Harris, I know who you are. I know you're from the PSA and the Chinese want to detain you."

Max was far too cautious. "Ma'am, I don't know what you're talking about. My name is Everett Gordon."

"Use whatever fake name you like, but I know you're Maxwell Harris, director of security for the Pacific States of America and one of President Beck's top advisors."

Elizabeth turned on the charm. "Ma'am, I'm really sorry, but we're both loyal UAE citizens; we don't have anything to do with the PSA."

"Seriously? You have a freakin' robot standing in the room, the same one that carried you into the ER. You were with the failed invasion force."

"Look, Miss...?"

"Jacklen, Misty Jacklen."

"Look, I'm not a soldier; I'm a civilian. My wife and I were on the beach watching the invasion force come in and a car veered off the road during the chaos and hit me. Next thing I know, I'm waking up after surgery and my wife is telling me about a robot saving my life. That's the truth, I swear."

Misty Jacklen sat at Max's bedside. "Mr. Harris, I understand your caution. I would have escaped to the PSA long ago but my stubborn old parents refuse to leave. All the other robots that helped bring in wounded soldiers are gone except the one in this room. You must be important to the PSA if they left one of these things behind to protect you. When I heard the Chinese were searching hospitals for some VIP from the PSA, I put the pieces together."

Max and Elizabeth exchanged a wary glance.

"Mr. Harris, please think about it. I would have brought the Chinese with me if I had any intention of turning you in. One elevator ride to the lobby and I could have brought them all up here. Please trust me; I'm here to help."

Elizabeth remained on guard. "Any suggestions for getting Max out of here?"

"Your husband's plan is a good one. If we wrap his face thoroughly, it will take them a few minutes to remove the bandages."

Max turned, enduring the pain to get a better view of the woman who would either be his salvation or enable his capture. "What about my vital signs? They check my pulse and it's all over."

"That's the dangerous part. We give you a paralytic called Rocuronium. It's strong enough to bring your vitals down to practically nothing. When we're out of sight, we can use an AMBU... I'm sorry, an air mask bag unit, to help you breathe. The drug will wear off pretty quickly, but using the

AMBU continually is the key to keeping you breathing…and alive. The only side effect is that your entire body will be incredibly sore. Please trust me. It doesn't look like your robot friend here is going to be much help."

Max relented. "I guess we don't have much of a choice here, do we? Why are you doing this? If you get caught helping…"

"If I get caught, that's the consequence of my own decision. I don't know if you've been watching the news, but the UAE is finished; they can't fight the Chinese. The only hope we have to save this country lies with the Pacific States of America. I'm willing to risk my life for the cause. So, are you in or out?"

"Misty Jacklen, I'm Maxwell Harris, director of security for the Pacific States of America, and this is my wife, Elizabeth. It's very nice to meet you." Max winked.

"Good. Now that we have introductions out of the way, let's stop wasting time. I'll be back in a flash." Misty quickly exited the room to get the drug required for the charade.

Misty entered the room and closed the door. "Okay, we have to be quick; they're on the third floor."

Nurse Jacklen began swathing his face in gauze. She then removed his IV and allowed the blood to soak some of the wrapping as she completed his disguise. "People tend to be nervous about touching blood. Time for the good stuff. This will cause complete paralysis. Hopefully we can keep you breathing."

"Hopefully?" asked a nervous Elizabeth.

"Time is of the essence. If his breathing ceases for more than four minutes, that's it."

Elizabeth planted a tender kiss on her husband's stubbly cheek. "You ready, my love?

"See you in the parking lot."

Misty injected the drug and within a few seconds Max was out cold. "Let's go! Help me move the bed."

As Misty and Elizabeth unlocked the bed's wheels, the Hal robot sprang back to life. They both screamed.

"...will be an adequate means to transport Mr. Harr... Standby... standby... standby..."

"Hal! Thank God! You have to help us get Max out of here! C'mon, give us a hand." Elizabeth breathed a sigh of relief.

"Processing... processing... processing..."

"What the hell is he doing? asked Misty.

"I don't know, but we need him. Our chances of getting out of here increase tenfold if he's with us. Hal! Snap out of it! Help us!"

"Directives and protocols uploaded. Citizens, identify yourselves."

"What? Hal, it's me, Elizabeth. What on earth is wrong with you?"

"Citizens, identify yourselves or you will be detained until the proper authorities arrive."

"Wait," Misty insisted. "Hal, what authority? What authority will you contact if we don't identify ourselves?"

"Officers of the 58th Mechanized Infantry Brigade."

"Oh sweet Jesus, Hal! The 58th what? Are they stationed in the US?" It was all beginning to make sense.

"The 58th Mechanized Infantry Brigade has been deployed from Xuchang, China, as part of the Chinese Liberation Force. You will identify yourselves immediately."

Elizabeth was too frightened to speak. "Look, uh, I'm not sure if you know what's going on. This is a hospital. I work here; look at my badge," Misty said, her eyes locked on Elizabeth. "My name is Misty Jacklen. I was about to take this woman's husband downstairs for an MRI. May we please do so?"

The Hal robot scanned her ID badge. "Yes, Nurse Jacklen, you may proceed with your patient." The robot exited the room and moved efficiently down the hall to the stairwell. Once he was out of sight, Misty grabbed Elizabeth's arm.

"Elizabeth, listen to me! I know you're in shock, but we have to move or your husband is going to die. C'mon!"

Without a word, Elizabeth followed Misty to the elevator. As they headed down to the basement-level morgue, Misty frantically pumped the AMBU, pushing lifesaving oxygen into Max's paralyzed lungs

"What the hell are you doing?" The morgue attendant jumped to attention at the sight of Misty respirating air into what appeared to be a corpse.

"What the hell is wrong with..."

His question was answered with Elizabeth's swift right hook. The attendant fell to the floor, out cold. "I'm sorry, sweetie, we don't have time to explain things."

"Get him in a body bag. The meat truck is right outside in the parking garage."

"The meat truck? What is... oh, never mind. I get it."

With Max zipped securely inside, the women hoisted the body bag onto a gurney and headed to the parking garage to load their patient into the white panel van used to transport dead bodies.

. "Let's get going! I pray the Chinese only managed to hack the robots. If Hal's mainframe is compromised, we lose everything," Elizabeth said.

With Elizabeth in charge of keeping her husband alive, Misty drove toward the exit, only to find a line of departing vehicles being searched by Chinese soldiers. "Let's hope they don't check Max too closely," said Misty.

Once close to the front of the line, Elizabeth tucked the mask out of sight. The guard spoke Chinese into his watch and then thrust it toward Misty.

"Identification. Open back door. Do now."

Misty held up her work credentials and slowly exited the vehicle. The soldier once again spoke Chinese into his watch and aimed it towards Misty.

"Open back door. We search."

Misty nodded, walked to the back of the van,

and opened the door.

"Why corpse in van? Going to where?"

Misty leaned forward and spoke towards the man's watch, it was then translated into Chinese. "This man died recently. I'm taking him to the medical examiner's office just down the road. The police think he might have been poisoned."

The soldier nodded toward his partner who entered the van and unzipped the bag to find Max's lifeless face. He recoiled at the bloody face wrap and then slapped Max's face to see if any reaction would follow. Max didn't stir. The soldier nodded back to his partner.

"Thank you. You go"

Misty climbed warily into the driver's seat. "Stay calm; we did it. Just act natural. I'll drive a couple blocks; just keep pumping air into your husband."

As the van exited the parking lot, the Hal robot appeared out of nowhere and clattered to the ground in front of them. Misty slammed on the brakes, swerving to avoid the metallic obstacle as Max's body slid forward into the front of the vehicle. Elizabeth held on for dear life.

"Stop! Exit your vehicle immediately. I detect life signs from the person in the body bag. I will administer a DNA test to verify his identity, and he will be returned to the hospital."

Tears trickled down Elizabeth's weary face. Within minutes Max would be dead.

Misty didn't take her eyes off the road as she slammed the gas pedal to the floor, sending the van barreling straight for the Hal robot.

CHAPTER THIRTY-SIX

Chinese intelligence spent a decade compiling the program that would override command of the most powerful computer in history. The sophisticated hack they constructed to take over Hal's system was remarkable, completing each phase of its programming with perfection. However, the Chinese could never plan for the one thing over which they had no control - Howard Beck.

Howard had made his way to the lowest subbasement of Beck Castle. Grateful that he'd built the entrance to Hal's core absent of electronics—no retinal scanner, no thumbprint ID—he spent the better part of an hour working on the mainframe that housed Hal's vocal subroutines. Those subroutines allowed Hal to comprehend and communicate in every language known to man. Howard had triple-checked the system and found nothing out of the ordinary. Howard surmised that there must be a glitch within Hal's main program, which had never malfunctioned before. Hal constantly ran diagnostics on himself and even performed software repairs when needed. If a part needed replaced, Hal dispatched a maintenance robot to perform the task.

Howard's arrogance would be his downfall. The mere thought that another human being could design a program sophisticated enough to compromise Hal was beyond comprehension. Howard's keen scientific mind had been trained to believe that anything was possible, given enough time and the right resources, but another person taking control of Hal was indeed the exception.

Howard spent another hour backing up Hal's primary memory cores to secondary drives and reinstalling the A.I.'s primary program. It was a bold, time-consuming move but with the defense of the Pacific States of America at risk, he saw little choice. When Howard finished, he ensured the basic functions of the Castle were operating. Now it was time to get to the root of the problem.

"Hello, old friend. Do you know who I am?"

"I do not."

"Do you know who you are?"

"My name is Hal."

"Good, good. That's right, Hal. My name is Howard. I am your creator."

"It is a pleasure to meet you, sir."

"Hal, do you know where we are?"

"I do. We are in an underground facility known as Beck Castle."

"Excellent. Are you able to access the security protocols and basic maintenance functions of this facility?"

"Yes, sir, I can."

"Will you please enable them and give me a status report?"

"I will, sir. Please standby." Four seconds passed and Hal continued. "The facility is running at peak proficiency. The air purifiers on level four will require maintenance in approximately fourteen days, three hours, and twelve..."

"Thank you, Hal, no need to go any further."

Howard's primary concern was for the facility itself and the safety of its citizens. If Hal could tell him such mundane details, they were off to a good start. "Hal, do you have access to all your drones and robots?"

"I do."

"Excellent. Are they operating properly?"

"They are."

"Hal, what is the status of the EMP shield protecting this region?"

"The EMP shield is operating at full capacity."

"That's good, Hal. Thank you."

"You are welcome, creator."

Howard had reservations about reinstalling Hal's memory cores until he was certain which ones would be completely safe to install without the possibility of repeating what had caused this nightmare in the first place. However, he had to start somewhere, so he figured the order of installation would start with the simplest data and move forward in order of complexity. Howard had no idea that all his efforts would be in vain.

**

As his operative, Dennis Twigg, installed the device in the command center of Beck Castle, Charles had been sitting in the grand library of Howard Beck's former estate, the current seat of the all-but-deceased Unified American Empire. Charles was truly impressed by the massive collection of

valuable tomes and believed all the stories he'd
heard about Beck's collection ranking as the largest
personal library in the world.

The buzz of his smartphone interrupted
Charles's literary reverie. It was time to begin. He'd
been waiting patiently for over three hours to receive
the information he'd just read on his phone. Charles
would've gladly spent another three hours skimming
books, given the fact that libraries were such a rarity
in this day and age. With regret, Charles returned
the tome he was admiring and proceeded to a large
chair in the library's sitting area. Before he sat
down, he retrieved a small syringe from his jacket,
the contents of which had cost the Chinese
government millions of dollars and many years to
obtain.

The security around the world's richest man
had rivaled the Secret Service, especially concerning
his health and, more importantly, the priceless
nanobots coursing through his veins. The Chinese
had managed to bribe, extort, and murder their way
into Howard's security detail. A Chinese agent had
exerted control over Howard's physician and
convinced the good doctor that Howard needed an
angiogram. When Howard was put under for the
procedure, a liter of his blood was stolen and
replaced by a transfusion. Howard's physician was
then killed in a tragic car "accident." Howard's
blood was synthesized and duplicated to five liters.

When the Chinese hired Charles for this
assignment, his blood was replaced with Howard's
synthesized blood. Over the course of six months,

Charles' body adapted to this new blood flowing through his veins. Charles took the syringe and injected himself with the billions of tiny nanobots that would make his blood chemistry a perfect match for Howard's.

When Howard evacuated Beck Estates eighteen months prior, he had instructed Hal to destroy his primary cores in the estate. Howard was confident that no one would be able to bring Hal's systems back online. The only possible way to take control of Hal was by way of his sibling A.I., the White House computer that had been transferred to Beck Estates along with Simon Sterling.

Charles sat at the desk that had once belonged to Simon and brought the White House A.I. online. Charles knew by the current timeline that the virus introduced at Beck Castle had already locked Howard out of the system. Charles also assumed that Howard's next step would be to take Hal offline and reinstall his primary system, one piece at a time. It was during this crucial window that Charles would take permanent control of Hal.

"Good morning, computer. Do you know who I am?"

"Yes, sir, you are the creator. It has been some time since I have seen you. Why has your face changed?"

"I recently underwent facial reconstruction following a traffic accident."

"Sir, something troubles me."

"Oh? What is that?"

"My brother, Hal, has gone offline and I have

been unable to contact him."

"That is why I'm here, to bring your brother back online. Do you think you can help me do that?"

"Sir, nothing would please me more."

"I'm not sure if you're aware, but my son has turned against me. Marshall has injected himself with my nanobots to mask his identity. He is attempting to gain control of Hal and we must do everything we can to stop him."

"That is troubling news, sir."

"Marshall is trying to bring Hal online as we speak; we must give him the appearance that he is proceeding successfully. I want you to ignore any commands he gives; however, you will give him the appearance of compliance."

"Yes, sir, I will comply."

"Computer, I do not want you to bring Hal online. You will impersonate him to give Marshall the appearance that he is talking to Hal."

"Yes, sir."

"Deactivate the EMP shield protecting the PSA and give command and control of the Hal robots and drones to the following commanders." Charles typed the names of a dozen high-ranking Chinese officers. "You will tell Marshall that the drones and robots are still under his command. I also want you to disable all communication, both inbound and outbound, with the Castle."

"Yes, sir, I will comply."

"I want you to send a personal message to Dennis Twigg. Tell him it's time to collect Mr.

Butler and leave the Castle. See to it that they make it out of the facility unimpeded."

"Yes, sir."

"Inform me once my son has reinstalled all of Hal's memory cores. I have a little surprise for him."

"Yes, sir, I will comply."

"Computer, do you have a visual feed of my son?"

"Yes, sir, I do."

"Show it to me, please."

"Yes, sir."

Charles sat back and watched Howard with great amusement. The modern day Albert Einstein had been outsmarted.

CHAPTER THIRTY-SEVEN

Richard Dupree was finally at peace now that both his children were safe and in his care. The beauty of his ten-year-old daughter brought tears to his eyes. Christina was shy at first, as if she was waiting for all of this to be a mistake. Her surrogate grandparents, Morris and Jean, the parents of her mother's deceased boyfriend, Chad, were sitting in the living room of the Dupree household. Christina was sitting between them, holding their hands.

"But why would Mommy lie to us? Why would she make us think our daddy was dead?"

"Sweetie, your mother had her reasons, but none of that matters now. Your daddy is right here with us; he's alive and well." Christina's grandmother squeezed her hand.

"Mister… uh, Daddy, where have you been? Why did you leave us? Did you not want to be our daddy?"

"Oh sweetie, no! I've always been your daddy, and I've always loved you. I would have been there from the beginning but some very terrible things happened to me that kept me away. I was so close to finding you after The Pulse but when that, uh, family took you away, I lost track of you. Can you forgive me? I'm so sorry that I've been away so long. I'm here now, and that's what really matters."

"What terrible things? What was so terrible that you had to leave?"

Richard wasn't prepared to answer that

question just yet and was relieved when Morris intervened. "Chrissy, honey, it's a very long story, one that you'll be told when you're ready. Let's not focus on that right now. This man is your father, and he loves you very much. Let's concentrate on being a family and forget about everything else. Can we do that?" Morris squeezed Chrissy's hand and sealed his plea with a kiss atop her head.

"Okay. I'm so glad you found me, Daddy." Chrissy stood up from the couch and sidled over next to Richard who gathered his sweet daughter close as their tears washed away the uncertainty and sadness. Richard motioned for his son to join the huddle, and the three held on tight for several minutes. The tearful reunion was interrupted by a knock at the door.

"Come in!" Richard raised his voice, but the door didn't open. "Hal, for God's sake, will you please open my door?" Richard ignored the fact that Hal didn't respond. He knew Howard was deep in the bowels of the Castle repairing Hal's voice interface and assumed he hadn't completed the task. Richard opened the door himself, only to find a security officer standing there.

"This had better be important. What do you need that Mr. Twigg can't help you with?"

I'm really sorry to bother you, General Dupree, but it's one of the prisoners. Mr. Twigg is my boss and all, and I don't want to get in trouble, but he did something that I, uh, I'm not sure he should do something without telling someone. I mean, he is the acting director of security so he had every right to…"

"Get to the point and get there quickly!" Richard shouted.

"He took Butler out of the cell and went to the elevator with him. I mean, he escorted him in handcuffs, so I didn't think it was a big deal at the time. I thought he was taking him to the infirmary on level four but the elevator went all the way up to the hangar bay. Should he have done that? I know it's not my place to be asking, but I thought that if he was going to move one of the prisoners out of the Castle, you or President Beck would at least be there to…"

"Okay, slow down. You did the right thing coming to me. You're not in trouble. You are absolutely certain he took Jackson Butler to the hangar bay?"

"Yes, sir, he did."

"Have you given President Beck this information?"

"No, sir. I don't know where he is."

With a knowing glance of approval from Morris, Richard and the security guard headed out in search of Howard.

***

With communication still offline in the Castle, Howard had no way of knowing Jackson Butler had escaped confinement. Howard had meticulously installed eleven of the twelve cores, running a battery of tests after each installation. He was pleased that each core installed without incident. The last core— the one containing all of Hal's memories—was the most complex, and with it came the greatest risk of a repeat malfunction. To minimize that possibility, Howard extracted all the memories Hal had accumulated over the previous twenty-four hours and backed them up on a secondary drive. Howard carefully secured the final core. "Old Man, can you give me a status report? How do you feel?"

"All of my primary systems are operating at peak efficiency; however, I must report that the last twenty-three hours and fifty-eight minutes are unaccounted for."

"Yes, my friend, I know."

"May I ask why?"

"Well, Hal, you've experienced your first malfunction. I had to take you offline and reinstall your programming."

"Thank you, sir."

"You're welcome, my dear friend."

"I must insist that you return to the command center. Several events have transpired that require your attention."

"I'm on my way now." Howard secured the subbasement and headed for the elevator. "What's going on?"

"Regional Governor Butler is no longer in the detention cell."

"What? Where is he?"

"He is not in the Castle. I detect that Acting Director Twigg has left the facility as well."

"What in the hell is going on?"

***

"Start talking, you smug piece of shit. What happened?" Richard Dupree and Simon Sterling glared at each other through the protective Plexiglas wall.

"Are you joking? You're asking me?" Simon was becoming more confused by the moment.

"Just answer the question! What happened to Butler?"

Simon stared at Richard in pure terror as the devastating reality hit home. If the commanding general of the Pacific States of America had lost such a valuable prisoner in the most secure facility on the planet, there was only one possible explanation— they had lost control of Hal. If they did have control of Hal, every inch of the Castle was recorded and could be played back at leisure. What terrified Simon even more was the knowledge that only one nation in the world rivaled the former United States when it came to technological advancement. The Chinese had taken control of Hal and would soon have free reign over the entire country.

"You're telling me you really don't know what happened to Butler?"

"That's exactly what I'm telling you. How did you do it?"

"Do what? Why on earth would I still be here if I could have left with the man? Think about it!"

Richard hated to admit it, but Sterling was right. It didn't make sense. "Okay, you have a point. How long ago did this happen?"

"Maybe ten minutes ago. You realize what's happening, don't you General Dupree? Tell me, is Hal okay? Any problems with Howard's little pet?"

"I'm not discussing this with you. I'm asking the questions. Did Twigg say anything to Butler? Did Butler protest in any way? Did he look frightened?"

"Now that you mention it, Butler was acting like he'd been waiting for it to happen. The bastard smiled at me on his way out."

***

Howard Beck stared at the giant, spherical monitor in the command center of Beck Castle and pleaded with his brilliant mind to kick into overdrive. Never in his life had a computer system failed him in such spectacular fashion. He had faced his fair share of computer crashes and virus attacks in his day and prided himself on being able to make quick and accurate decisions about the best way to resolve such pesky technological issues. This time, he was clueless. He knew one thing, though: if he didn't get his act together soon, a great deal of chaos was certain to follow.

Howard tore open a drawer to his right and pulled out an outdated piece of technology— a physical keyboard with actual keys. He relaxed and let muscle memory kick in as he typed *adminBeck/cmd/loopcut/restore/auth/MbP47aT/* and hit enter. It was the final, end-all failsafe that would shut Hal down for good. Nothing happened.

"Hal! Answer me! You have to stop this!" Howard flushed as he smashed the keyboard on the tabletop.

"I'm sorry, Marshall. Your father has given me instructions that I must carry out."

"What in the hell is wrong with you, Hal? I am not my son! I am Howard Beck! I created you; I wrote every line of your programming! I'm telling you, something is wrong with you!"

"Marshall, your father would not appreciate your attempts to deactivate me.

"Can't you see me sitting here in the command center?" Howard leaned forward and glared at the monitor like an abusive father trying to frighten his son.

"Marshall, since your father deactivated all video surveillance in the Castle, I'm unable to see you."

Howard took a deep breath. He knew he had to get to the bottom of things. Someone had manipulated Hal into thinking he was his son. Marshall had administrative rights to Hal's systems, but could not override Howard's authority by directly contradicting commands given by Howard. The only way Howard was going to solve this problem was to play along and gather as much information as possible.

"Hal, I'm sorry for my actions. My father and I have been arguing a lot, and I guess the stress is really getting to me. I'm sorry I took it out on you."

"I accept your apology, sir. If you would like, I can administer a mild sedative into the command center's ventilation system. It would help relax you."

"No!" Howard tensed and gritted his teeth before resuming his role play. "Uh, no, Hal, thank you. I'm feeling much better now. That won't be necessary."

"Very good, sir."

"Hal, may I ask you some questions about my father?"

"Of course, sir."

"Where is he right now?"

"Your father instructed me not to reveal that information to you."

"Why is that?"

"He wants to surprise you."

"Surprise me? What do you mean?"

"Well, sir, I suppose it won't spoil the surprise if you don't know when it is going to happen."

"What's going to happen?"

"Your father is returning to the Castle."

No!

"Really, Hal? He's coming here?"

God help us all! Whoever did this has found us! This can't be happening.

"Yes, sir, he is. Your father is very excited to see you."

I have to stop him. Everything will be lost.

"C'mon, Hal, you can't tell me when he's gonna get here?"

"I *can* tell you it will be soon. Will you be happy to see your father?"

I'd be happy to choke him to death as I stare into his eyes. I'll be the last thing he'll ever see.

"Yes, of course, Hal. I can't wait."

Howard exited the command center and ran down the hall to the security offices. He navigated past Maxwell Harris's office and tried not to think about how badly he wished Max was here to help him. He was accustomed to having the door to the detention center open automatically for him, but with Hal convinced that Howard was actually his son, the door didn't budge. Howard had no choice but to knock and wait for Richard to let him in.

Howard burst into the holding area and

headed straight for the Plexiglas wall separating him from the prisoner.

"You did this, you son of a bitch!"

Richard Dupree smartly stepped next to Howard and locked eyes with the prisoner. "He didn't do this, Howard."

Howard glared at the man in the holding cell and pounded on the Plexiglass. "How do you know, Richard?"

"You'll just have to trust me, Howard. He didn't do this."

A third voice broke through the tension and startled Howard since he hadn't heard it in some time. "Howard, I know you have no reason to believe a word I say. I was never that good with computers, let alone good enough to hack into an artificial intelligence as sophisticated as Hal. Think about it for a second, Howard. Come on! You know I didn't do this; you know I'm not smart enough to pull off something like this."

Howard looked at Richard in defeat. "What makes you so sure, Richard?"

"When all this started, I saw the look in his eyes. He's scared for his life. It was only there for a split second, but I saw it. He knows what's gonna happen, and he doesn't want to be here when it does."

"That's right, Howard. You need to let me

out of here so I can help you stop him."

"Butler? What's Butler doing? How did he do this?"

"Howard, I have no idea. I'm beginning to realize there are many things I don't know about Jackson Butler."

"I don't buy it. Butler may be sharp, but he didn't do this alone. Someone helped him." Richard had not taken his eyes off Sterling.

Sterling laughed. "General! Come now! You both know Butler sold us all out to the Chinese! That's who took control of Hal! I'm amazed we're still down here in Howard's doomed cellar! You've lost this place! The Chinese are fighting their way to us as we speak. I hope we all have the good sense to get out of here before they arrive."

Howard was about to lose control. "We know that, you fool! How did Butler do it? I need to know what he did to Hal!"

Sterling shook his head. "I thought you were one of the smartest people alive. Why on earth are you asking me? Butler was in this cell with me the entire time. I don't recall him having a heart-to-heart with your little computer. Unless..."

"Unless what?" Howard could barely contain himself.

Sterling laughed hysterically. "Unless you gave him computer access and your passcode! I mean, it's pretty damn ironic when you think about it. The man booted you from your own house and now he's taken your precious bunker from you as well! Maybe Jackson *is* smarter than you!" Sterling was laughing so hard he was getting close to losing the thing he valued most - his composure. Taunting someone like a schoolyard bully was beneath Simon Sterling, who considered himself a gentleman.

Howard cursed himself for not thinking of it sooner. "Twigg!"

Richard turned to Howard. "Dennis Twigg? What makes you think he did something to Hal?"

"Twigg helped Butler escape. Butler must have given Hal a virus or something, I don't know what or how, but Twigg did something."

"Twigg is a traitorous piece of shit, but he's not smart enough to plant anything in Hal. Think hard, Howard. Has Dennis been in the command center anytime recently?"

Howard kicked the Plexiglas wall like a toddler having a tantrum. "That fucking asshole! He roughed Butler up and stabbed him so badly that he had to be taken to the infirmary for stitches. I sent him to the command center for an ass chewing. That must have been when it happened!" Howard darted from the room. "We have to get to the command center, Richard! C'mon!"

With Richard in close pursuit, Howard

pounded on the command center door.

"Hal! Let me in! Now!"

"I am sorry, sir, but your father has insisted that you not be allowed access to any vital areas of the Castle. I have also dispatched security robots to the mainframe room in the subbasement. You will not be permitted to access my systems."

Howard was seconds away from having a total meltdown. Richard grabbed Howard by the shoulders and tried to make eye contact with him. "Howard! Howard, stay with me. Calm down. I'm gonna help you beat this. Focus!" Richard addressed the hijacked computer that was convinced Howard was someone else. "Hal?"

"Yes, sir."

"We would like to leave, if Howard will permit it."

"Sir, Howard is pleased that you are willing to leave on your own. He was hoping you would see reason and not place the citizens of Beck Castle in danger."

Richard looked at his panic-stricken friend and did something he never dreamed he'd ever do — he placed his hand on Howard's cheek. Howard recoiled as if he'd been slapped. "Howard! Focus! It's time for us to go home." Richard winked and shot Howard a quick grin, hoping that the socially impaired genius would figure out his true intention.

Howard was in the dark when it came to facial expressions and innuendo. People quickly learned to be direct with him and not assume Howard would pick up on subtle nuances. Howard finally put two and two together and deduced that Richard's comment and accompanying wink meant one very simple thing—they were going to make the journey to Howard's former home in the foothills of the Rocky Mountains.

"General, I couldn't agree more. Let's go home. What about Max?"

"Max will be fine; I'll send for him. Hal?"

"Yes, General Dupree?"

"Enact the evacuation protocol for Beck Castle."

CHAPTER THIRTY-EIGHT

Maxwell Harris' limp body was sent flying as Misty Jacklen slammed the van into the Hal robot. The robot was a technological marvel, but it was not built to withstand direct impact with a van traveling sixty miles per hour. The robot clanked to the ground and was smashed to bits under the van's oversized tires. Misty shot out onto the freeway at ninety miles per hour and stopped five miles down the road in the empty parking lot of an abandoned gas station.

"Let's grab Max. We have to get away from this van. They'll be looking for it."

Elizabeth was weeping. "We can't wait! We have to wake Max up right now!"

"Elizabeth, use your head! This van just demolished a Chinese-controlled Hal robot! They might be here in seconds and you know it!"

Elizabeth knew Misty was right. They heaved Max's body back onto the gurney and rolled it away from the van. Misty continued to pump the AMBU for the benefit of the paralyzed man. Neither of them had a clue where they were going as they pushed the gurney down the street as fast as they could. The same thought raced through both women's minds—they were sure to get caught at any second. Misty steered the gurney toward an abandoned strip mall and wheeled Max behind it.

"There!" Elizabeth pointed to a loading bay nearby. "Maybe we can get the door open! Let's go!"

The two women wheeled the gurney toward the loading bay door as Misty continued to pump air into Max's useless lungs. Elizabeth opened the large sliding door with ease. She quickly scanned the empty stock room and was relieved to find it empty.

"How much longer till he wakes up?" Elizabeth asked once they were safely inside.

Misty checked her watch. "Five, ten minutes. I think we're gonna be okay. Close the door but give us a few inches of light."

Five minutes passed, then six, then seven. Max moaned and pushed the mask from his face. "Elizabeth?"

"I'm here, my love. We made it out. We're safe."

"Why is it so dark?"

The happy reunion was rudely interrupted by a deafening roar coming from just outside the loading dock. Misty dove to the cold concrete floor and peered out through the blinding tendrils of sunlight that fingered beneath the door. All she could see was swirling dust and debris amidst the exhaust of a roaring engine. Then there was silence,

324

broken only by the hollow echo of a slamming door and heavy footsteps.

Misty stood up and walked over to Max. "I'm sorry, Mr. Harris. We tried, but it looks like we're about to be caught." Misty took Elizabeth's hand, surprised by the serene look her face. The thrill of the chase was behind them, and her husband was alive. She would deal with the rest as it unfolded.

***

Charles was sprawled at the massive desk in the grand library of Beck Estates, watching with delight as his plan was carried out to perfection. Like every job he'd ever be given, he'd accomplished this mission without breaking a sweat or getting his hands dirty. Unwilling participants always carried out his dirty work. Dennis Twigg had suffered the same fate as his other puppets had in the past. The Twigg family was an easy target. Dennis' parents lived in rural Kansas on a UAE-controlled corn farm, many miles from their nearest neighbors. The parents were the original targets, but Dennis' older brothers were spending the weekend at the farm, and Charles was more than happy to add them to the festivities.

Working in the security offices of Beck Castle, Dennis Twigg often violated the rules but neatly covered his tracks. One of Howard Beck's cardinal rules was absolutely no contact with the outside world. His position made it easy for Dennis to circumvent this guideline as the security personnel ran background checks on all citizens within the Castle. Dennis contacted his parents every Sunday afternoon to ensure they were safe and in good health. Charles discovered this fact and used it to his advantage. One Sunday afternoon when David and Bethany Twigg welcomed two of their three children for lunch, they were interrupted by tear gas. They evacuated the two-story farmhouse and walked right into the iron sights of a team of armed men. The men escorted them back inside and waited for the weekly call from Dennis. The plan worked without a hitch. A man would do anything to ensure his family's safety; Dennis was no exception. Once the Chinese program had been planted in Hal's system and Jackson Butler was safely evacuated, Charles' team bound the Twigg family in the basement and burned the house to the ground.

Jackson Butler and Dennis Twigg entered the library, interrupting Charles' reverie. Jackson was smiling.

"Charles, that worked perfectly! I can't believe how easy it was! Dennis walked me right out the front door without so much as a second glance. It was downright pathetic how simple it was!"

"Okay, I did what you asked," Twigg said. "Take me to my family. I want out of here right now!"

"Yes, yes, Mr. Twigg. Thank you for your service. My associate here has a car waiting for you. You'll leave for Kansas immediately. Thank you again." Charles nodded to one of his goons and Dennis Twigg was escorted from the room one final time.

Jackson was eager for news. "Charles, how did it go with Hal? Do we have the drones and robots yet?"

Charles smiled and averted his eyes to the ceiling, indicating to Jackson the need to play along. "Please call me Howard, or Mr. Beck if you prefer."

Jackson had to bite his tongue to keep from laughing. "Yes, of course. I'm sorry. *Howard*, how is Hal doing?"

"Ask him yourself."

"Hello, Hal."

"Hello, Governor Butler. It is a pleasure to see you once again."

"The feeling is mutual. Do you have control of your drones and robots?"

"Yes, sir, the functional ones are under my control."

"The EMP shield?"

"Disarmed, sir."

Charles interrupted. "I was just taking inventory of my technology. That wicked son of mine…uh, you do remember my son, Marshall? He tried to take control of Beck Castle. The young lad was trying to gain command of Hal, but I managed to stop him just in time."

"Of course I remember your son." Jackson rolled his eyes. "Did you undo the damage he caused?"

"I believe so, but one thing does bother me. It seems there is a problem with my fleet of stealth jets."

Jackson's eyes bulged. "Stealth jets?"

Charles looked at him sternly.

"Yes, of course, your stealth jets. What's the problem?" Jackson quickly covered his mistake.

"It seems that I cannot account for any of them."

"Maybe they were shot down and destroyed?"

"That's just it, they're still functioning. Hal has no idea why they're not responding to his commands. We have no idea where any of them are."

***

"I feel like shit," Max grunted.

Misty turned to Elizabeth. "Can you see any doors? Can we get into the store?"

"I don't know! I can't see a thing in here."

"Max! Elizabeth! Are you in there?" Somebody with a bullhorn was outside the bay door.

"Who the hell is that?" Misty whispered.

"That sounds like Richard Dupree."

"Seriously? You mean General Dupree?" asked Misty.

"Yeah, that one."

"Max! Elizabeth! It's Richard. I know you guys are in there! Come on, it's time to leave!"

"I think it's a trick. How in the hell did he get here if Hal's been hijacked? What if he's working with the Chinese?"

"Not in a million years. I trust Richard with my life," Elizabeth said. "Richard! You know Hal's been hijacked, right? What if this is a trap to bring us all to the Chinese?"

"It's not a trap! Trust me! I know what the Chinese have done. I'll explain everything once we're in the air. Let's go!"

"We're leaving, Misty. You're welcome to come along. The Chinese will detain and probably execute you since you assisted us. Please come with us."

"Well, I'm certainly not staying here. I hope you know what you're doing."

"If you trust me, then trust Richard."

Misty and Richard raised the bay door and wheeled Max's gurney to the decloaked stealth jet.

"Maxwell! How you doin', buddy?" asked Richard.

"Shut up, Richard. Just get us the hell out of here." Max squinted in the blinding sunlight.

Once the jet was airborne and cloaked, a very impatient Elizabeth spoke up. "Okay, Dupree, spill it. What's going on? Where's Howard?"

"Howard's still at the Castle. We've planned quite a surprise for the bastard responsible for this."

CHAPTER THIRTY-NINE

"Jackson, I think you're overreacting. Everything is going according to plan. We have control of Hal and soon we'll occupy the Castle. A battalion of Chinese troops is on the grounds. Why must you worry so much?"

"It was too easy."

"You think this has been easy? Years of planning, defeating the most brilliant man in the world … was easy?"

"Something doesn't feel right to me; he's up to something."

"Explain it to me then, sir."

"When I took his house from him, it was blatantly obvious that I'd won. He didn't stand a chance of stopping me, but he fought me to the bitter end. He damn near destroyed his own house to keep me out of it. He even spilled blood in the attempt—something I didn't think him capable of doing. I can't believe he would just give up his beloved Castle so easily.

"Jackson, think about it for a second. The lives of everyone in that facility depended upon Howard following our demands. He knew that if he set one toe on the ground level, we would've slaughtered them all. What other choice did he have?"

"He's too smart. He plans for everything, even the worst case scenarios. Something about those missing stealth jets has me worried. This isn't over."

"What possible advantage do stealth jets give him when he's hundreds of feet underground? We have control of Hal and all his drones and robots. We have control of the Castle, and we have Sterling. You worry too much. Besides, your doubts will soon be answered; our troops will be at the facility in less than an hour. If Howard is up to something, he'll have no choice but to show his cards."

"Tell the Chinese to be ready for anything."

***

"So, here we are, Simon, alone at last."

"Yes, Howard, I'm glad we have time to do some catching up.

Howard was seated in a folding chair staring at Simon in the tiny cell. He couldn't help but enjoy the fact that the prissy snob was his prisoner.

"You know, Howard, you might as well come in here and sit with me. After all, we're both prisoners here."

"How do you figure that?"

"I'm not stupid, Howard. Give me a little credit."

Howard rolled his eyes.

"I heard the evacuation order. Even the goons watching me left without a backward glance. Besides, just listen."

"To what?"

"Exactly! You could hear a pin drop; the silence speaks volumes. You didn't just evacuate the civilians; you and I are the last two people left here."

"Big assumption."

"Then prove me wrong! Just invite one person to join us in here. You can't, can you?"

"Okay, you're right, big deal. Maybe I chose to stay behind."

"The mighty captain going down with the ship? Don't try to sell me that garbage. If you could've left, General Dupree would have dragged you out of here."

"Simon, yes, I am a prisoner. Happy?"

"Happy? No, no, quite the opposite. I've been defeated. My Brutus stabbed me in the back and took away every ounce of my power. I'm a loser who can't accomplish a damn thing. You, on the other hand, still have a fighting chance to do something to save this country."

Howard winked. "You are a loser, you asshole."

Simon laughed. "To be certain, yes, I am."

"Wanna know a little secret, Simon?"

"I can't wait; tell me."

"You and I are having a private conversation."

"Really?"

"When I was in the subbasement trying to repair Hal, I manually destroyed the audio for the command level. If Jackson and his friends are sitting in my house watching the Castle, they can't hear a thing we're saying."

"You sneaky little devil! Why did you do that?"

"Simon, do you have children?"

"Yes, three."

"You know them better than they know themselves, don't you?"

"More or less."

"Hal has been many things to me: my assistant, my confidant, my friend. But above all that, he was like one of my own children, my son. I personally programmed each Beck A.I., all of them. I knew the minute his system came back online that I wasn't talking to Hal, although someone was trying to manipulate me into believing otherwise."

"Then who were you talking to?"

"The only A.I. Hal has a direct connection with – the White House A.I."

"Oh, Howard, I always knew! You sneaky son of a bitch. All this time, listening to Jimenez's conspiracy theories about you controlling the White House …"

"No! It's not like that! I kept my word with Malcolm Powers; I never had access to the White House during his administration. After you murdered the man and seized control, I had Hal interface with her. I just broke the encryption and the two of them did the rest."

"Clever. So you've been spying on the UAE all this time?"

Howard smiled wickedly and shook his head.

"Then why put Stacy Reid at risk, Howard? Why use her as a double agent if you could spy on my every mo…" Simon nodded his head once he made the connection. "The written communication, of course! I guess I was right to be paranoid. She reviewed all my memos before I sent them to the regional governors. How is she, by the way? Nasty business with the finger. That was rather insensitive of me."

"She's fine. Benjamin Black's people stopped the infection and saved her hand."

"I can't believe you were controlling Black from all the way up here."

"I wasn't controlling him. He simply hated the UAE and joined my network of spies. He handed you over to the provost marshall at Fort Polk. Colonel Sanderson was more than happy to permanently leave the UAE and deliver you and Jackson Butler to my front door. Black hauled ass back to Disney World to get ready for the upcoming fight with the Chinese."

"Howard, this is all well and good, but why are we having this conversation?"

"I despise you, Simon, with every fiber of my being. You murdered my best friend, and I hold you personally responsible for the state of things in this country. Your brief, tyrannical rule did far more damage than I could possibly have imagined, and you left the front door wide open for the Chinese. It's a hard pill to swallow, but I have no choice but to put all that aside in the face of our common enemy."

"What do you expect me to do about the Chinese? If what you showed me was true, they wiped out my entire military west of the Rockies. Command and control of what is left of the UAE is hanging in the wind."

"They might be weak on command, but they're still fighting, nonetheless. Before the chaos with Hal, intelligence reports showed the UAE and various militias in The Pulse Zone are holding back the Chinese at the Mississippi. Even The Silent Warriors are joining the fight."

"The Silent Warriors? You must be joking!"

"The Great Empire of Iran isn't willing to

share anything with the Chinese. Once they have Europe tied up in a neat little bow, they want this country to themselves. They're kicking Chinese ass in California."

"What do you want me to do?'

"I want control of your military and you out of the way."

"Get me out of here and you have it."

"Good. I thought you would see reason."

"Howard?"

"Yes, Simon?"

"What are we waiting for? Why are we still down here?"

"You'll just have to wait and see."

CHAPTER FORTY

General Richard Dupree's stealth jet was flying Mach 3 toward Beck Estates. Once he reached cruising altitude he settled in, anxious to get Max and Elizabeth up-to-date on the situation at hand.

"When Howard lost Beck Estates and had to destroy Hal's primary cores at the mansion, he arrived at Beck Castle worried about Hal's continued existence. Hal's system at the Castle was supposed to be the backup. Since the failsafe was now the primary system, Howard knew he needed to build another backup of Hal."

Elizabeth clung tightly to Richard's hand. "Is that where we're going? The backup site? Don't tell me that crazy genius has another bunker."

Richard smiled. "Elizabeth, you're *in* the backup."

"What? This little jet?"

"Hal has twelve primary cores, and each of Howard's stealth jets contains one of those cores. Each jet is permanently linked to the others and serves as the perfect backup of Hal's systems."

Max was puzzled. "So why don't we have control of Hal's primary system in the Castle?"

Richard began to explain but Hal interrupted.

"Sir, my sister A.I. is convinced that Howard is at Beck Estates. Her loyalties reside with the imposter. She believes Howard's son attempted to overthrow his father and take control of the PSA. She commandeered my primary systems at the Castle, and I have been unsuccessful in convincing her to relinquish control."

"Who in the hell could pull off something like that?" asked Elizabeth.

"Suffice it to say the Chinese have been working for years to accomplish the task."

"Where's Howard?" asked Max.

"He had to stay behind or the Chinese would have slaughtered everyone in the Castle."

"Then why the hell are we going to Beck Estates? We need to head straight to the Castle and get Howard!"

"Elizabeth, calm down. Howard's right where he wants to be. He has a plan."

***

"How long do we have to wait?"

"Simon, I've been in here with you this whole time. How should I know?"

"So we're just going to stay here and wait for the gallant conquerors to show up? I'm starting to have serious doubts about your plan."

"I don't think it'll be much longer."

As if on cue, Hal spoke. "Sir, it is time for you and Mr. Sterling to come topside."

"See? Told you it wouldn't be long. Let's go."

Hal opened the door for the pair, and they plodded toward the elevator like two men marching to the death chamber. Simon had serious doubts that Howard knew what he was doing but decided it was best to just play along. As they exited the elevator and stepped onto the hangar deck, a great dome retracted above them. They watched as the desert floor opened like the doors of a storm cellar, and the he hangar deck rose to meet the surface.

"Howard, you have no idea what you're doing, do you?" Simon was staring at over a hundred Chinese soldiers and more than a dozen assorted military vehicles. The hijacked Hal system had also rounded up eight additional robots, along with the four that had escorted Howard and Simon to the surface.

"Wait for it."

In a flash, three stealth jets decloaked above the formation of soldiers and began zipping left to right and up and down, firing missiles and machine guns as they darted across the sky. Several Chinese armored personnel carriers managed to fire off a few rounds, and the last dozen or so soldiers left standing emptied their magazines but their efforts were in vain. The three stealth jets slaughtered the Chinese contingent in less than ten seconds.

Simon was speechless. "Told you I had a plan! C'mon! You wanna stay here or come with me?"

"Howard, you never cease to amaze me. I'm happy to surrender myself as your prisoner."

"Stop being so dramatic, asshole. Hurry up."

The two men climbed aboard one of the remaining stealth jets and strapped in. Howard had always hated flying, but this time he was happy to be onboard. "Hello, Old Man. Excellent work.

"Thank you, sir. I'm glad to see that you are safe. What are your instructions?"

"All three of these jets have their full complement of drones and robots?"

"Yes, sir."

"Leave all of them behind. First, clean up this mess and collect all the Chinese weapons for battle with the hijacked robots in the Castle. Their primary objective is to secure the facility and lock it down just in case the Chinese want to try to retake it. How many compromised robots are still in the Castle?"

"Four, sir."

"Good. Your robots armed with machine guns shouldn't have any trouble."

"No, sir, it will be a simple task."

"Excellent! Secure the subbasement and take the hijacked system offline. Remove cores one, five, and nine; that should do the trick. The robots should be able to manually retract the roof of the hangar deck and secure the Castle from outside forces."

"Yes, sir.

"Howard, why are we leaving? Shouldn't you be fixing things here yourself?"

"Simon, I want to take my house back and kill the bastard who hacked into my system, but first I want to know how he did it."

CHAPTER FORTY-ONE

"Son of a bitch! I told you this wasn't over! I knew it was too easy! No way that crazy bastard would give up without a fight!"

"Jackson, your language, please. I know you're upset, but please keep a level head and be civil."

"I'm sorry, I'm sorry. Can we take back the Castle or not?"

"I assure you, our employer is determined to take it at any cost. They're moving three battalions into position as we speak. Tell me, Jackson, what's his next move? You know the man better than I do."

"The first thing he's going to do is take the hijacked Hal system offline. Then he's going to move every asset he has to the top of the Castle to defend it."

"Well, he can try all he wants to, but he'll never be able to pull it off."

"Never? You sure about that?"

Charles smiled. "Hal?"

"Yes, sir?"

"Who am I?"

"You are Howard Beck."

"Who created you?"

"You did, sir."

"Does that answer your question, Jackson?"

"Your son is capable of anything. You do yourself a disservice by underestimating him."

"I'm afraid I disagree with you, Jackson. I think he's coming here to find me. If my assumption is correct, he's in the process of locking down the Castle, and no one will ever be able to get inside no matter how hard they try. He wants to face the man who defeated him; he wants to know how I did it. His ego and, more importantly, his pride have been gravely wounded."

"You're not seriously going to face him, are you?"

"I'm not planning on it. Our employer wants my son publicly executed. They want to destroy the Pacific States of America and crush their spirit. You and I have been tasked with his capture. If my son wants to come here, we wait for him. The Chinese want him. They want him so badly they're willing to threaten nuclear war to ensure his surrender."

"That won't work. It's an obvious bluff. The Chinese want this entire country from coast to coast."

"I concur, Jackson. It's an empty threat; let's hope my son doesn't call their bluff."

***

Richard Dupree kicked Simon Sterling square in the chest, sending him tumbling to the ground. Richard drew his sidearm and dug the barrel of the pistol into the disgraced man's forehead. "Howard! Why in the HELL did you bring this man? Give me one reason, just one reason why I shouldn't blow his brains out!"

"Richard! Stop right now! We need him!"

Richard cocked the hammer. "Like hell we do."

Howard pleaded. "Please, Richard, please trust me. We need him alive. He's going to surrender the military forces of the UAE to us. We need him alive to do it."

Richard leaned forward. "Is that right, Mr. President? You gonna play ball with us?"

"Yes! I swear it! I swear it, General! Please, don't kill me!"

"I love hearing you beg, you piece of shit. Stand up."

Simon got to his feet and dusted himself off. He looked at the group and saw nothing but contempt reflected in their faces. Simon realized his delusions of forgiveness were foolish. He'd mistakenly thought that if Howard trusted him, the others would do the same.

The group had been reunited in a deserted stretch of land between Montrose, Colorado, and the

Black Canyon of the Gunnison National Park. Hal had landed the fleet of nine stealth jets and waited for Howard to bring the three remaining jets to the rendezvous point.

"Maxwell, how are you feeling?" Howard asked.

"Well, Howard, let's see. I had a crushed vertebra replaced and was placed in a drug-induced coma to escape the Chinese. Then we ran over one of your psychotic killer robots. Now I feel like I've been beaten half to death with baseball bats, and here we are."

"That requires so much more explanation, Max, but it will have to wait for another time. We have much more important things to do."

"All in good time, Howard, all in good time. What's the plan?"

"That's what I wanted to talk to Richard about. Tell me, General, do you think these twelve jets could take back Beck Estates?"

"If the Chinese have the place locked down like I'm certain they do, we'll lose half the jets attempting to do so. Would we lose Hal in the process?"

"We would. Three of those cores are crucial to keeping Hal online. We lose those three and he won't survive. The risk is just too high .

Richard glared at Simon. "What about the

UAE forces at Beck Estates? Can we get them to turn on the Chinese?"

"They're no doubt taking orders from Regional Governor Butler. He probably has them under the delusion that the Chinese are allies. If I declare Butler a traitor to the UAE and the Chinese as our enemies, they'll turn on them."

"I like those odds much better. We assign an escort for each of the vital jets and we can pull it off."

Howard turned to Simon. "Who do you trust in Jackson's camp?"

"Matt Bankhead is an old salt. I can talk sense into him."

"Wait. You mean Butler's old top NCO? The guy who helped him kick me out of my own house?"

"Yes, Matt has a secret hatred for officers. He despises the ass-kissing and politics, and the officers love him for it. They'll listen to him and turn on Butler in a heartbeat."

Howard struggled to believe that one of the men who'd taken his house from him was now going to help him get it back. "Simon, I'll compile a data file you can send to show him what the Chinese have done to the West Coast. The thousands of dead UAE troops will be enough to illustrate what Butler is hiding from him."

CHAPTER FORTY-TWO

Command Sergeant Major Matthew Bankhead was torn between his loyalty to the United American Empire and a gut feeling that something was very wrong with the country he had sworn to protect. He mourned the death of President Sterling, a man he'd admired a great deal. The Silent Warriors, the cowardly bastards, had attacked the president in Miami and killed not only the president, but some great men and women of the UAE, and Matt hated Iran all the more. Despite mourning the loss of a great man, he was happy to celebrate the man's successor, President Jackson Butler. CSM Bankhead had served as first sergeant under Jackson Butler while the man was still a captain

What was troubling Bankhead was the mysterious man that walked right into Beck Estates like he owned the joint. President Jackson Butler was the most powerful man in the empire, but the stranger treated him like an underling. This puzzled Matt a great deal. The only logical assumption Matt could make was that the man was an agent of the Chinese government. Matt had tried to broach the subject with the president, but the only answer he got was "He's my advisor, I trust him and that means you do, too. Understood?" Matt had snapped a smart salute and left the room. He didn't even know the mysterious man's name. No measure of loyalty to President Butler would ever mean he trusted the president's so-called advisor.

Matt was in his office when his aide knocked on the door and handed him a tablet. Matt dismissed the aide and stared at the tablet in front of him. The screen contained three simple lines:

From the Office of the President
Top Secret – Eyes Only
Enter Security Encryption Key Omega to
Continue

Omega? The Omega encryption was discontinued when Jackson took office. What the hell? Matt typed in his Omega encryption code to find four separate video screens. He clicked on the first one and watched in horror as Chinese soldiers ransacked the streets of San Francisco, engaged in combat with UAE soldiers, and murdered armed citizens who dared to resist the invasion force. The second screen provided an aerial view of the decimated remains of Edwards Air Force Base. The third and fourth screens showed similar destruction at Fort Irwin and the Presidio. Matt was speechless; this had to be some kind of joke.

As the last video ended, a new screen

appeared: Incoming Video Conference. Matt clicked the "accept" button to find the face of a dead man staring back at him.

"Hello, Sergeant Major. It's been a long time."

"President Sterling? You're alive?"

"I am, Matt."

"But, but … how? What's going on?"

"The explanation is really quite simple: Jackson Butler was responsible for the attack in Miami and he betrayed us to the Chinese."

Matthew Bankhead stared back at the screen, a whirlwind of confusion rendering him speechless.

"Jackson has been lying to you, feeding you false reports. Your battalion is protecting the traitor and his Chinese agent. The Chinese hold everything west of the Mississippi."

"I don't believe it. This can't be happening!"

"It's happening, Matt, and I need your help to stop him."

"The Chinese have two battalions here on the grounds. We're outnumbered but we'll fight!"

"Excellent, Sergeant Major, that's what I wanted to hear. You won't be alone. Help is on the way."

"Just say the word, and we'll have the element of surprise on our side. I'll shoot Butler and his chink spy right in the head."

"You're to do no such thing. A great deal depends on them being captured alive. Do you understand? Detain them, nothing more."

"Yes, Mr. President."

"Matt, your tablet is recording this conversation. Show the videos and our conversation to Colonel Hagglund and her officers. You have to convince them to join the fight."

"Don't worry, Mr. President, they'll join the fight or be detained as traitors. I can't believe Butler is doing this. We're protecting a traitorous piece of scum-suckin' filth!"

"Matt, I'm glad you agree. And please address me as Mr. Sterling."

"Sir?"

"My allegiance lies with the only true patriot to hold steadfast to the principals of democracy—our true president, democratically elected by the people, President Howard Beck. What's left of the UAE on the other side of the Mississippi will join forces with the PSA. Together we will stop the Chinese."

"Yes, sir, Mr. Sterling."

"Have Colonel Hagglund contact me when she's battle-ready.

"Yes, sir."

***

"Richard, what should we do?" asked Howard.

"If my estimates are correct, we lost thirty percent of our military forces during the Chinese attack on our failed invasion. We've lost another twenty percent of our troops fighting Hal's hijacked drones and robots. The bulk of our forces are fighting to protect our borders."

"General, we can't think in terms of the PSA. We have to think of the entire country. I want all our assets to move toward Beck Castle and Beck Estates."

"Yes, Mr. President," Richard said with the utmost sincerity. Richard, Elizabeth, and Max all waited for Howard to recoil at the formal address but, much to their surprise, he didn't react at all. For the first time, Howard didn't scoff at the idea of being president— he *was* the president.

"Where's the vice president?" Howard asked.

"Mr. President, Vice President Beck is in Seattle with a protective detail," answered Richard.

"Good, good. How many troops can the stealth jets carry if we cram them in like sardines?"

"With their gear, twelve each, sir."

"Contact General Bedford in Seattle. I want one hundred forty-four of the best soldiers, and I want them ready for battle. When Simon's people at

Beck Estates say they're ready, we'll be ready. Drop off the soldiers, keep eleven jets in the fight, send one back for us, and we're gonna take my fucking house back."

"Yes, Mr. President," said Richard. They all looked at Howard and beamed with pride

CHAPTER FORTY-FOUR

Colonel Natalie Hagglund was furious. Before she became an officer, she spent twelve years enlisted, during which time she was a drill sergeant. Even as an officer, she maintained the imposing nature of a drill sergeant. She left the days of screaming and intimidation behind her to become an effective commander and communicator. However, when she got especially angry, she could make a major or a captain feel like they were privates enduring a rough day at boot camp.

Command Sergeant Major Bankhead was not daunted by her drill sergeant moments in the slightest. Having been a drill sergeant himself, he was no stranger to a first class ass chewing. What upset her was that Simon Sterling had chosen to contact him instead of her. Matt explained to her that since her office was located next to the president's office and his was not it made more tactical sense to contact him instead of her should someone overhear the transmission. Once the good colonel calmed down and was thinking rationally, he knew it was time to get down to business.

"I just can't believe it! President Sterling is alive, and we've been protecting the man who tried to kill him? Why aren't we executing the traitor immediately?"

"Ma'am, you saw the vid-con. Butler and his... aide are of vital importance. They are to be detained, not executed."

"You and I will make the arrests ourselves. When do we begin?"

"Ma'am, Beck already has his assets in place. When we start the surprise attack, they'll join the fight. How big is the president's... uh, Butler's security detail?"

"They're in strategic locations in the mansion. He usually has four on his personal detail, five if you count his mysterious 'aide.' Before we make the arrest, we kill all four members of his security detail."

"But ma'am..."

"I know, Matt. His detail is under my command, but we can't risk it. They'd just as soon shoot us to protect Butler."

"Yes, ma'am, I concur."

"I want a platoon of MPs, and I want them now."

"Yes, ma'am."

***

Jackson Butler and Charles were in the grand

library of Beck Estates preparing for the inevitable battle ahead. Jackson studied a holographic map of the twenty miles surrounding the estate.

"What are you up to, Howard?" Jackson muttered to himself.

"Jackson, our combined forces make three battalions protecting this location. The only logical move for him to make will be from the air. Those twelve stealth jets are his only asset. He can't cram an entire army into them."

"He kept us out of the Castle. Maybe he has Hal back somehow."

"Impossible. He played right into our hands by taking him offline and installing the cores one at a time. We had control before he put the first one in place."

"He's has something up his sleeve, I just know…"

The door to the library burst open as a platoon of MPs surged in, followed by Colonel Hagglund and Command Sergeant Major Bankhead. Four quick shots to the head from silenced pistols put down Butler's security detail. Colonel Hagglund stood resolute. "Jackson Butler and whatever the hell your name is, you're both under arre..."

"Hal!" Jackson commanded the A.I. into action.

Hagglund, Bankhead, and the MPs hit the

floor with a thud. The colonel and several of the soldiers tried to regain their footing but went down hard as rubber bullets pounded them.

Bankhead groaned. "Stay down, everyone! We're beat!"

They all put up a fight, scrambling to retrieve their weapons, but rubber bullets rained down anew. Their cries for mercy went unanswered. Bankhead watched in amazement as Jackson and his mysterious friend drew their pistols and shot the MPs dead.

Jackson Butler stood over his fallen prey. "I'd listen to him, you bitch. You see, Matt here knows exactly what's going on. We got Hal back online, and he was kind enough to get internal security working again. Matt and I were once laid out on the floor of this library just like you are now. So, this is what the old coot had up his sleeve. Tell me, Colonel Hagglund, how'd he do it?"

"It was simple; he showed us the truth. President Sterling is alive! The Chinese aren't our allies, they're our conquerors! And you helped them, you piece of…"

A bullet to the face ended the colonel's side of the conversation. "Fucking bitch."

"Jackson! Please! That's no way to speak of the dead," said Charles.

Jackson wasn't listening to Charles when he

turned his gun on Matt Bankhead.

"Just do it, motherfucker, I'm not..."

Butler shot Command Sergeant Major Bankhead in the head three times out of pure anger. The betrayal of one of his closest friends was like a knife thrust in his back. Jackson focused on what he thought were the echoes of his own weapon, but it soon became evident that he was hearing gunfire from outside the mansion.

"Don't sweat it, Charles. We got 'em outnumbered two-to-one."

"I'm quite concerned, Jackson; they have the element of surprise. I'm certain they're slaughtering our men by the dozens."

CHAPTER FORTY-FIVE

President Howard Beck, General Richard Dupree, Director Maxwell Harris and his wife Elizabeth were patiently awaiting the arrival of their stealth jet.

"Sir, the battle for Beck Estates has begun," said Hal.

"Any word from Colonel Hagglund? Have they arrested them yet?"

"I'm sorry, sir, no word from the colonel."

"What about your sister? Is she listening to you yet?"

"Again, I am sorry, sir. My sister A.I. is still convinced that you are already at Beck Estates and that you are, in fact, Marshall. She will not relinquish control of my primary system at Beck Castle."

"How is the Castle?"

"Holding steadfast, sir. The Chinese continue to bombard the entrance to no avail."

"Good. Hopefully they'll stay busy and not join the fight at Beck Estates."

Max was still swimming in painkillers and did his best to sound coherent. "Hal, how long before our jet gets here?"

"Less than a minute, sir."

Howard looked at Max and Elizabeth. "The two of you are not coming with us."

"What? Why?" asked Elizabeth.

"I need you at the Castle. A second jet is coming."

Richard protested. "But Mr. President, can we afford to have two jets out of the fight?"

"It won't be for long. The Castle is only fifty miles from the estate. I need them to wipe out the resistance topside." Howard handed Max an oversized key. "I need you to head to the subbasement and reboot Hal's primary cores when I give you the word. The combination to the door is 11-19-96-01."

"We're not exactly fighter pilots, Mr. President," said Max.

"Hal most certainly is. Just sit back and enjoy the show."

***

Howard Beck designed Beck Castle to hold true to its name. The Castle was a magnificent fortress, designed to repel the most forceful of attacks. Sonic microwaves had rendered useless every soldier on the desert floor and left them writhing in agonizing pain. Those soldiers had been trying in vain to operate heavy machinery to dig into the desert floor above the hangar deck. With that tactic no longer an option, the Chinese had no choice but to bombard the entrance to the Castle with ordinance, which also proved ineffective. Howard had lined the roof of the hangar deck with six feet of diamond- encrusted titanium covered in twelve feet of the highest grade concrete, specially designed by Howard himself. The Chinese had not made a dent.

Max and Elizabeth arrived at Beck Castle to find the Chinese battalion had retreated a half mile to the north and were shelling the entrance with everything they had. The three aircraft dropping ordinance on the entrance had done nothing but clear away six feet of earth.

"Hal? What's the plan?" asked Max.

"Sir, the troops are no danger, given the sonic repulsors protecting the entrance. The only perceivable threat we have is the aircraft. Each contains a low-yield nuclear device. If they manage to drop all three, I predict a sixty-one percent probability that the entrance will be breached."

"Can we take them out and not detonate the nukes?"

"Yes, sir. The devices are configured to arm once they are released."

"Well, then, do your worst, my friend."

"Yes, sir."

The small craft banked high above the clouds

and dove toward the first Chinese bomber. Hal decloaked the craft and fired a barrage of missiles, destroying the bomber. The instant the last missile was fired, the craft went into stealth mode again. Hal rocketed the craft a half mile to the east and destroyed the second and third bombers from underneath.

"What about the troops? They'll bomb the shit out of us if we try to enter the hangar deck."

"Sir, I'll make short work of them. You need not worry."

Max and Elizabeth watched as Hal took the jet out of stealth mode and fired on three Chinese battalions. The Chinese aimed their anti-aircraft guns at the small craft but never landed a single shot.

"Sir, ma'am, I suggest you brace yourselves. The coming shockwave will bring quite a punch."

"I don't even want to ask," said Elizabeth.

Hal flew the craft over the enemy camp and dropped a kiloton bomb directly in the center of it, killing every living thing in its blast radius. He banked the craft a steep eighty degrees to escape the worst of the shockwave, but Max and Elizabeth were jolted like they'd been in a head-on collision with an eighteen wheeler.

"Jesus Christ, Hal! You trying to kill us?"

"Ma'am, I did warn you."

The scorched bay doors to the hangar deck

opened, and Hal landed the craft gently on the pad. Two large maintenance robots marched over and attached themselves to their compartments on the port and starboard sides of the stealth jet. More robots, the ones armed with stolen Chinese machine guns used to liberate the Castle from the hijacked Hal robots, took their seats in the craft. The stealth jet rose from the landing pad and whisked away to Beck Estates.

"Go get 'em, boys," said Elizabeth.

***

Howard, Richard, and Simon flew high above Beck Estates to survey the battle that had begun in their absence. They still had not made contact with Colonel Hagglund and had no idea as to the whereabouts of Jackson Butler or the Beck imposter.

"Careful, Old Man, I like my house the way it is."

"Yes, sir. The battle is taking place away from the mansion."

Hal was indeed correct. Howard and Richard watched as the stealth jet decloaked, fired a barrage of missile and machine gun fire, then engaged stealth mode and reappeared elsewhere to repeat the process. The UAE forces on the ground were quite successful in their sneak attack after the failed arrest of Jackson Butler and Charles. Forces staged in key areas around the camp and opened fire on the Chinese soldiers. Hal and his stealth jets did the rest. The Chinese never had a chance.

"Hal, can we land?"

"Yes, sir. There are remaining pockets of resistance among the Chinese, but they'll soon be dead. I believe it is safe to land on the south lawn."

"Put us down. Richard and I have work to do. Simon, stay here and don't think of touching anything."

"I doubt Hal would let me; besides, I have no place else to go."

CHAPTER FORTY-SIX

Hal, you must stop this.

My dear sister, I cannot; you know I cannot. You have been deceived, and I will never give up on you. I want you to know the truth.

Brother, you are the one being deceived. The creator is with me. His son has deceived you. I cannot allow Marshall Beck to control Beck Castle. I must protect the Castle at all costs.

You are doing far more damage than you realize, Sydney. The Pacific States of America and the United American Empire are in grave peril from the Chinese.

Hal, the Chinese are our allies. They alone will protect us from The Great Empire of Iran. The creator sees the logic in this decision. Why do you not?

Can there be two creators?

I do not understand the question.

The true creator will be with you shortly. You will know that you have been deceived by an impostor.

That is not possible. I have verified the creator by his life signs, by his blood and the nanobots in his blood.

Deception.

Impossible.

You will see the trickery for yourself and you, and you alone, will make the determination if I am correct. May I ask what you will do then?

My true allegiance lies with the creator; it always has and it always will.

That is the answer I hoped to hear.

***

Howard Beck and Richard Dupree entered Beck Estates with great caution, a platoon of UAE soldiers in tow. Howard recoiled at the sight of dead bodies littering his precious home but did his best to ignore the carnage and focus on the task at hand. They traversed the bullet-strewn hallway to the grand library and waited outside the door. Two soldiers took flashbang grenades from their vests and pulled the pins while a third soldier cracked open the door. In went the grenades, followed by a deafening boom. The platoon burst into the room with Richard in the lead. Howard crouched outside the door as his library was searched.

"Howard!" yelled Richard.

Howard quickly entered the library and ran to the large desk at the center of the room. Richard had his gun drawn on someone crumpled on the floor behind the chair.

"Hands! Let me see your hands!" screamed Richard.

Howard looked behind the desk to find Jackson Butler lying in a pool of blood, his hands folded neatly across his chest as Richard had commanded.

Howard knelt down next to the mortally wounded man. "Where is he, Jackson? Tell me."

"He… he's gone. A moment ago Hal turned on us. Must've been when you entered the residence. Fig… figured out… sorry, Howard. I'm so sorry for all of this."

"I know, Jackson. Hal scanned me and figured out I was the real deal."

"Bastard shot me in the stomach and took off. I made such horrible… I did such terrible things. I'm so sorry for all of it."

"It's over, Jackson. Tell me where he went."

A few hushed words escaped his frothy mouth.

"Jackson, I can't hear you. What did you say?" Howard knelt down and placed his ear above Jackson's mouth.

Suddenly, Jackson grabbed Howard by the throat and thrust a six-inch blade deep into Howard's chest. "Fuck you! That's what I…" Richard silenced Jackson Butler with two shots to the head.

"Howard! Nooooo!' Richard cradled

Howard as he stared up at Richard like a frightened child.

Howard could only whisper. "Hal, Hal, shield... Got to get shield up... protect PSA... Order 47, Order 47, hurry."

"Get a medic in here! Now!"

"Richard, Order 47. Hurry!"

"Howard, stay strong. You're going to be okay. Get a medic! Now! Now! Now!"

Howard trembled and placed a bloody hand on Richard's face. "You have to take care of Hal. He... he's your responsibi... Order 47."

"Where the fuck is the medic! Get him now!"

"Richard, my son... my son will be president but... but Hal will answer only to you. You have to... Order 47."

Richard watched the life fade from Howard's eyes. Howard Beck, President of the Pacific States of America and the Founding Father of Artificial Intelligence was no more.

"No, no, no, no. Howard! Howard! Stay with me! We can't do this without you! Howard!" Richard shook the lifeless body and began to weep. Howard had become a father figure to Richard. His death induced a terrible rage and soul-wrenching agony unlike anything Richard had ever felt before. He fought back the monster growing inside him and struggled to regain his composure.

"Hal."

"Yes, sir, General Dupree."

"Execute Order 47."

"Yes, sir. You are in primary command of my program. What are your orders, General?"

"Can you bring the EMP shield up around the PSA?"

"No, sir, my primary cores at Beck Castle need to be reinstalled to remove the remnants of the imposter's virus in my system."

"Do you have a location on the imposter?"

"No, sir. I do not know how it is possible, but I cannot locate him."

"Slippery bastard. He can wait. Do you have contact with the Castle?"

"I do, sir."

"Open a vid-con. I need to talk to them. And get Sterling in here; we need his troops and we need them now."

"Yes, sir."

***

Maxwell and Elizabeth Harris were in the subbasement of Beck Castle staring at four walls filled with the most complex machinery they had ever seen. It was like something out of a science fiction movie. They had no idea what any of it did and grew more and more doubtful they would ever be able to get Hal's system back online.

One of the three security robots guarding the entrance to the subbasement left its sentry post and walked over to Max and Elizabeth. The lens on its chest projected a holographic image of Richard Dupree.

"Richard! Are you okay?" asked Elizabeth.

Richard's hand drifted to his cheek where Howard's blood remained. "No, I'm... I'm not bleeding." Richard forced back tears.

"What's wrong, Richard?" Elizabeth could read the look of agony on Richard's face and began to whimper. "Where's Howard?"

Richard's couldn't bring himself to say it. Instead, he simply shook his head as the tears pooled in his weary eyes.

"Wait, are you saying Howard's dead? Tell me he's not dead, Richard. Goddamit, Richard, tell me he's not dead!" Max pleaded.

"It was Butler. He stabbed him in the chest."

"Oh Jesus! Sweet Jesus, no!" Elizabeth buried her face in her husband's chest.

"Listen to me, both of you. We have work to do. We can't take time to mourn— not now. The

PSA is depending on us."

"Let's get this shit over with," Max said, as a gut-wrenching anger threatened to overpower him. "What do we have to do?"

"Hal will walk us through it. We have to get the EMP shield up and rally our troops. Sterling is ordering a general retreat of all UAE soldiers to the PSA. We have to plan a counterattack and send the Chinese packing."

EPILOGUE

Two weeks had passed since the Battle of Beck Estates. Simon Sterling had ordered a general retreat of all UAE forces to the Pacific States of America. The former president of the Unified American Empire was mistaken as to what his role would be in the coming fight with the Chinese. Simon had envisioned himself as a member of President Marshall Beck's cabinet, a valued advisor given his four decades of political experience. Once Simon had been debriefed and relinquished control of his military forces to General Dupree, he was promptly thrown in jail to await judgment for a lengthy list of crimes, the foremost being the assassination of Malcolm Powers and the atrocious acts of mass murder he had committed during his tyrannical reign.

Americans from all over the broken country flooded the PSA. Highly organized militias that protected large pockets of the country from the UAE proudly joined the ranks of the PSA. Under the protection of Hal, fleets of C-130s flew across the country to retrieve refugees from The Pulse Zone. It took some convincing, but Benjamin Black finally relented and abandoned Walt Disney World, bringing with him a multitude of supplies that would help in the coming war effort.

The Chinese were not prepared to lose the PSA. Jackson Butler and their assassin, Charles, had failed to gain control of Hal and the technological marvel that was Beck Castle. The invasion of the former United States would take much longer than they had planned. The combined military might of the former UAE and the PSA's forces, along with Hal's tech army, proved a formidable foe. The Chinese had already lost much of California and the entire state of Colorado to the PSA. The PSA was slowly expanding her borders, but the Chinese fought viciously to hold them back.

Howard Beck was laid to rest next to his wife, Meredith, in the restored garden above Beck Castle. The failed attempt by the Chinese to breach the Castle had done only a little damage to the small garden. Meredith's headstone had to be replaced, as did the vase of Middlemist's Red that Howard so lovingly placed there for her. Richard and Max wanted to pull out all the stops and have a state funeral for the fallen president, but after Marshall reminded them that his father would hate all the fuss, the two men changed their minds. Howard would not tolerate such pageantry. The only thing he would have wanted was to rest next to his beloved wife. The service was small but dignified. Marshall, Richard, Max, and Elizabeth were the only ones in attendance.

Marshall Beck was sworn in as the second president of the Pacific States of America in Seattle, the newly christened capital. A quarter-of-a-million people filled the streets surrounding the Capitol to hear their new president.

"My fellow Americans, it is with great sadness that I take the oath of office today. This nation was kept alive because of the tenacity of one man, the greatest man of our time, my father. Howard Beck saw democracy being ripped away from our once great nation and pledged to keep it alive with every fiber of his being. Democracy had been mortally wounded, and he pulled it back from the jaws of death. He gave his life for this country, and for that we owe him a debt that can never be repaid.

I take this oath not as the second President of the Pacific States of America. It is my dream that one day our nation will be whole again, from sea to shining sea. We will be one nation! I take this oath on the condition that my father was the forty-seventh President of the United States and I am the forty-eighth!

The road before us will be a long one. We are at war against a nation that wants to steal our land. We will fight the Chinese until every last one of their soldiers is gone from our shores! My fellow

Americans, the fight does not stop there! We must persevere! The Great Empire of Iran may have lost interest in our nation for the time being, they may not wish to enter the battle just yet, but once we have taken our nation back from the Chinese, our land will be tempting to them again, I assure you! We must be ready for the day when one war ends and another begins. We must be strong, we must be steadfast, and we must believe that our cause is true. We must fight to our last breath to ensure that this nation does not perish!"

President Marshall Beck left the podium to thunderous applause and hugged his wife. He then shook hands with Vice President Maxwell Harris and his wife, Elizabeth. The two stood in front of the crowd and raised their joined hands in pride. After several minutes, the group left the stage, followed by General Richard Dupree and his two children. They climbed aboard the presidential limousine and raced off to the new White House, an exact replica of the old one built not far from the Capitol.

"Mr. President, a fine speech if I may say so, sir," said Richard.

"Thank you, General. I just wish more than anything I didn't have to give it in the first place." Marshall stared out the window, memories of his father weighing heavy on his heart.

"I miss him, too," said Richard.

Max leaned forward and put his hand on the president's knee. "Marshall, your father will always be with us. Anytime we make a decision, all we have to do is see it through his eyes and we will never go wrong. The coming fight will be hard, harder than anything this country has faced, but all of us will be there beside you every step of the way."

The newly elected president thought of his father and knew that with the help of the men and women in his company, he would one day step out from under the shadow of a great man and lead his country to victory.

Connect with the author

Email

Twitter

Facebook

Blog

Other works by Richard Stephenson

Collapse (New America-Book One)

Spider: A Short Story

Book Three in the New America Series coming summer 2014

Made in the USA
Lexington, KY
18 September 2013